"I don't know what you're talking about."

Jedidiah growled, "You use your beauty the same way a gunfighter uses his gun, Susannah Calhoun. And if you've got any ideas about working your wiles on me while you're in custody, you can just forget it. It's not going to work, because I know how you are. Do we understand each other?"

She stared at him for a long moment. "You don't know how I am, marshal," she said quietly. "All my life, people have overreacted to the way I look. Don't condemn me for using a gift like that to my advantage. Everyone does it. It's called survival."

"There's more to you than your looks," he scoffed. "You're intelligent and resourceful, too, so don't act like you don't know it."

She looked as surprised as if he had just handed her the sun. "I wouldn't dream of it," she finally whispered.

"Good. Everyone else may underestimate you, but I don't. Understand?"

"Perfectly," she said softly.

Other AVON ROMANCES

Coming Soon

And Don't Miss These
ROMANTIC TREASURES
from Avon Books

DEBRA MULLINS

THE LAWMAN'S SURRENDER

AVON BOOKS
An Imprint of HarperCollinsPublishers

This is a work of fiction. Names, characters, places, and incidents are products of the author's imagination or are used fictitiously and are not to be construed as real. Any resemblance to actual events, locales, organizations, or persons, living or dead, is entirely coincidental.

AVON BOOKS
An Imprint of HarperCollins*Publishers*
10 East 53rd Street
New York, New York 10022-5299

First Avon Books paperback printing: March 2001

Avon Trademark Reg. U.S. Pat. Off. and in Other Countries, Marca Registrada, Hecho en U.S.A.
HarperCollins® is a trademark of HarperCollins Publishers Inc.

Printed in the U.S.A.

10 9 8 7 6 5 4 3 2 1

This book is dedicated to
my wonderful and talented editor,
Micki Nuding,
and to
Colleen Admirand and Michele Richter,
for their kind words and support

The Lawman's Surrender

Prologue

Wyoming Territory
July, 1882

That man was watching her again.

Susannah Calhoun peered over her dance partner's shoulder at the figure standing in the shadow of the huge crabapple tree. He stood unmoving near the white picket fence that encircled the yard, isolated from the revelry of the barbecue. She had sensed his eyes on her during the last three hours, and no matter how hard she tried, she couldn't seem to ignore him.

Matt Gomez, her partner in the Virginia reel, probably attributed her flushed cheeks to the vigor of the dance. But she knew her racing pulse had nothing to do with dancing.

1

And so did *he*—the rogue who stared so boldly at her.

The music stopped. Matt released her and turned to applaud the musicians, and Susannah did the same, smiling automatically. But all her attention was on the shadowy figure who watched her.

"May I fetch you some punch?" Matt's dark gaze warmed with masculine appreciation as he scanned her face.

"That would be lovely, thank you," she replied. He walked off the dance floor and headed for the refreshment table, but Susannah barely noticed his departure. After a long moment of hesitation, she started across the wooden floor toward the crabapple tree.

Where U.S. Marshal Jedidiah Brown awaited her.

The whole thing was ridiculous. The man was as stubborn as a mule and had the manners to match. She thought him rude and impossible; he had called her selfish and vain. Yet the memory of their one and only kiss lingered in her mind. Something had shifted inside her the day he had touched his mouth to hers, and she knew that if she didn't explore this strange and unsettling bond between them, she would regret it for the rest of her life.

As she stepped beneath the branches of the

crabapple tree, the flickering light of the lamps illuminated his features. Tall and lean, he had the coloring of a mountain lion: a mane of sun-streaked, tawny hair, sun-darkened skin, and brandy-colored eyes. His long, angular face was a fascinating combination of aristocratic cheekbones, sensual lips beneath a neatly trimmed mustache, and peaked eyebrows that gave him a look of perpetual amusement. Lines creased the tanned skin around his eyes and mouth, adding character. Hatless, he wore a plain white shirt and a brown coat and trousers that made him look almost like every other man there—except for the air of danger that he wore like an enticing cologne.

Susannah's pulse skipped wildly as she stopped in front of him, as if he were indeed a mountain lion and she a mere field mouse that would make a tasty morsel.

"Evening, Miss Calhoun." His slow Southern drawl reminded her of molasses in summertime; it made her knees weak and her breathing hitch. He affected her as no other man ever had, but she would die before admitting that to him.

"Good evening, Marshal Brown," she replied with her best company smile. "Are you enjoying yourself?"

"Donovan and your sister surely know how to throw a party," he replied.

"They do indeed. I haven't seen you dancing, marshal. Does your injury still bother you?"

"Not at all. It was just a scratch." He flexed his shoulder, where he had been shot a few weeks ago, and his white shirt stretched taut over the muscles of his upper body.

Her pulse stumbled, and she had difficulty tearing her gaze away from the smooth ripple of sinew beneath the snowy fabric. "It's a beautiful night, isn't it?" she quickly said.

He flashed his teeth in a grin. "Small talk, Miss Calhoun?"

"Most people consider it polite conversation," she replied with just a hint of tartness. "Perhaps you've heard of it?"

"Polite conversation. Let me see." He rubbed his chin. "That would be where I tell you how beautiful you are and you keep agreeing with me, right?"

"Must you always come back to that?" she snapped. "I'm trying to be civil, and you keep insulting me."

He arched his eyebrows. "Maybe if you were to have a real conversation with me instead of all this 'civilized' beating around the bush, I might be more accommodating."

"And what have we got to talk about?" she asked. "I think you're rude. You think I'm conceited. End of conversation."

"I was raised to be a gentleman under most circumstances," he said softly. "The thing is, I don't think you're the kind of woman who wants a gentleman as a lover."

Susannah stiffened. "Who said anything about a lover?"

"Why not a lover?" His deep voice rumbled like a lion's purr. "All your life you've been surrounded by men telling you how beautiful you are. And what good has all that gentlemanly conduct done your admirers? No good at all." He leaned closer. "You like it that I talk straight. That I treat you differently than the others do."

She sniffed disdainfully. "You're crazy."

"I don't think so. They treat you like a pretty china doll. I treat you like a real woman." He eyed her with consideration. "But maybe you're not ready for that yet."

A hot-tempered retort rose to her lips, but she bit it back. Why was it that this man could make such a mess of her emotions? Anger at his presumption made her steam with temper. But there was also a surge of pure, unladylike lust at the images his words conjured in her mind. She took refuge in disdain. "Your opinion hardly matters to me, marshal."

"I think it does." He took her hand and brought it to his mouth before she could pull away. As he pressed his lips to her palm, his mustache tickled the sensitive flesh, sending ripples skimming along her nerve endings. Her pulse leaped into double-time as his dark eyes met hers, and he deliberately nipped the heel of her hand.

Her entire body felt as if it were wax, and he the flame. His touch melted her protests until she wanted nothing more than to surrender herself to his tender care. She had finally met her match, and part of her rejoiced in the discovery.

She knew he could feel her thundering pulse as he brushed his lips against her wrist. The knowledge of what he could do to her was there in his eyes. For a moment, he seemed to know everything there was to know about men and women, and she wanted desperately for him to teach her. Then he smiled and pressed her hand to his cheek.

"Ah, Susannah," he murmured. "What a sweet temptation. A ripe fruit waiting to be plucked by an experienced hand."

The confidence in his tone snapped her back to reality.

"Not by yours," she retorted, jerking her hand away from his face. He laughed out loud, and she curled her fingers into her palm, her flesh still tingling from the slight roughness of his skin.

"We'll see about that," he murmured, his eyes warm with unashamed desire.

Someone called her name. Her mind registered it even as her heart protested the interruption. Even though he infuriated her, he also made her feel more alive than she ever had before.

"Your sister wants you," he pointed out.

"I hear her." Yet she didn't move.

"You'd better go on," he urged. His smile tempted her to ignore the summons. She wished she had the courage to step into his arms and accept that silent invitation, but the knowing gleam in his eyes made her hold her ground.

Without another word, she turned her back on temptation and left.

They didn't speak again that night.

The next morning, when Susannah went into town, toying with the idea of goading Jedidiah into kissing her again, she learned that he was gone. He had left town at dawn, without a word to anyone.

She refused to cry. A man like Jedidiah Brown didn't deserve her tears. And he surely didn't deserve her heart. Obviously, she had narrowly escaped making a fool of herself. If she ever saw the rotten scoundrel again, she would thank him.

Susannah returned home, eyes dry, firm in her decision to never again let her heart tempt her head.

Chapter 1

~~~◦◯◦~~~

Silver Flats, Colorado
One year later

S he wondered if she'd killed him.

Susannah Calhoun stared down at her employer, who lay unconscious on the sumptuous carpet of his dining room, and felt a twinge of remorse for hitting him with the very ugly statuette of the naked woman. But damn his hide, Brick Caldwell had gone too far in his amorous pursuit this time.

Gathering the skirts of her sky blue gown, she pushed back her silver blond hair and crouched beside his body, placing a hand on his neck. A pulse beat there, and she sighed with relief. But since he owned the opera house where

9

she sang every night, she felt certain that she was now unemployed.

He moaned, and she quickly straightened. Brick was likely to awaken with the temperament of a wounded bull. It would be much healthier all around if she wasn't present when he opened his eyes.

As a matter of fact, the sooner she got out of Silver Flats—and beyond Brick Caldwell's reach—the better.

As if he read her thoughts, his eyelids flickered, then opened.

For a moment he stared blankly at her shoes. Susannah took a quick step back. With a groan, he rolled over onto his back and raised a hand to his head. His gaze slid to her face and stayed there for a long, breathless moment. Rage followed recognition.

"You!" he thundered, then winced and rubbed his head.

Brick's body blocked her escape, but if she timed it right, she might be able to get past him.

He suddenly sat up and grabbed for her, and only her quick maneuver prevented him from snagging her skirt with his fingers.

"Now, Brick," she cajoled. "I realize you're probably a bit angry—"

"Angry?" he roared. "I'll teach you a lesson you'll never forget." He staggered to his feet.

"No woman is going to get the best of Brick Caldwell! And certainly not some opera house whore."

"Whore!" Incensed, Susannah propped her hands on her hips. "As I recall, you pig of a man, it was my refusal to *be* your whore that got us to this point!"

"You'll never work in this town again," Brick warned as if she hadn't spoken. Then his lascivious gaze came to rest on her generous bosom, and his expression took on a sly cast. "Unless you decide to mend your ways, that is."

"And I suppose your idea of mending my ways involves spending time in your bed? I don't think so." She glanced down his body. "The benefits appear to be very . . . small."

Brick's face flushed with fury. "You'll do what I tell you, Susannah Calhoun!"

"Get out of my way." She gave him a shove that upset his unsteady balance and sent him crashing into a mahogany table, and he fell heavily to the floor. The vase of flowers atop it wobbled and then smashed over his head, soaking his expensive pin-striped suit with water. Susannah eyed the daffodil that sat perched atop his balding pate. "By the way, Mr. Caldwell—I quit."

She skirted around his outstretched legs and hurried out into the hallway, his enraged bellow following her. As Susannah yanked open the front door, the housekeeper, Abigail Hawkins, came scurrying out of the kitchen.

"Better get your rifle, Mrs. Hawkins," she said. "Seems like there's a wounded bear in there. You might have to shoot him."

The housekeeper looked startled at first; then a smile flashed across her face. Susannah gave the woman a cheeky salute and hurried out into the night.

The sooner she saw the last of Silver Flats, the better.

Forty-eight hours later, Susannah watched Sheriff John Benning of Silver Flats turn the key to her jail cell. She had taken the early stage out of Silver Flats and made it halfway to Colorado Springs, before the local lawmen had caught up to the coach in search of her. They had called her a murderess and made a big scene of dragging her off the stage and back to Silver Flats.

To add insult to injury, the sketch on the wanted poster they had brought with them had been *most* unflattering.

"Sheriff Benning, this is the most ridiculous thing I have ever heard!" Susannah exclaimed as the lawman hung the key on a peg on the wall. "I did *not* kill Brick Caldwell!"

The sheriff sighed. "Look, Miss Calhoun, a

neighbor saw you run out of the house after midnight that night."

Miss Calhoun. Susannah's heart clenched at his formality. Over the past few months, she and the sheriff's family had been developing a close friendship. Now the suspicion of murder put distance between them. "I won't deny that I was there, sheriff," she said, pride stiffening her spine.

His expression wavered between apology and duty. "From what Miss Anne Blanchard says, you had a supper with Mr. Caldwell after the show."

"Anne Blanchard!" Susannah snorted. "She wanted my spot on stage. And she wanted Brick for herself. Darn it, sheriff, she just wanted to be *me*!"

"Miss Calhoun, I don't think you appreciate the gravity of your situation here." Sheriff Benning pushed a hand through his dark hair and gave her a sympathetic look. "You're the only one we can place at the murder scene that night. Since he was killed with a knife from the dinner table . . . and since you left town early the next morning . . ."

"You think I killed him." Fear curled in the pit of her stomach. "But I didn't. Brick was alive when I left. Alive and cursing, as a matter of fact, since I'd just hit him over the head with a statue."

"Now, why would you go and do a thing like that?"

"Because he was trying to force me to become his mistress," she said bluntly. "Ask Abigail Hawkins, his housekeeper. She was there when I left. She heard Brick shouting after me."

"Mrs. Hawkins left town yesterday morning," the sheriff informed her.

"Left?" The world spun for a moment as Susannah realized her best hope had taken the morning stage to who-knows-where. "You let her go? How do you know *she* didn't kill Brick?"

"Mrs. Hawkins stated that she left that night at seven o'clock, as she always did," the sheriff said. "Mr. Caldwell's neighbor saw her leave. She's not a suspect at this time."

"But she was there," Susannah said softly, then lifted her gaze to the sheriff's as fear clogged her throat. "I didn't kill him."

He sighed. "That's for a jury to decide, Miss Calhoun."

Susannah leaned weakly against the bars. "When is the trial?"

"In two weeks."

"Two weeks!" She stood up straight. "Why so long? Can't you just get a jury together so I can prove my innocence and get this over with?"

"It's not that simple." Sheriff Benning scratched his chin. "You know Mr. Caldwell's family owns that big mining company out of Denver, and his uncle, the Senator, asked the governor if the trial could be in Denver to make it easier for them to attend. A U.S. Marshal is on his way to escort you there."

"A U.S. Marshal? Oh, that's just what I need." A vision rose up from the past of wicked dark eyes beneath peaked brows, but she forced the memory from her mind.

"Is there no way we can just have the trial here, Sheriff Benning? After all, this is where the crime occurred." She gave him her most winning smile.

"Sorry, Miss Calhoun." John Benning swallowed hard and shuffled his feet. "I've got my orders straight from the governor. You're going to Denver. There's nothing I can do."

He turned to walk away.

"Sheriff." When he looked back at her, she asked, "What's my supposed motive for killing him?"

"Maybe self-defense," he replied. "You said he was pressing his attentions on you. But it doesn't really matter; according to the evidence, you're the only one who was there."

As he left the room, Susannah sank down on

the stark cot in her cell. One moment she was the star performer at the Silver Dollar Opera House, the next she was a murder suspect. She wracked her brain for a way to prove her innocence.

She had indeed dined with Brick after the eleven o'clock show the night before last; he had made it clear that to refuse the invitation was to lose her job. While she had rebuffed Brick's attentions many times without repercussions, that night he had seemed determined that she would end up in his bed—willing or not. Things had escalated, and she had been forced to defend herself.

Susannah got up and paced the length of the tiny cell. It wasn't the first time she had been forced to fight for her virtue, and it probably wouldn't be the last. She knew that men found her beautiful, but some of them lost all sense of reason in their desire to pursue her. She would have cursed fate for giving her such stunning looks, but it was hard to feel remorseful when she had deliberately cultivated a lethal charm to go with her striking appearance. Many a time she had used her attractiveness to get out of tight situations, but it didn't look as if she'd be able to charm her way out of this one.

Fear rose again, and she fought it back with pure strength of will. If she gave in to her rising panic, she wouldn't be able to think. She had to figure out what to do next.

The only flaw in Sheriff Benning's case was his assumption that she had been the only one there that night. There was one other person who had been at the scene, the only person who could clear her name—Abigail Hawkins. But now that the woman had left town, the chances of getting her to change her testimony were slim.

She remembered Abigail's smile and wondered what had been behind it. Why had the housekeeper lied to the sheriff? What was she hiding? Had she killed Brick? These questions had to be answered.

John Benning was as honest as the day was long, and just as stubborn, once he made up his mind. Since he wouldn't bring Abigail back in for more questioning, the task fell to Susannah. She would have to find the housekeeper herself and clear her own name. Obviously the law wasn't going to help her do it.

With a thoughtful expression, Susannah regarded the small, barred window of her cell and started to plan a jail break.

"Marshal Brown!"

Jedidiah groaned and, half-awake, reached across the bed, as if searching for someone even in slumber.

The call came again, louder. "Marshal Brown!" Then there was a pounding noise, like thunder. Was it going to rain?

"Marshal Brown!"

With a start, Jedidiah sat up in the bed. Daylight streamed into his hotel room, a rude contrast to the moonlight that lingered in his memories. Scowling, he glanced at the pillow beside him, but there was no evidence that anyone had shared the bed with him.

He let out a gusty sigh and rubbed both hands over his face. Another dream.

"Marshal Brown!" Someone continued to shout his name and pound on the door.

With a muttered curse, he shoved aside the sweat-dampened sheets, grabbed his gun from beneath the pillow, and stalked across the room, unconcerned with his naked state. He positioned himself to the side of the door, then reached over and yanked it open, leveling his Colt at the startled hotel clerk. "What?"

The young man's eyes bulged, and his mouth worked for a few moments without any sound coming out of it. He shoved a piece of paper at Jedidiah and ran.

Jedidiah slammed the door, then turned to face his empty bed. Crumpling the paper in his hand, he leaned back and pounded his fist against the sturdy wood in frustration. The damned dream was always so real. He hated to wake up to the truth.

Even the memory of the dream was enough to stir his flesh. He glanced at the paper, but the words blurred before his sleep-heavy eyes. With a muttered curse, he went to the washstand and put down the paper, then poured water into the basin. It was cold from sitting out all night, and he gratefully sponged off his overheated skin, his mind still awhirl with the images the night had brought.

If it had just been an ordinary erotic dream, he would have shrugged it off as the normal fantasies of a healthy, thirty-nine-year-old man. But *she* was in it again, and that wasn't so easily pushed aside.

Damn Susannah Calhoun, anyway.

He finished washing and reached for his clothes. Ever since he had met the woman last year, he hadn't been able to get her out of his mind. Lord knew she was a beauty, but it wasn't just her looks that drew him. The first time he had seen her, he'd been struck by a feeling of recognition, as if she were a part of himself looking back at him.

That still disturbed him.

Uncomfortable with the feeling, he had tried to avoid her. But it was a small town, and their paths inevitably crossed. When they did, conversation became a battlefield of dagger-sharp insults and strategic retorts that grew more heated each time they met.

Perhaps if he'd never kissed her—or better yet, if they'd just ripped up the sheets a time or two—he'd be getting more sleep.

Jedidiah grabbed a plain white shirt, buttoned it up, and tucked it into the waistband of his buckskin-colored pants. The woman had haunted him ever since he'd left that one-saloon town.

Now he found himself dreaming of her nearly every night. More than once he had considered riding through Burr again just to see if he had imagined the whole thing. But he had managed to stop himself before he did something so foolish.

One thing he had learned in life was that caring brought pain. So except for his older sister Lottie, he made it a policy never to open his heart to anyone.

Jedidiah sat on the bed and reached for his boots. He hadn't seen his sister in a while, and now that the Slater gang was safely behind bars, he planned to go home to Charleston for a visit. He looked forward to seeing his nieces and nephews.

He lifted his leg to yank on his boot, and his gaze fell on the message still sitting on the washstand. He stomped his foot into the worn leather, then reached for the crumpled piece of paper. He frowned as he smoothed it out. It had better not be more orders; he needed a break.

The telegram was short and sweet. So was the curse he uttered.

BABY DUE ANY DAY. CAN'T LEAVE SARAH. STOP. SUSANNAH IN JAIL FOR MURDER SILVER FLATS, COLORADO. STOP. PLEASE HELP. DONOVAN.

Damnation, he was going to have to put off Charleston, after all. And the reason made even a cynic like him appreciate fate's sense of humor.

He shoved the telegram into his pocket. Jack Donovan was perhaps the only real friend he had in the world, and he was real fond of Jack's wife Sarah, too. Now her sister, Susannah, was in trouble, and there was no way Donovan could possibly go help. Which left it up to him.

He grabbed his other boot and stamped his foot into it, then quickly donned his dark duster and worn tan hat. He packed his things by the expedient method of sweeping them off the bureau and into his satchel. Then he headed toward the door. He had telegrams of his own to send.

Chapter 2

⁓⟡⟡⁓

Susannah had decided to make the best of things while waiting for the right moment to escape from jail. Over the past two days, Sheriff Benning had allowed her some small comforts while they awaited the U.S. Marshal who would escort her to Denver. She was grateful for his compassionate nature when a visitor arrived that afternoon.

Anne Blanchard was a beautiful woman with ivory skin and jet black hair set off by blue eyes that glittered like gemstones. She swept into the jailhouse as if it were a palace, dressed to impress in a gown of sapphire blue silk and snowy lace with a matching parasol. From the disappointed look on her face, she had obviously expected to see Susannah unkempt and in rags, not well groomed and dressed in a clean dress of pink dimity.

"Susannah, my dear, how are you?" she trilled in insincere tones. "This whole ordeal must be simply dreadful for you!"

"Anne, how nice of you to come," Susannah replied, not meaning a word of it. "How is everyone at the Silver Dollar?"

"Everything is quite disorganized." Anne gestured with her hands as she spoke, her accent one of upper class snobbery, though Susannah knew she had been born a sharecropper's daughter in Kansas. "Brick's brother is coming to take charge soon, and then everything should get back to normal." She sent Susannah a sly glance. "Of course, it won't be the same without you performing."

Susannah gave Anne a sugar-sweet smile. "I'm certain you'll get along without me."

"I suppose we'll have to," Anne replied, patting her stylish raven curls. "After all, it wouldn't do to have Brick Caldwell's murderer performing in his opera house."

"I didn't do it, Anne," Susannah said, dropping the polite facade. "Not that you care. I'm sure you just came here to rub my nose in the fact that you're probably going to be the new star of the Silver Dollar."

"I *am* going to be the new star. And you, Susannah Calhoun, are going to be hanged for murder."

At the glee in the woman's voice, Susannah raised her eyebrows and said coolly, "Why, Anne, if I didn't know you had spent that night bouncing on Mayor Rafferty's mattress, I'd swear that you killed Brick just to get me out of the way."

Anne's ivory cheeks turned crimson, and her eyes narrowed in fury. "You don't know what you're talking about!"

Susannah laughed. "Anne, *everyone* knows about you and Mayor Rafferty. And he's how much older than you? Thirty years? Thirty-five?" She scanned the woman from head to toes. "Then again, maybe twenty."

"You think you're so much better than everyone else," Anne hissed. "Well, it looks like you finally got your just desserts, doesn't it?"

"When you pinch your face up like that, Anne," Susannah replied blandly, "it makes you look old enough to be Mayor Rafferty's mother."

With a sound of fury, Anne turned and stormed from the jailhouse, shoving past a tall man who was entering the sheriff's office. He nimbly sidestepped the furious woman, then turned to face Susannah. Her heart skipped a beat as she recognized Jedidiah Brown's familiar lopsided grin.

"You do have a way with people," he drawled.

Susannah closed her eyes, then opened them again. No, he wasn't a figment of her imagination. He was there in the flesh: all six-foot-plus of lean, ain't-I-charming, devastating male.

Jedidiah got a real bad feeling from the gleam in Susannah's lovely blue eyes. From the look on her face, he was probably lucky that she was unarmed and behind bars.

"What are *you* doing here?" she demanded.

"Your family's worried about you," he replied, approaching her cell. "And I hear you need an escort to Denver. I called in a few favors and managed to get myself the assignment."

Susannah propped her hands on her hips. "I knew I shouldn't have wired home. I suppose I'm lucky Sarah didn't come tearing up here in her condition."

"Instead they sent me." He almost laughed at the sour expression that crossed her face. "Your family trusts me. You might consider doing the same."

"Trust is usually earned, marshal. And with the tab you're running, you're already way behind."

"I'll catch up." He studied her accommodations with raised eyebrows. The plain cot had been topped with a luxuriously thick mattress, complete with pillows and a ruffled coverlet. Makeshift curtains hung from the window, and a vase of wildflowers stood on the small washstand next to a silver-backed brush and mirror set.

She followed his gaze. "Something wrong, marshal?"

All the way here, Jedidiah had imagined her scared and lonely in a stark cell. He ought to have remembered that Susannah Calhoun always landed on her feet. And if he'd remembered what a spoiled brat she was, he would never have lost a moment's sleep.

"You seem to have adapted well to your situation, princess," he drawled, and watched her eyes spark with temper.

"The sheriff was kind enough to let me have some of my things," she said tightly.

He leaned against the steel bars separating them. She was still beautiful enough to stop a man's heart. Her silver-gilt hair was done up in fancy curls and ribbons, as if she were going to a ball instead of living in a jailhouse. A mixture of emotions, the most prominent of which was annoyance, lit her exotically slanted smoky blue eyes. Her peaches and cream complexion took on a becoming flush as he scanned her from head to toe, noting with masculine appreciation how her store-bought pink dress showcased the body that had inspired his lustful dreams.

Susannah Calhoun was a hell of a woman. But had she killed a man?

"Are you finished staring at me, marshal? It's quite rude." She looked down her nose at him, though he was a head taller. "But then, you always were lacking in manners."

"I seem to get along well enough." He tapped one of the cell bars. "I can't say the same for you."

She made a vexed sound and threw up her hands. "Of all the U.S. Marshals, why did it have to be you?"

"Your family didn't want you rotting in jail." He tipped back his hat. "So, did you kill him?"

"Of course not. Do I look like a murderess?"

"No, you look like every man's fantasy come to life. But you know that already." He ignored her huff of outrage. "Actually, I believe we're all capable of killing, but the circumstances would have to be right. I imagine that if someone's life were in danger, or the life of a loved one, anyone could kill without losing sleep over it. But we're not talking about what other folks could or couldn't do. We're talking about whether or not you killed Brick Caldwell. And that's a whole other question."

Susannah stared at Jedidiah in surprised silence. There he stood, calmly stating that he believed she was capable of murder. She had somehow expected he would immediately leap to her defense, though why she should feel such a thing, she didn't know. After all, except for one kiss, she barely knew the man.

Then again, he was a man few women would forget.

She started to pace, slanting a sidelong glance at him. He still looked the same, tall and well muscled, sun-kissed from head to toe. He never seemed to be in a hurry and did things in his own time. Once upon a time she even had wondered if he made love with the same studied slowness . . . She jerked her thoughts back from that path.

He continued to watch her with those hawk-like eyes that revealed no clue to his thoughts. She had seen those eyes hard and predatory, as well as hot with passion, but Jedidiah Brown was very good at hiding his feelings when it suited him. After all, he'd revealed nothing the last time she'd seen him that indicated he would be gone by the next morning. The sting of his abrupt departure had lingered with her for a long time.

But she had to admit that he was right. She knew she wouldn't hesitate to kill in order to protect her life or someone else's. However, she hadn't killed Brick Caldwell.

"I didn't kill him," she said out loud.

He raised his brows. "I've heard that before."

"I didn't," she repeated. "But believe what you want."

"It's not my job to judge you, just to get you to the courthouse for trial."

Her eyes narrowed. It was on the tip of her tongue to tell him about Mrs. Hawkins, but why bother? The man didn't seem inclined to believe in her innocence, and she was damned if she'd beg. "If that's the way you want it to be, marshal."

"That's the way it has to be." He centered his hat on his head. "Now, where's the sheriff?"

"Next door, having his supper."

"Good, I think I'll join him." He tapped one steel bar with his finger. "Stay out of trouble."

"And here I was planning on going over to the saloon to start a brawl."

"Resist temptation," he advised with a chuckle, then turned away and strode from the room.

She leaned against the bars, watching his retreating form with reluctant appreciation. "Don't you worry, marshal," she said softly. "I will."

* * *

Maudeen's Restaurant was crowded and noisy—and the smells coming from the kitchen were so heavenly that Jedidiah's mouth started to water as soon as he set foot in the door. Miners and businessmen alike crowded together at the tables, roaring at each other's tall tales and eyeing the pretty waitresses that nimbly wove through the maze of humanity.

Jedidiah spotted the sheriff at a table in the corner, a dark-haired man with a silver star pinned to his vest. As Jedidiah approached, John Benning looked neither right nor left, merely concentrated on his roast beef dinner in a single-minded way that Jedidiah's empty stomach could appreciate.

"Evening, sheriff," he said, reaching the table. "I'm U.S. Marshal Jedidiah Brown. I've come to escort your prisoner to Denver."

Sheriff Benning shook Jedidiah's outstretched hand, still chewing his roast beef. He gestured to an empty chair, swallowed, and said, "You're welcome to join me, marshal. I expect you're hungry."

"You're right." Jedidiah slipped into the empty seat. He took off his hat and laid it on the chair next to him, then caught the eye of the pretty brunette waitress and signaled her over.

Sheriff Benning continued to work on his meat and potatoes as Jedidiah ordered fried chicken and biscuits, with a pitcher of buttermilk to wash it all down.

"Buttermilk?" the sheriff asked, raising his eyebrows as he forked up more roast beef.

Jedidiah sent him a look that discouraged further questions. "I *like* buttermilk."

Sheriff Benning shrugged. "To each his own."

Jedidiah settled back in his chair. "I went by the jailhouse on my way in, sheriff. Your prisoner looks right at home."

Benning chuckled and reached for his cup of coffee. "I didn't see as it would harm anyone to let the gal have a few things to make herself more comfortable."

"I noticed that your deputy's letting in a lot of visitors. Do you think that's wise?"

"I don't see the harm in it."

"Even if the prisoner's been accused of murder?"

Benning just shrugged and helped himself to more roast beef. "That little slip of a female isn't going anywhere."

Jedidiah believed that Susannah Calhoun could sweet talk any visitor into helping her escape if she decided to, but he kept his feelings to himself. He didn't want Benning inquiring as to how he happened to know Susannah quite so well. "I hope you're right," he said instead.

Benning sighed. "Accused murderers are normally guarded more closely, marshal, but I have to admit, I sure hated to lock that pretty thing up. The wife and I sat with Miss Calhoun at the town picnic a while back, and we all got friendly after that. Even the children took to her. Then this mess happened."

"Why don't you tell me about it?" The brunette returned bearing Jedidiah's supper, and he sat back so she could set the food down in front of him.

"Seems pretty clear," Benning said. "She sang at Brick Caldwell's opera house, the Silver Dollar Opera. Caldwell ran a decent place—no whoring going on. Miss Calhoun is a respectable woman, and I never heard tell of her doing anything a decent woman shouldn't."

"Until now," Jedidiah said.

"Until now." Settling into his story, Benning scooped up a forkful of potatoes and gravy. "Brick had his eye on her and invited her to his house after the show for a midnight supper. Next morning he turns up dead. Stabbed with a knife from the supper table."

"No other suspects?" Jedidiah bit into a chicken leg.

"Not a one. Closest we came was the house-keeper, Abigail Hawkins. I talked to her myself. Caldwell's neighbor saw the housekeeper leave at seven that night, just like she always does. The same neighbor saw Miss Calhoun running out of Caldwell's house just after midnight like the place was on fire. The way I see it, she was there at the right time and had access to the murder weapon. And if you figure that she might have been fighting off some unwanted attention, it all fits."

"Sounds pretty straightforward." Jedidiah poured himself a glass of buttermilk. "So why is she going to Denver?"

"Caldwell's relatives are rich folks—they own Caldwell Mining and Ore out there. And his uncle is Senator Morris Caldwell. The gover-nor personally asked that Miss Calhoun be ex-tradited to Denver for trial so they can attend."

Jedidiah's lips twisted. "Politics."

"Yeah." Benning sopped up the last of the gravy with a piece of bread. "I wish I could do something for that gal. She claims Caldwell was trying to force her into his bed, and I believe her. Maybe they'll rule it as self-defense."

"But Miss Calhoun claims she didn't kill Caldwell at all, not that she did it in self-de-fense," Jedidiah pointed out.

Benning's expression turned grim. "Unless

another suspect comes into the picture, that gal's in big trouble. I've got a feeling Caldwell's family means to see her hang."

A vision of Susannah swinging from a rope made the chicken stick in Jedidiah's throat. He forced himself to swallow. "You may be right," he murmured.

"Funny about that housekeeper, though," Benning said a moment later. "Miss Calhoun swears that Abigail Hawkins was there when she left that night."

Jedidiah put down the chicken leg. "What?"

"Miss Calhoun says that Mrs. Hawkins was still there when she left that night. Can't see how that could be, since the witness saw Mrs. Hawkins leave the Caldwell place at seven o'clock."

"What did Mrs. Hawkins have to say?"

"Just what the witness said. That she left at seven, like always. I've crossed her off the list of suspects."

"Already?"

"She was real upset, seeing as how she found the body," Benning said. "Since there's a witness to back up her story, I let her go. She left town the next morning."

"Where'd she go?"

"To a friend's house in over in Placerville. She said she wanted to take a few days before looking for work somewhere else. Can't say as I blame her."

"Do you have the friend's name?"

Benning glared. "Of course I do. What's with all the questions, Marshal Brown? I know how to do my job."

"No offense meant, sheriff." Jedidiah managed a smile. "As a lawman myself, I tend to be curious."

The sheriff relaxed his stiff posture. "All right, then. When are you fixing to leave for Denver?"

"The day after tomorrow."

"I'll see that Miss Calhoun is ready."

"I'd appreciate it." The conversation drifted into more neutral topics, and Jedidiah laughed in all the right places and kept a smile on his face. But all through the evening, one thought played over and over in his mind.

Why hadn't she told him about the housekeeper?

Chapter 3

Susannah didn't see Jedidiah again that day, nor did he wander into the jailhouse to annoy her the next morning. She was beginning to think she had imagined him.

In between visitors, she passed the day by flirting with Joe Horner, the deputy who sat in the outer office. Joe was a homely creature, and he blushed like a schoolboy whenever she teased him. Her plan was to distract him enough that she could lift the keys from his belt. Unfortunately, his shyness made him keep his distance from the cell.

She felt only the tiniest bit guilty for using his infatuation with her, since this was a matter of life and death: hers.

The only person who could clear her name

was Abigail Hawkins, and for some reason the woman had lied to the sheriff. Either she had killed Brick herself, or else she had seen the real murderer. Why else would she have left town like that? Susannah intended to find the woman, one way or another, and get the truth from her.

And obviously, she would do so alone.

As she packed her belongings in the small carpet bag the sheriff had brought for her trip to Denver, she tried not to resent Jedidiah for not believing her. It wasn't that he didn't deserve her resentment—he did. But she was a firm believer in not wasting emotion on useless causes, and Jedidiah Brown was the most useless cause she had ever encountered. He didn't deserve an ounce of her attention. He was beneath her. If he thought she would murder a man in cold blood, then he didn't know her at all.

Susannah wasn't certain why she felt hurt that he hadn't even tried to get to know her better.

She closed the carpetbag with a decisive snap. It certainly wasn't the first time a man had shown interest in her attractive outside without making an effort to get to know the person on the inside. Indeed, it was the story of her life. But for some reason, she had thought

Jedidiah would be different. And he just kept disappointing her.

"Going somewhere, Miss Calhoun?"

She looked up at the unfamiliar voice. A beefy, broad-shouldered man stood just outside her cell, with three other men standing just behind him. His clothes were store-bought and tailored, and he wore a gold watch and a thick gold pinky ring. His boots were shiny and unscuffed.

Money, was her first thought. This fellow had a lot of it.

"Do I know you?" she asked.

The man laughed, and it wasn't a nice sound. His small eyes narrowed above his bulbous nose as he gave her a toothy smile. "You may not know me, but you know my family. I'm Wayne Caldwell, Brick's brother."

Susannah stiffened. "I'm sorry about your brother, Mr. Caldwell."

"You ought to be sorry, you two-bit whore, since you killed him!"

Protestations of innocence died unspoken on her tongue. "That's to be determined by a trial."

"I heard all about how my parents are having you hauled back to Denver." He gripped the bars of her cell so tightly that she took a step back, half expecting him to bend them. "I'm not as patient as the rest of my family, sweetheart. I just want to see you hang."

His hostility was a live thing that threatened to choke her. Fear rose up, but she hid it behind a calm expression. She'd seen his kind before; men like him thrived on the dread they inspired in others.

"I'm sorry to disappoint you, Mr. Caldwell, but the law says I have to be tried before I can be hanged."

"Not my law." He signaled to one of his men, who came forward and slipped a key in the lock of the cell door.

The little snick of the door unlocking made her heart freeze in her breast. Then it pounded faster as terror shrieked through her veins. "What are you doing? Where's Deputy Horner?"

"He had a little accident." Wayne Caldwell opened the cell door and reached for her. "Just like you're going to."

She was going to die! She calculated the three-to-one odds as meaty hands gripped her arms and dragged her out of the cell. Unarmed, she had no chance of defending herself against them.

But at least she would go down fighting.

* * *

Jedidiah rode back into Silver Flats with a frown on his face. He didn't like the smell of things—not one bit.

He had gotten the address of Brick Caldwell's former housekeeper from the sheriff, and ridden over to have a talk with the woman who ran the boardinghouse where Mrs. Hawkins had lived. But Harriet Coleman hadn't been able to help him much. She had stated that Mrs. Hawkins had been agitated and in a hurry to leave Silver Flats. As soon as she had gotten the okay from the sheriff, she had lit out for Placerville to visit with her friend, Mrs. Rachelle Jenkins.

That was all he had been able to get out of her, and it was basically the same information the sheriff had given him.

Nothing was adding up the way it should. Susannah had insisted Abigail Hawkins had been present the night she had had supper with Brick Caldwell. Yet Mrs. Hawkins had testified that she had gone home hours before that incident, and her story had been verified by a witness. But the woman had been extremely jumpy during the investigation, and then she had lit out of town like the place was on fire. Perhaps it was simply the horror of finding her employer murdered that had upset her so, but Jedidiah had a feeling it was more than that.

He reined in outside the sheriff's office and tied up his horse, then entered the jailhouse to question Susannah about her side of the story. A groan drew his attention, and all thoughts of Mrs. Hawkins fled his mind when he saw a pair of booted feet sticking out from behind the desk.

Drawing his Colt, he knelt on the floor beside the fallen Deputy Horner. The man had been hit over the head, but it looked like he was coming around.

"I'm not going to make it easy for you!" he heard Susannah shout from the jail area.

There was a thud and then a screech. Jedidiah leaped to his feet and pressed himself against the wall next to the jailhouse door. Cautiously, he peered into the room.

Susannah's cell stood open, and three men were trying to subdue the enraged woman, who wielded her carpet bag like a weapon. She swung the bag at one man's head, then bit the hand of another who tried to grab her. A fourth man, dressed more richly than the other three, called out orders.

"Grab her, Clem! Goddammit, she's only a woman!"

"She's slippery," the man complained.

"She's a goddamn whore," the one in charge growled. "And she's gonna hang for killing my baby brother."

Jedidiah slipped through the doorway and aimed his gun at the fancy-dressed fellow. "Let the lady go, boys."

All heads turned toward him. The expression of surprise on the faces of the men holding Susannah would have been comical in a less critical situation. Susannah herself cast him a look of profound relief, then kicked one of her assailants in the leg, forcing him to release her arm to grab his own injured limb. The fellow holding her other arm followed suit before she could maim him. Head held high, Susannah marched over to stand beside Jedidiah.

"Don't just stand there," she hissed. "Shoot them!"

"Hush," was all he said, but the tone of it had her shutting her mouth and folding her arms across her chest. He never took his eyes from the four men across the room.

"Who the hell are you?" demanded the big fellow who was obviously the leader of the group.

"U.S. Marshal Jedidiah Brown," Jedidiah responded. "I don't believe I caught your name."

"Caldwell. Wayne Caldwell."

"A relation to Brick Caldwell, I assume?"

Caldwell puffed out his chest belligerently. "He was my brother."

"I see." Jedidiah looked from one man to the other, his gaze finally coming to rest on Caldwell once more. "Would you care to explain what's going on here?"

"Justice," Caldwell snarled.

"Justice? You consider four men against one woman to be justice?"

"That murdering bitch killed my brother in cold blood," Caldwell roared, pointing a finger at Susannah. "I mean to see that she pays for what she did."

Jedidiah stepped in front of Susannah. "That's the law's job, Mr. Caldwell."

"Then how come the law's not doing its job? How come my brother's killer is still alive?"

Jedidiah softened his voice. "Mr. Caldwell, I know you're grieving, but this isn't the way to see that justice is served. Why don't you and your men go on home, and we'll just forget this little incident."

Caldwell scowled and hesitated. There was a long moment of silence while Jedidiah held Caldwell's gaze. Then the other man looked away, obviously realizing the wisdom in letting the matter drop. "Fine," he grumbled. "I'll go on home. But I'll see *you* in Denver." He again pointed at Susannah, his narrowed eyes gleaming with hate. "And I'll wear my Sunday clothes to your hanging!"

Susannah stayed behind Jedidiah as Caldwell and his men passed by. Once they heard the door slam behind them, Jedidiah turned to face her.

"You're just a magnet for trouble, aren't you?"

She gaped. "Surely you're not blaming *me* for this?"

He took her chin in his hand and studied her face. "A woman as beautiful as you makes a man do crazy things. Did they hurt you?"

"No." She stepped back, and his hand dropped to his side. "So you *are* blaming me. How typical."

"There's nothing typical about me, princess. I'm surprised you haven't figured that out yet."

She gave him a haughty look that seemed to suit her exotic features. "On the contrary, Marshal Brown, I find you utterly typical."

He chuckled. "Don't make me prove you wrong. You might like it a little too much."

"Savage!" She dismissed him with a look. "I see your manners haven't improved over the past few months."

"And I see you're just as spoiled and conceited as ever."

She made a sound halfway between a squeak and a scream. "Spoiled? Conceited?"

"Exactly." Sliding his pistol back into the holster, he took her arm and pulled her toward the empty cell. "Time to go back in your cage, Miss Calhoun."

She dug in her heels, but he managed to shove her into the cell and slam the door. She surged forward, gripping the bars as he grabbed the keys off the wall and locked the cell. "Is this how you treat all your prisoners, marshal? I'm surprised they haven't arrested *you* yet!"

"No, princess, you're a special case."

"I'm so flattered," she said with biting sarcasm.

"You ought to be," he replied. "You're lucky I don't tan your hide for holding out on me."

"I don't know what you're talking about."

Jedidiah leaned close to the bars. "Why didn't you tell me about Mrs. Hawkins?"

She stiffened. "What about her?"

"Sheriff Benning says that you told him that Mrs. Hawkins was there the night you had supper with Caldwell. Is that true?"

"What does it matter?" she retorted. "The sheriff has a witness who says otherwise. And what's the word of a suspected killer against a reliable witness?"

"You should have told me."

"Why?" she shot back. "So that you could ac-

cuse me of making up stories to save my skin?
I'd do better without your help, Marshal
Brown."

"Let me tell you something, princess," he
said softly. "Right now, I'm the best friend you
have in the world."

"Then I'm in worse trouble than I thought."

He stared at her for a long time. "I don't
know why I waste my time with you. If it
weren't for your sister . . ."

"Feel free to leave any time, marshal," she
said, her eyes icy with disdain.

"I will leave . . . when I take you to Denver."
He turned toward the office, where faint sounds
of movement told him that Deputy Horner was
regaining consciousness.

"And when will that be?" she called after him.

He didn't even glance over his shoulder. "I'll
let you know."

Susannah waited, but though voices drifted
back to the jail, Jedidiah didn't return.

She stared out the window at the setting sun,
still shaken by the encounter with Caldwell. If
Jedidiah hadn't returned when he had, she knew
she'd have been dangling from a tree somewhere. She raised a hand to her throat, fully
aware that only chance—and Jedidiah Brown—
had saved her from a hangman's noose.

Or had her execution merely been delayed?

She had no choice; she had to escape tonight.

Caldwell would return; she had no doubt about that. And he would bring more men with him next time. She had no intention of being there when he did.

She looked down at the keys in her hand, the keys she had picked up off the floor during the struggle. The keys she had slipped into her bodice to hide from Jedidiah.

These were the keys to her freedom. And later that night, as the town slept, she would use them.

Jedidiah had planned to take Susannah on the stage to Colorado Springs, and from there catch the train to Denver. Now that Wayne Caldwell had entered the picture, he discarded that plan.

Wayne had shown some smarts by backing off, but Jedidiah knew he'd be back. His kind always came back. The trick was to get Susannah out of town before Caldwell regrouped.

Jedidiah yanked on the straps of his saddlebags, double checking that all his gear was secure and buckled tight. His Palomino stood patiently, used to such behavior. A second horse, a sturdy little paint, waited nearby, saddled and ready to go. After Jedidiah finished, he led both horses out of the livery and into the night.

Trains and stages ran on schedules. They were predictable and could be intercepted. But two people on horseback, picking their own winding trail to Denver, would be a lot harder to track.

He'd already spoken to Benning about his plan to leave in the middle of the night and gotten his agreement. He only hoped Susannah didn't give him any trouble. If she did, he'd be forced to bind and gag her, and darned if part of him wouldn't enjoy the experience. The woman had a mouth on her that could bring a man the utmost pleasure or tear him to ribbons. Unfortunately, she seemed oblivious to the first and far too inclined to the second.

He left the horses tied up behind the dry goods store and crept over to the jail, keeping to the shadows. He wouldn't put it past Caldwell to have a man watching the jailhouse.

It's what he would have done.

The creak of a door made him freeze in the shadow of the building. He drew his gun and watched as a figure slipped out of the sheriff's office. The person was too small to be Deputy Horner or Sheriff Benning, and it certainly wasn't Caldwell.

The swish of a skirt reached his ears as the person approached. Jedidiah muttered a curse and shoved his gun back in its holster. He reached into his pocket, then stepped out in front of the obviously feminine figure. Her perfume reached him before she did, the sweetness of jasmine sprinkled with a hint of spice.

He grinned at her shocked gasp, and she dropped the carpetbag she carried. He took her wrist.

"Evening, Miss Calhoun," he said, slapping the handcuffs closed. "I see you're ready to go."

Chapter 4

"**W**hat are you doing here?" Susannah hissed, her pulse pounding from the scare he'd given her when he'd stepped out of the darkness. "Get these things off me!"

He smiled, his teeth a flash of white in the shadowed planes of his face. "I told you I was going to escort you to Denver. And here you are, all packed and ready to go."

"I'm not going anywhere with you. Now, take these things off!"

"You know I can't do that." He took her arm, then bent down and scooped her bag from the ground. "You wouldn't want me to lose my job, would you?"

"If you don't let me go, I'll lose my *life*!" She

51

dug in her heels as he half-dragged her behind the dry goods store where the horses stood waiting. "Darn it, Jedidiah Brown, don't you hear what I'm saying?"

"I hear." Keeping his grip on her arm, he hooked her bag over the saddlehorn, then turned his complete attention on her. "Listen up, princess—I'm going to see justice done, no matter what. That's my job. Do you understand me?"

Fear streaked through her. Jedidiah Brown always got his man—or woman—and his efficiency did not bode well for her escape plans. Perhaps if she annoyed him enough he might turn his back on her, and she could break away.

"You don't let yourself feel anything, do you, marshal?" she jeered. "I'm just one more prisoner to bring in, one more fugitive retrieved to add to your impressive record. You don't even care that I didn't do it."

He stilled, and though she couldn't see his face in the darkness, she knew she had hit her mark.

"It's not my job to judge," he said softly.

"I don't much like your job, marshal."

"You don't have to like it," he replied. "Now, get up on this horse before the whole town wakes up. Or do you want Wayne Caldwell riding over here to see what all the commotion is?"

Her next remark died on her lips. As long as

she was on her own, she would be easy prey for Wayne Caldwell and his brand of justice. But if she went with Jedidiah, she would be able to get beyond Wayne Caldwell's reach. Then she could slip away from Jedidiah and go find Abigail Hawkins.

Her chances of escaping Marshal Brown were very slim, but they were definitely better than her chances of surviving another encounter with Wayne Caldwell.

Which meant she would have to change her game plan and go with Jedidiah after all. Surrender didn't sit well with her, so she stuck her nose in the air and gave Jedidiah her best princess-to-peasant attitude. "And just how do you expect me to mount with handcuffs on?"

Cupping his hands together, he drawled, "Luckily you have a gentleman on hand to assist you, ma'am."

"That's a matter of opinion." She grabbed the pommel with both hands and set her foot into his cupped palms. He boosted her easily into the saddle, as if she weighed no more than her carpet bag, and she tried to ignore the skip in her pulse at his strength.

The man was a boor, she reminded herself, and brute strength often went hand in hand with boorishness. Then he guided her feet into the stirrups as gently as if they were made of glass, and a warm flush of weakness swept through her. She fought to hold onto her negative opinion of him.

Jedidiah mounted his Palomino with fluid ease, then leaned over and caught the reins of her horse.

"I am fully capable of managing my own mount, marshal," she said, annoyed that she wouldn't be able to kick into a gallop and leave him in the dust.

He chuckled. "I'm well aware of that—which is why I'll be leading you until we get to Denver."

"Why couldn't they have sent a stupid one?" she muttered beneath her breath.

Jedidiah's deep chuckle echoed in her ears as he led her out of the sleeping town and into the night.

Silence reigned between them for hours as the first rosy fingers of dawn crept over the horizon. Several times, Jedidiah looked behind him to make sure Susannah was still there. He had never known her to be so quiet. But there she was, calmly sitting astride her horse as if she were out for a leisurely Sunday ride, instead of being escorted to a murder trial. He thought she was engrossed in her own thoughts, but then she lifted her gaze to his, and he was drawn to her despite himself.

He pulled up a little and let her horse fall into step with his. Even at this early hour of the morning, the woman looked stunning. The pink glow of early dawn lent radiance to her complexion, and a certain softness that made her look like an angel. She wore her blond hair loosely tied back from her face, but a few curls brushed her cheeks and brow in enticing disarray. Her china doll looks could make the harshest judge believe in her innocence, if not for the keen intelligence that lurked in her smoky blue eyes, and that stubborn line to her pouty mouth.

She was a smart one all right, and had dressed for her escape in a sensible brown skirt and matching jacket over a white shirtwaist, with a wide-brimmed hat and brown kid boots. She arched one golden brow as Jedidiah continued to stare at her.

"Something wrong, marshal?"

"Not a thing," he answered with a grin. "I was just thinking how pretty you look today."

Her lips curved and a sly gleam came into her eyes. "Why, thank you, marshal. I must admit, you look quite handsome yourself."

He touched his hat brim. "Nice of you to say so." He paused. "Yes, ma'am, mighty pretty— no one would ever figure you for a killer."

In the blink of an eye, her sweet smile changed to a furious scowl, and her eyes took on a chill that would have made the most vicious gunfighter fall back. No angel here—except perhaps the angel of vengeance.

He laughed at her fury. "Yes indeed, unless you get that look on your face, a body would think you couldn't even crush an ant without crying. Luckily, I know you better."

"You barely know me at all, marshal," she corrected tightly. "As I recall, we didn't have enough time to get to know each other. You left Burr that morning without a word to anyone."

He tipped back his hat. "I'm a marshal, princess, and I had a prisoner in custody. I couldn't stick around Wyoming Territory even if I'd wanted to."

"A convenient excuse, marshal. You didn't even have the manners to say good-bye before you took off in the middle of the night!"

"What's the matter? Did you miss me?"

She stiffened in the saddle. "Don't be ridiculous. Sarah and Jack, however, were disappointed that you hadn't stopped in to say good-bye."

"You didn't miss me at all? Not even after that sweet kiss we shared?"

"I don't know what you're talking about."

"Oh, you know, all right," he growled. "But if you've got any ideas about working your wiles on me while you're in custody, you can just forget them."

Her mouth fell open, and her eyes widened. "Marshal Brown, I thought no such thing!"

"Didn't you?" He pulled up, stopping both their mounts in the middle of the road, and leaned toward her "You use that beauty of yours to get your way the same way a gunfighter uses his gun, Susannah Calhoun. It's not going to work on me, because I know how you are. Do we understand each other?"

She stared at him for a long moment. "You don't know how I am, marshal," she finally said quietly. "All my life, people have overreacted to the way I look. Don't condemn me for using a gift like that to my advantage. Everyone does it. It's called survival."

"There's more to you than your looks," he scoffed. "You're intelligent and resourceful, too, so don't act like you don't know it."

She looked as surprised as if he had just plucked the sun from the sky and handed it to her. "I wouldn't dream of it," she finally whispered.

"Good. Everyone else may underestimate you, but I don't. Do we understand each other?"

"Perfectly," she said softly.

She looked almost vulnerable, but Susannah

Calhoun was a consummate actress. He wouldn't put it past her to try and lull him into a false sense of security with her lost little girl expression.

Well, he wasn't about to fall for that. He kicked the horses back into an easy trot, letting her mount fall into line behind his. Susannah had gotten too used to manipulating other people with her looks. She knew she was in more trouble than she could handle, but had she asked for his help? No. Had she told him there was a witness who might be able to clear her name? No.

If she had simply asked for his help, sincerely and without any games, he would have told her that he planned to locate Abigail Hawkins and find out the truth. But instead she had alternately insulted him and cajoled him, never once just talking straight with him.

If he were a different kind of man, he might be bedazzled by that siren's face and body. But he was U.S. Marshal Jedidiah Brown, and he always moved on when the job was done.

No woman, not even one who looked like an angel and had the cunning of the devil, could keep him tied down.

The sooner he cleared her name and got the hell away from her, the better it would be for both of them.

* * *

He thought she was intelligent.

Susannah stared blindly at Jedidiah's back as he rode ahead. She had been complimented on her eyes, her hair, her complexion, and her figure countless times, but never had anyone complimented her mind.

Intelligent and resourceful, he had said.

She placed a hand over her pounding heart and took a deep breath. This melting feeling could not be good, or this desire to get closer to this contradictory man. Just because he was perceptive enough to see past her looks as no one else ever had was no reason to get all excited.

But all her life she had been looking for a man who would go beyond the pretty face and care for the person she was inside. How ironic that she should find such a man here, now. Jedidiah was wrong for her in every way—yet that didn't stop her from wanting to explore this new attraction.

She didn't know how to approach him. Flirtatious smiles and coy glances didn't work with this man. And she knew that he would doubt her sincerity if she tried to get to know him better.

The best thing to do was to stay away from him. Not only was he a distraction, but he had the power to hurt her as no man had ever had before.

She had to escape as soon as she had the opportunity. No matter what it took.

They stopped to eat at mid-afternoon and shared a simple meal of sandwiches and fruit in silence. Susannah was tiring. She had left the jail in the middle of the night, and they had ridden straight through the morning. Jedidiah, on the other hand, didn't seem to feel fatigued at all. He sat with his back to a rock, biting into an apple while scanning the area, his rifle across his lap.

She studied him as she bit into her own apple. Even though she was irritated with him, she was also very much aware of him as a man. What was it about him that drew her so? He was attractive, to be sure, but there were many attractive men in the world. Men who didn't scramble her thinking or incite this disturbing push and pull of emotion. Jedidiah had lingered in her thoughts long after he had left Burr, and she was beginning to suspect he had lingered in her heart as well, despite her best efforts to dislodge him.

He turned his head to look at her with those cool, dark eyes that saw so much more than she intended, and her heart gave one slow roll of yearning in her chest.

Panic surged through her. She couldn't start feeling this way again. Not here. Not now. She turned her gaze away and studied the distant mountains.

When they were done eating, Jedidiah wordlessly cleaned up the camp so there was no evidence that anyone had ever been there. He once more helped Susannah to mount, and she felt that fluttering of her pulse again at his casual strength. This time she allowed herself to enjoy the thrill, reminding herself that after tomorrow, she would have left him far behind.

They rode several more hours in silence. As the sun sank lower toward the horizon, Susannah drooped in her saddle. At this rate, she'd be in no condition to make her escape, only to sleep!

Just when she was about to ask Jedidiah to stop, he pulled up, reaching out a hand to halt her horse as well. Just over the rise ahead of them, she spotted a wispy curl of smoke.

"Looks like we've got company," he said in a low tone. "Be ready."

"For what?"

He sent her a cold-eyed glance that sent a trickle of fear through her. "If it's Caldwell, be ready to run for your life."

"What would he be doing out here?" she asked, hating the apprehension that gripped her.

"Looking for you." He flipped her horse's reins back over the paint's head, giving her control of her mount. Then he slid his rifle out of the saddle holster and held it barrel down along the length of his leg. "Stay behind me. If there's shooting, you run."

"I thought you were taking me to Denver," she joked half-heartedly.

"I am. But I'd like you to be alive when I do." He pulled his hat low on his head and glanced over his shoulder at her. "Remember, stay behind me."

"No problem there, marshal." She clenched her fingers around the reins. As tempted as she was to bolt, she knew that if it *was* Caldwell up ahead, she was much safer with Jedidiah than on her own.

He gave her a small smile, then set his horse to a slow amble over the rise. Susannah followed.

As they came up over the hill, the source of the smoke became visible. A covered wagon sat at the side of the road, and there were a couple of rabbits roasting on a spit over a nearby fire. No one was in evidence.

Susannah glanced at Jedidiah. His entire posture was tense with readiness, and she knew that he would give his life to defend hers. The knowledge added to the confusing mass of feelings that she had for Jedidiah Brown.

How could a man be so hateful and yet so noble? How could he be so strong but so gentle, too? How could he be so uncaring of her innocence, yet be willing to protect her life, even if it meant sacrificing his? Jedidiah was like a chameleon who changed to adapt to any situation in which he found himself. No doubt that talent had kept him alive all these years, but keeping up with his changeable moods was driving her to distraction.

A high-pitched giggle echoed around them, and Jedidiah's head snapped toward the camp. A little girl ran from behind the wagon. A man chased after her, catching her up in his arms, making growling noises as he buried his face in her belly to her shrieks of laughter.

"The Papa-monster's got you, Lizzie!" He tickled her and made exaggerated chomping noises. "The Papa-monster loves little girls for supper!"

Susannah watched Jedidiah's posture relax as the little girl giggled hysterically. A woman climbed out of the covered wagon, wiping her hands on her apron.

"Samuel, don't you get her all churned up before supper," the woman said. "Otherwise she won't go to sleep when she's supposed to!"

"Aw, Maggie . . ." the man began. Then he caught sight of Jedidiah. He put the little girl on the ground and pushed her behind him. "Evening, folks," he said to them, his expression wary.

"Evening," Jedidiah replied. "Sorry to intrude. We saw your campfire. I'm U.S. Marshal Jedidiah Brown." He pulled open his duster so the man could see the star pinned to his chest.

"Sam Ferguson," the man said, visibly relaxing. "Can we help you with something, Marshal Brown?"

"We were just looking for a place to stop for the night."

"You're welcome to bed down here if you want," Ferguson said. "Would you care for some supper?"

"That's mighty kind of you." Jedidiah doffed his hat and smiled at the woman with all the charm of his Southern upbringing. "That is, if it's not an imposition on your lovely wife."

The woman blushed. "Not at all, marshal. Do set with us a spell."

"Thank you kindly, ma'am." Jedidiah dismounted and grabbed the bridle of Susannah's horse, leading them both forward.

"That your missus?" Ferguson asked, staring at Susannah. The man's eyes widened with admiration, and his mouth fell slackly open. Mrs. Ferguson nervously smoothed her skirts and patted her hair. Little Lizzie came out from behind her father and ran up to Susannah's horse.

"Are you an angel?" she asked with wonder.

Susannah smiled down at the child. "No, I'm Susannah."

Jedidiah glanced at the Fergusons with ill-concealed irritation. They'd never be able to keep Caldwell off their trail if every mother's son in the state reacted like these people. The woman was too darned memorable!

"She's not my wife and she's certainly no angel. She's my prisoner," he announced.

Susannah flushed with mortification as he came over and made a show of helping her down off the horse. The clink of the handcuffs seemed to shake the family from their fog of admiration.

"Hard to believe someone that pretty is a criminal, marshal," Ferguson said.

"Believe me, looks can be deceiving," Jedidiah said. "What we have here is the Black Widow of Barton Falls. She did away with three husbands, so if I were you, I'd keep the eating knives away from her."

Chapter 5

For the first time in her life, Susannah Calhoun was being ignored.

Jedidiah sat with the Fergusons, eating roast rabbit and conversing amiably, while she, Susannah, sat on the other side of the fire eating supper with her hands. Thanks to Jedidiah's ridiculous tall tale, they hadn't even allowed her a spoon!

She grew even more infuriated. The Black Widow of Barton Falls? What kind of nonsense was that? His labeling her a three-time husband killer made it perfectly clear what Jedidiah really thought of her: he thought she was the type of woman who led men on and then broke their hearts.

A bite of rabbit stuck in her throat as emotion

67

welled up. She had no idea why she should even care what he thought of her. As much as he fascinated her, he also irritated her beyond belief. All her life, she had been able to get men to do exactly what she wanted. But not Jedidiah Brown. He seemed determined to do the opposite of what she wanted him to do.

Clearly she was wasting her time staying with him for his dubious protection. They were far enough away from Silver Flats that she should be able to make it on her own. She knew Abigail Hawkins had headed for Placerville, which wasn't far from where they were now. She would find a way to sneak off tonight.

As Susannah swallowed the last bite of supper, Mrs. Ferguson produced dessert—a batch of cookies they had traded for in the last town. Though she wasn't offered any, Susannah couldn't help but smile as she watched Jedidiah eagerly reach for one. She'd never known a man yet who hadn't fallen into a sound sleep after eating a hearty meal. Once the marshal had bedded down for the night, she would make her escape.

Jedidiah knew that if looks could kill, he'd have been dead already.

Susannah was sitting isolated on the other side of the fire and had been sending him dagger-like glances throughout the entire meal. No doubt she wasn't used to being ignored, but the sooner she learned to keep a low profile, the better off they'd be. Hopefully, the story he'd told Ferguson would help to keep Caldwell off their trail.

But he doubted it.

He'd told the story partly to protect them from Caldwell, but also to rile Susannah. He loved the way her eyes glittered and her cheeks flushed when she was annoyed at him. Though he had no business getting involved with the woman, he just couldn't seem to help himself.

She sent him another of those looks, then she smiled as he reached for another molasses cookie. He didn't trust that smile. What deviltry was the woman planning now?

He finished the cookie in short order, then stood and stretched.

"Ma'am, that was a delicious supper," he said to Mrs. Ferguson, who beamed at him. "But we need to be going now."

Sam Ferguson sent Susannah a wary look. "You keep that dangerous criminal under close watch, marshal."

Susannah glared at the man, who flinched. Jedidiah reached over and took Susannah's arm, tugging her to her feet.

"Don't worry, Sam," he said. "She only kills her own husbands. Your family is safe."

Susannah's mouth fell open, and Jedidiah squeezed her arm in warning. The last thing he needed was Susannah ruining the false trail he had left for Caldwell.

"Come on," he said, tugging her toward the mounts. "I'm tired."

Susannah let him lead her along, then paused before Mrs. Ferguson. "Thank you for supper," she said.

The woman gave a curt nod in response. The evident disapproval brought a look of distress to Susannah's face. Then, holding her head high, she followed Jedidiah from the camp.

They reached the horses, and Jedidiah stopped her as she raised her foot to the stirrup. "Are you all right?"

"Fine, marshal," she replied frostily. "Will you help me mount or will you leave me to further humiliation?"

He stared down at her, so proud even in adversity, and something shifted inside him. Gently, he reached out and brushed a loosened curl from her brow. She stood still beneath his touch, staring stonily at him.

"I'm sorry," he said quietly. He had meant only to protect her with his ridiculous tale, not to hurt her.

She nodded stiffly. Jedidiah started to say more, but then thought better of it. Without another word, he bent and cupped his hands, boosting her into the saddle. She took up the reins, staring ahead like a queen awaiting her entourage. He mounted and brought his horse alongside hers.

She extended her reins to him.

"You know how to ride," he said shortly, then urged the Palomino to a trot. Susannah sat there for a long moment before following.

They made camp up in the hills. Jedidiah built a small fire as Susannah sat on a nearby boulder.

The sun had set, and the first tiny stars already twinkled in the black velvet sky. Susannah watched as Jedidiah removed the tack from each animal, his movements sure and smooth, his voice low as he murmured to them.

The fire flickered over his face as he rubbed down each horse. Despite herself, Susannah started to relax. Yes, she was annoyed at the man for humiliating her, but there was something soothing about his slow, steady movements as he performed so mundane a task. Fatigue weighed on her. She was simply so tired—physically, mentally, emotionally. All she wanted now was rest—and her good name back.

She frowned down at the handcuffs on her wrists. To make up a story like he had told the Fergusons . . . it still stung that he had such a low opinion of her. Now she wasn't only considered a killer, but a man-hater as well!

She turned her gaze once more on Jedidiah. The man confused her.

She tried to hate him. She wished he weren't so intelligent, neatly anticipating and intercepting every attempt to escape him, yet she grudgingly respected his quick wits. She wished he weren't so strong, since he could easily overpower her physically. But she had to admit that his strength also made her feel protected. She really shouldn't feel so attracted to him—but she did.

He moved around the camp, setting out the bedrolls with an efficiency that bespoke years of experience. She watched as he smoothed the blankets with strong hands—hands that could manage a gun or a woman with equal expertise. Either way, Jedidiah Brown was lethal.

He sat down on the bedroll and took off his hat, running a hand through his long hair. The flames played over the wheat-colored strands and shadowed the sharp planes of his face as he glanced up at the night sky. In the flickering light, she could see the lines around his eyes and mouth. How much of it was from years of riding the trail beneath the merciless sun, and how much from hard living? He turned to look at her suddenly, his sherry-colored eyes seeming dark and mysterious as he met her gaze across the fire.

The seconds ticked by. Susannah's heart pounded and her mouth grew dry as awareness pulsed between them. Slowly he rose and came around to her side of the fire. Her pulse skipped erratically as he approached, and she wondered what was wrong with her. She had been in the company of men much more attractive than Jedidiah without feeling as if her heart were about to explode from her chest!

Yet as he stopped before her, prickles of sensation swept across her flesh, making her feel as if her skin were suddenly too small for her body. He stood there for a moment, looking down at her, then he crouched so that their faces were level.

Reaching into his pocket, he pulled out the key to the handcuffs and unlocked them. He removed the metal bracelets, setting them on the ground at his feet, then took her hands in his, rubbing her chafed wrists with his thumbs.

Her breath caught at his gentle caress. The tiny sound caught his attention, and he met her gaze.

"I'm sorry about today," he said quietly. "I told that story to throw Caldwell off our trail. I didn't realize it would hurt you."

She only nodded, so confused by her own emotions that anything she said was sure to come out horribly wrong.

He continued to stroke his thumbs over the red marks left by the handcuffs. "You're such a strong woman," he continued. "It's hard to remember sometimes that you have feelings just like the rest of us."

Strong? He thought her strong? A sob escaped Susannah's lips, and tears stung her eyes. She had never felt more vulnerable in her entire life!

"Hey now, what's this?" He brushed a lone tear from her cheek. "Come on now, angel, don't cry. Yell at me. Insult me like you always do. I'll even let you kick me, but *please* don't cry!"

She sniffled, trying desperately to control herself. She refused to break down in front of him; her pride wouldn't allow it. "I'm *not* crying."

He eyed her skeptically. "All right, you're not crying."

She took a deep breath and sat up straight, hoping her nose wasn't red as a beet from the brief sniffle. "I'm not crying," she repeated. "I'm fine."

"Susannah, you're more than fine," he said with admiration. "Any other woman would have been leaking buckets by now."

"Well, I'm not any other woman," she said.

He reached out a hand to gently touch her hair, her face. "You can say that again."

She swallowed, and her lips parted as his fingers lingered, trailed along her jaw. She didn't dare move, didn't dare breathe, lest she disturb the strange current that flowed between them. She looked into his eyes and saw the same need, the same confusion, that she felt.

"I must be crazy," he murmured, sliding a hand beneath her hair at her nape. Then he leaned forward and kissed her, his lips soft and sweet, clinging to hers with a tenderness that shook both of them.

Her eyes slid closed. She should push him away. But the kiss wasn't threatening, and the passion she sensed inside him remained firmly under his control. Still, the magic of his touch seduced her, and for just a moment she indulged her need for the comfort of his caress.

She grazed her fingers along his arm, needing to touch him.

He broke the kiss and stared into her eyes for a long moment. Then he stood. "This is not a good idea," he said, his voice a rough whisper. "Why don't you go on over behind those rocks and take care of your private needs, while I finish setting up camp?"

"All right." She slowly rose and smoothed her skirts with trembling fingers. The sweetness of the kiss had shaken her down to her soul, and she struggled to go on as if everything was normal. "It's been a long day, marshal."

"You can say that again," he agreed. "Go on and do what you have to do, then we can both get some sleep."

He turned away and went to finish laying out the bedrolls. Susannah stared after him for a moment, then went to relieve herself behind the rocks.

His pretty apology and the toe-curling impact of his kiss hadn't changed things a bit. She still intended to escape custody and find Abigail Hawkins. Nothing could be permitted to distract her from that goal.

Any other path—including the one toward Jedidiah—would only lead to the hangman's noose.

* * *

Jedidiah took care of his own needs behind a nearby boulder, then returned to the camp and prepared to retrieve Susannah if necessary. But she surprised him; she promptly returned.

She settled down on the bedroll next to his. He handed her the carpet bag—from which he had already removed such dangerous articles as a jeweled brooch and some hat pins—and watched out of the corner of his eye as she rummaged around and came up with the silver-backed hairbrush he'd seen in the jail cell. She gave a sigh of pleasure as she released her hair from its confines. It settled over her shoulders in a soft cloud of moonlit blond that fell to the middle of her back. Eyes closed, she began brushing her hair, a half smile of pleasure on her lips.

Jedidiah felt a tightening in his groin as he watched her. She looked like some sort of fairy creature, with her porcelain-smooth skin and silver-gilt hair. Her lips curved in a private, feminine smile that made him want to touch her intimately and learn all her secrets.

He could still taste her.

A man couldn't live almost forty years on this earth and not have seen his share of beautiful women. He'd even bedded a few of them. But there was something about this woman, something intrinsic to who she was and *how* she was, that made her damned near irresistible to him.

The fact that she had the face of an angel and the body of a sinner only added icing to the cake.

She turned her head this way and that, brushing her hair until every snarl and tangle was gone. He wanted to take the brush from her hand, wanted to feel the silky strands slip through his fingers as he ran the brush through her hair. It was all he could do not to reach across and make his fantasy a reality.

If he weren't a lawman and she weren't his prisoner, he could have indulged all his passions without a qualm. As it was, he had already overstepped his boundaries. She was his responsibility, and he wouldn't take advantage of that.

But he was surely tempted.

She put the brush back in the carpetbag and pulled out a mirror and a handkerchief. Peering into the mirror, she delicately dabbed at the dust on her face. Jedidiah watched her in silence for a moment before he held out his hand for the handkerchief.

Her expression puzzled, she handed it to him. He splashed a bit of water from his canteen on the lacy white scrap, then handed it back to her. She gave him a delighted smile and used the dampened cloth to wash the trail dust from her face and throat.

When she turned away and flicked open a couple of the buttons on her shirtwaist and ran the cloth over her bosom, Jedidiah grew even more aroused. He shifted, trying to make himself more comfortable, and wondered what she would do if he offered to hold her clothes while she washed the rest of her body. He grinned at the thought of her maidenly outrage. He was tempted to suggest it just to see what she'd do.

Susannah turned toward him, suspicion on her face. "What are you chuckling about?"

"Not a thing. I sure am beat, though. Are you done prettying yourself up, or are you going to put on more of a show for me?" He gestured at her shirtwaist.

She glanced down at her open buttons, gasped, and quickly began to close her blouse. A becoming flush crept over her cheeks as she kept her eyes steadily on her task.

"Sure is a shame to cover up such a pretty sight," he drawled.

"You are a hideous man," she snapped.

"Now, princess, there are women from here to Texas who would disagree with you on that."

"I really have no interest in your women, marshal." She set the carpetbag aside and made a show of adjusting her skirts as she prepared to lay down on the bedroll.

Good Lord, she was hard to resist when she was all snotty and in a temper. He reached out and took her hand. She whipped around to face him.

"What are you doing?" she asked haughtily, but he heard the breathlessness behind the question. Her fingers trembled in his. She wasn't as unaffected as she appeared to be.

"Looks like I'm holding your hand," he said.

"Well, stop it." She tried to pull her hand from his, but he didn't release her. "Jedidiah, let me go right now!"

He grinned at her. "Say that again."

"Let me go."

He arched his brows. "Not that. My name."

She rolled her eyes.

He stroked her palm with his thumb. "Say it, Susannah."

She sighed in exasperation. "Marshal Brown—"

"Not like that." He turned her hand over and splayed open her fingers so that he could trace lazy circles over her palm. "Say my name, Susannah. Please."

She closed her eyes and whispered, "Jedidiah."

He pressed his thumb against the pulse at her

wrist and found it racing. "I'll take care of you, Susannah. You just have to trust me."

Her eyes opened. "How can I?" she whispered. "You think I'm guilty."

"I think you're capable of doing it," he corrected. "That's a long way from guilty. I also think you're too beautiful and too smart for your own good. And I think that we had both best go to sleep, or else Caldwell will find us easy pickings when he catches up with us."

"Do you think he *will* catch up?"

"Eventually." Jedidiah rubbed the fading red mark the handcuff had left on her wrist. "The problem is, no matter what story I spread around to cover our trail, everyone is going to remember you. And Caldwell doesn't strike me as stupid."

"Sometimes I wish I had been born ugly," she said bitterly. "This face gets me into too much trouble."

"I think you're putting too much store in your looks," he said. "There's more to you than pretty packaging."

"My entire life, all I've heard about is how pretty I am and how easily I'd be able to catch a husband," she said bitterly. "But what if I don't want a husband? What if I want to do something with my life besides become some man's ornament?"

"From what I've seen, you have the brains and guts to do whatever you set your mind to."

"Why are you the only one who can see that?" she asked, her voice uneven with emotion. "Everyone has always been more preoccupied with the color of my eyes than with any opinions I might have. Sarah was always considered the smart one. I was the pretty one."

He snorted. "No one in this world is just any one thing. Your sister is as pretty as you are, just in a different way. And you're both smart enough to give a man fits. Look at all the trouble you're giving me!"

She raised her brows. "I beg to differ. I've been a model prisoner, marshal."

"You've been a pain in the—suffice it to say that you are one hell of a woman, Susannah Calhoun."

A blush of pleasure spread across her face. "Thank you."

"That said, you'll understand when I tell you that I don't underestimate a woman of your considerable talents."

He pulled the handcuffs from his pocket and closed one bracelet around her wrist with a final-sounding click. He locked the other cuff around his own wrist. "This is so you don't get any ideas about wandering off in the middle of the night," he said as her eyes started to simmer with thwarted anger. "Sweet dreams, now."

He lay back on the bedroll, the short chain pulling her down and tumbling her onto her own blanket with a squeak of surprise. He arranged his Colt beside him, then lay back and placed his hat on his face.

"Don't stay awake too late," he advised. "We have a long day ahead of us."

"Go to hell!" she snapped.

He chuckled and closed his eyes for some much-needed rest.

Chapter 6

❦

Placerville was a small but growing town whose economy depended on the nearby silver mines. The streets were crowded with miners, and every other building was a restaurant, boardinghouse, or saloon.

Susannah hoped Abigail Hawkins was still in the area. The sooner she cleared her name, the sooner she would be free of Jedidiah's constant company.

As she rode into town behind Jedidiah, she became aware of people staring and pointing. She was quite used to her appearance causing a stir, and turned a smile on the nearest male bystanders. To her shock, they glared at her in disgust and turned away to mutter amongst themselves. It was the same with every person she saw. She glanced at Jedidiah and saw that the townspeople's reaction hadn't escaped his notice; he frowned as he gazed from face to face.

She urged her mount forward until she rode beside him. "I don't like this," she whispered. "Why is everyone looking at me like that?"

"I don't know." Jedidiah flipped open the snap on his gun holster just in case. "There's the sheriff's office. Let's go talk to him."

Susannah fell back and let him lead her through the congested street. She kept her eyes on Jedidiah's back, but she could feel the hostility of the townspeople as if it were a living thing.

Outside the sheriff's office, Jedidiah dismounted and tied up both their horses, then helped Susannah down. They stepped up onto the wooden sidewalk, Jedidiah's hand on Susannah's arm. At this range, it was obvious to all who watched that she wore handcuffs.

"It's her!" someone whispered loudly.

"Easy to see how she led those men to their demise," another muttered.

"The Black Widow of Barton Falls here in our town!" a third exclaimed. "Think we'll be famous?"

Susannah's steps faltered. The Black Widow

of Barton Falls? She turned to look at Jedidiah, who wore an expression of startled guilt.

"*Now* look what you've done!" she hissed.

"Get inside." With a wary look at the crowd, Jedidiah shoved her into the sheriff's office, slamming the door behind them.

"What can I do for you, folks?" The sheriff rose from behind his desk. He was a big man, rather handsome, with slick black hair and dark eyes. A shiny silver badge adorned his white shirt, and a six gun nestled against his thigh.

Jedidiah stepped forward, hand extended. "I'm U.S. Marshal Jedidiah Brown," he said. "This is my prisoner. I was wondering if I could borrow your jail for a spell."

The sheriff shook Jedidiah's hand. "I'm Sheriff Barkley Jones. You must be the marshal we've heard tell about." He turned a considering glance on Susannah. "And you must be the Black Widow of Barton Falls. A lot of folks have gotten stirred up about the news of you passing through these parts."

Susannah waited for Jedidiah to correct the sheriff's mistaken impression.

"Then you can see why I'd like to borrow your jail for a bit," he said, to her astonishment. "I have business to attend to here in town, and I don't want a mob getting to my prisoner."

Susannah let out a squeak of dismay that made the sheriff stare at her.

Jedidiah pretended not to notice her.

"I don't blame you for wanting to lock this pretty thing up," the sheriff chuckled. "Fact is, a lot of men are all bent out of shape at the thought of a husband killer in town."

"I noticed that."

"You can bring her on back." Sheriff Jones took the keys off a hook on the wall and led them back toward the cells. "The jail's empty now except for old Homer Gatling, sleeping off a wild hair he found at the bottom of a whiskey bottle."

The sheriff unlocked a cell and opened the door. Jedidiah turned to Susannah. "Give me your hands," he said quietly.

She raised her hands, wishing him to the devil with every fiber of her being. Her thoughts must have shown on her face, for when he unlocked the handcuffs, his movements were as wary as if she were a keg of dynamite with a lit fuse.

Which wasn't far off the mark.

He slipped the handcuffs in his coat pocket and gestured for her to enter the cell. Head held high, she walked inside, then turned to stare at him defiantly, her arms crossed.

Sheriff Jones closed and locked the door. Jedidiah looked at the other lawman. "Would you give us a minute alone please, sheriff?"

Jones nodded, sent Susannah a speculative look, and headed back to his desk in the other room, keys jingling. Jedidiah stepped up to the bars.

"I'm sorry about this," he said. "But I need to leave you somewhere safe, and this was the best I could think of."

"And where are you going?" she shot back. "The saloon, I suppose?"

"You suppose wrong." He leaned toward the bars, his face taut with annoyance. "I've about had it with that mouth of yours, Susannah Calhoun."

"Please, just call me Black Widow," she replied with a sweet smile.

His lips thinned. "So I miscalculated. I've already apologized for that. If you weren't so conspicuous, none of this would be necessary!"

"Oh, do let's blame this on me!" Hands on her hips, she sauntered up to the bars until all that separated them was the cold, hard steel. "*You* are the one who came up with that ridiculous story!"

"I'm trying to help you."

Her eyes widened. "Into the hangman's noose, perhaps!"

He pointed a finger at her. "You're the one who got herself into trouble. I'm doing everything I can to keep a rope from around your pretty neck, so I suggest you forget the snotty remarks."

"Considering I am traveling with a man who thinks me guilty of murder, I believe I'm entitled to a few snotty remarks!" she scoffed.

"I thought you were capable—there's a difference," he shot back. "But no matter what I think, Brick Caldwell is dead. It's my job to find out who killed him and bring that person to justice. And I don't think it was you."

She gaped at him. "But . . . but you've been treating me horribly and acting as if you think I'm guilty. And you're taking me to Denver!"

"It's my duty to take you to Denver. But I am also sworn to see that justice is done. And that includes tracking down a witness who can prove your innocence."

Hope flickered in her breast. "You're going to help me?"

"I'm going to find Abigail Hawkins," he corrected. "I'm going to hear her testimony, and hopefully she'll swear to the fact that Brick Caldwell was alive when you left him."

Susannah's shoulders sagged with relief. "Why didn't you tell me?"

"Because you were acting so contrary," he replied. "But it's easier for me to do my job if you cooperate. Given the way this town has been acting, I wanted to clear the air before I leave you alone again. I'm on your side, Susannah. I care what happens to you."

She gave him a soft smile. "You do?"

"Sure." He shrugged casually and gave her a pleasant smile. "That's what a marshal does; he rights the wrongs so the bad men go to jail and innocent people can live in safety."

"I see." Her smile faded. "So that means when your job is done here, you'll be moving on."

"That's right."

"Then you'd best get going, marshal," she said in a falsely bright tone. "The sooner you get your man, the sooner you can be on your way."

"In a hurry to see the back of me, princess?"

"In a hurry to get out from behind these bars," she corrected. "Go on, marshal. I'll still be here when you get back."

"You'd better be." He tugged his hat low over his eyes, and with a last, warning look, he strode away.

The sun was well on its way to setting when Susannah left the jailhouse.

She knew Jedidiah would want to kill her when he discovered she was gone, but she really didn't have a choice.

Over the course of the day, a buzz of growing unrest had escalated among the townspeople. Several times, Sheriff Jones had stepped outside to calm what was turning into an angry mob of upset husbands who objected to having a "black widow" killer in their midst.

There had been a lull in the protesting around suppertime, as all the stalwart husbands of the town went home to fill their bellies at their wives' tables. Susannah's own stomach had started to growl when Sheriff Jones came back into the cell area followed by a petite woman carrying a dinner tray, whom he introduced as Mrs. Molly Pruitt.

The sheriff unlocked the cell door, allowing the diminutive woman to enter her cell. Mrs. Pruitt had smiled at Susannah, reminding her of a doe with her big brown eyes and delicate stature, and placed the covered tray on the small table next to the bed. Then, when the sheriff's back was turned, the sweet lady pulled a napkin away from the tray, grabbed the piece of pipe she had hidden there, and hit Sheriff Jones over the head with it.

Susannah had watched in stunned amazement as the lawman dropped like a stone.

Mrs. Pruitt grabbed the sheriff's gun and pointed it at Susannah. "It would be better if you came along quietly," she said in a small, whispery voice.

"I agree," Susannah said, and walked out of the cell ahead of Mrs. Pruitt.

And so it was that Susannah found herself in the cellar of Pruitt's Bed & Feed, a combination boardinghouse and restaurant only two doors down from the sheriff's office.

Mrs. Pruitt urged her into the cellar, lit a lamp, and closed the door, shutting out the sunlight. Then, with a squeak of disgust, she dropped the gun to the earthen floor.

"I hate guns," she said, wrinkling her nose.

Susannah gaped at the woman.

"Well, I do," Mrs. Pruitt insisted, obviously reading Susannah's puzzlement in her face. "They're so noisy and dangerous! I do so hate violence."

Susannah felt as if she'd stepped into some bizarre dream. "But you hit Sheriff Jones over the head with a pipe!"

Mrs. Pruitt twisted her slender fingers. "Well, he wouldn't have let me take you out of there otherwise," she reasoned. "Though I suppose I could have asked."

"No, I think you read the situation correctly." Susannah sat down on a pile of flour sacks. "Might I also mention that you led me here at gunpoint?"

"Oh, that was for your protection," the woman responded. "This way they can't say that you broke out of jail—not if I forced you to go!"

There was a convoluted logic there that Susannah had to acknowledge. "Why don't you tell me why you went through so much trouble?"

"I need your help," Mrs. Pruitt said. She glanced around as if expecting someone to leap from behind the stores piled around them.

"*My* help? What for?" The only help Susannah felt capable of providing was fashion advice, though that couldn't be what the woman referred to—even though her baggy gray gown was two sizes too big for her small frame.

"I want you to kill my husband," Mrs. Pruitt replied.

Susannah stared at the woman, noting the desperation in those doe-like eyes that seemed too big for her pale, delicate face. Molly Pruitt was serious—and Susannah was in big trouble.

"Damn you, Jedidiah Brown," she muttered beneath her breath.

Jedidiah stared at the fallen sheriff and the empty jail cell.

"Damn you, Susannah Calhoun," he muttered.

The sheriff groaned, and Jedidiah went over to help the man rise. Leaning him in a sitting position against the bars of the cell, he crouched down and waited for Sheriff Jones to regain his senses.

"What happened?" the lawman groaned, raising his hand to gingerly feel the back of his head.

"I was hoping *you* could tell *me*," Jedidiah replied.

"Where are we?" The sheriff looked around, then groaned again as he noticed the empty cell. "Don't tell me that husband killer got away?"

"Afraid so. Do you know who hit you?"

"Must have been her." Sheriff Jones squinted as he tried to focus his memory. "All I remember is letting in Mrs. Pruitt with the prisoner's dinner. Next thing I know, here we are."

"Who's Mrs. Pruitt?"

"Hal Pruitt's wife. Sweet little thing. They run the boardinghouse a couple doors down. I doubt she hit me; she's just a small woman and not given to violence. It was probably the other one, the one we know hates men."

Jedidiah believed the chances that Susannah had done it were negligible. Why would she escape, knowing Caldwell was out for her head and that Jedidiah was working to find the witness who might be able to prove her innocence?

Then again, anything was possible with Susannah Calhoun.

"Do you want me to fetch the doc?" Jedidiah asked.

"No, I'll be okay. Have a heck of a headache, is all. I spent the day keeping that mob at bay.

The husbands in town aren't real keen on having a woman like her around. It was getting ugly for a while there."

"Ugly enough that someone might break her out of here and try to take the law into his own hands?"

The sheriff's eyes widened. "I didn't think of that."

"What about this Mrs. Pruitt? Could her husband have put her up to something like this?" Jedidiah asked.

Sheriff Jones looked thoughtful. "That Hal Pruitt is a mean son-of-a-gun. Runs Pruitt's Bed & Feed and makes loans to a lot of the other businessmen. He owns a share in some of the mines hereabouts, too. If he weren't a respectable businessman, I'd be keeping my eye on him just cause he's so nasty. But all he's ever done that comes close to breaking the law is have a few too many over at the saloon now and again. You think he might have something to do with this?"

"Don't you?" Jedidiah countered. "His wife was the only one in here."

"I don't know what to think. Hal *did* seem to be shouting the loudest this afternoon. Something about teaching the woman a lesson. But that's just Hal. I figured he was just liquored up again."

"Maybe. Maybe not." Jedidiah stood and checked the bullets in his Colt army revolver. "I'm going to go over to Pruitt's."

"I should probably come with you." He started to rise, then winced and sat back down again. "Then again, you're a U.S. Marshal. You're not gonna go shoot up the place, are you?"

"Not unless I have to." Jedidiah grinned, dark humor coloring his words. "Just to sober up Mr. Pruitt, maybe."

The sheriff sighed. "All right, then. Just take it easy over there. Pruitt can be something of a hothead, and he's not real big on respecting law and order when he's had a few too many."

"He'll respect me. Take care of that head, sheriff."

Jedidiah turned and left the cell, hand resting on his Colt.

Chapter 7

"Mrs. Pruitt," Susannah said, "why would you want to kill your husband?"

"That's a private matter," the woman answered, turning away to fuss with some jars of preserves on a nearby shelf. "You've killed three of your own husbands. What's one more?"

"It's just not that simple," Susannah replied, stalling for time. "I mean, a woman has her reasons for doing these things."

"Indeed she does," murmured Mrs. Pruitt, though she seemed to be speaking to herself.

"Well, I simply can't kill a man without a reason." As soon as the words came out of her mouth, Susannah wanted to call them back.

Where had that come from? She had no intention of killing anyone! But Molly Pruitt's evident distress made her play the game until she could find out just what was going on.

Mrs. Pruitt spun around to face her, clutching her hands together in dismay. "Couldn't you just trust me on this? The man needs killing, and I can't do it myself."

"I'm sorry, but you're going to have to tell me why."

Mrs. Pruitt bit her lip. "How about you tell me why you killed your husbands, and then I'll tell you why I want you to kill mine?"

"All right." Jedidiah was never going to hear the end of this, Susannah vowed, even as she searched her imagination for a likely tale.

"My first husband was Winston," she began. Her gaze fell on the jars of preserves lining the shelves. "Winston Glass. He was a charming man, and I fell in love with him right away. Unfortunately, two months after our wedding, I found out that he was already married, so I kicked the lowdown skunk out of our bed and locked him out of the house. Unfortunately it was winter, and he froze to death."

"I would have done the same thing," Mrs. Pruitt said with admiration. "What about your second husband?"

"My second husband? That would be

Homer . . . ah . . ." She searched her mind for a name, then glanced down and noticed the flour sacks she rested upon. "Homer Flowers," she said triumphantly. "He drank too much and caused me no amount of embarrassment. One night I locked the door against him. He drowned in the horse trough."

"How awful," Mrs. Pruitt gasped. "But it seems to me that your husbands' deaths were more accidents than murder."

"Well, I thought so, too," Susannah agreed, getting into her tale. "And I have to admit, the townspeople let them both slide, seeing as how my only crime was to lock them out of my house. But then came . . . Jed. Jed Brown."

"What happened with Jed?" Mrs. Pruitt asked breathlessly.

"Jed was a different breed altogether," Susannah said with a mischievous grin, imagining Jedidiah's face in her mind. "He was a liar and a skunk. He had no manners at all—a complete and utter lout."

"Then why did you ever marry him?"

"Because he was handsome," Susannah replied truthfully. "He's . . . I mean, he *was* a man of the world who knew how to sweet talk a lady when he had a mind to."

"He sounds wonderful to me," Mrs. Pruitt sighed.

Susannah frowned, realizing her tone had softened from righteous to almost infatuated! "Well, uh . . . unfortunately, he had a mind to sweet talk a lot of ladies . . . none of whom were his wife."

"My goodness!" Mrs. Pruitt exclaimed in horrified fascination. "What did you do to him?"

"I poisoned him," Susannah replied with relish, imagining the scene. "I put poison in his supper one night. He died three days later—a long and lingering death with a lot of pain. Needless to say, that man never bothered me again."

"I'm sure he deserved it."

"Every second of it," Susannah muttered. "The fast-talking weasel!"

"And that was when they decided to prosecute you for all three murders?"

Susannah abandoned her mental image of Jedidiah writhing in pain and cleared her throat. "Well, three husbands in two years is quite a lot." She raised her eyebrows in expectation. "I've told you my story, Mrs. Pruitt. How about you tell me yours?"

"You're such a strong woman," Mrs. Pruitt said in admiration. "I wish I had your courage. And please, do call me Molly."

"All right, Molly. Why do you want me to kill your husband?"

Molly ducked her head and stared at her hands. "It's hard for me to talk about," she whispered.

A suspicion slipped into Susannah's mind, one that chased all humor from the situation. "Molly, does he hit you?"

Molly made a small whimpering sound and refused to meet Susannah's gaze.

Susannah reached out and took hold of the woman's arm. "Does he hurt you? Tell me, Molly."

Biting her lip, Molly gave a small nod.

"How long has this been going on?"

"Just since we've been married."

"And how long have you been married?"

Molly twisted her wedding band around on her finger. "Three years."

Susannah stared at Molly, noting her fragile build, and wondered what kind of monster would deliberately harm such a clearly kind-hearted woman?

"He's been beating you for three years?"

Molly nodded. "He doesn't mean it most of the time," she added quickly. "It's usually the drink that brings it out in him. And he's always sorry."

"I'm sure he is," Susannah muttered, anger simmering through her. She should have seen the signs sooner—the scared rabbit demeanor, the defensiveness, Molly's lack of interest in her appearance. But she had been so caught up in her own problems that she hadn't even noticed things that would normally have set off warning bells. She had encountered beaten wives before in her travels, and it never ceased to infuriate her that men who claimed to love, honor, and cherish could turn on their mates in such a brutal manner.

"It's just that I found out I'm expecting," Molly continued, resting a hand on her abdomen, "and I'm afraid if he keeps on with this, he'll hurt the baby. I've asked him to quit the drinking, but he just gets even madder. The only way to make sure my baby is safe is if Hal is dead. And I can't do it myself."

"So you figured that I could."

Molly shrugged. "Seems to me you've already killed so many husbands, what's one more? Maybe we could poison him, like you did to Jed."

"Have you gone to the sheriff, Molly?"

The smaller woman grew pale. "I couldn't do that! Then everyone would know. Besides, Hal told me lots of times that no one would believe me." She sniffled, her bony shoulders sagging. "You're my only hope, Miss Black Widow. Or should that be Mrs. Black Widow?"

"For heaven's sake, my name is Susannah."

"Susannah, then." Molly's voice trembled at Susannah's terse tone. "I suppose we should be on a first name basis since you're going to poison Hal for me and all."

Susannah rubbed her temples. "Did it occur to you that there might be another way? You could just leave him, you know."

"Leave my husband?" Molly exclaimed in shock. "I could never do that! It would be a sin against God!"

Susannah stared. "Leaving him because he beats you is a sin against God, but killing him wouldn't be?"

"Well, we're married only until death parts us. And besides, I wouldn't be doing the actual killing. You would."

Once again Susannah had to acknowledge the convoluted logic.

"What kind of poison did you use on Jed?" Molly asked, turning to rummage on a shelf full of cans and boxes. She pulled forth a brown bottle. "I managed to get some of this from the ore refinery. It's arsenic."

Susannah looked from the bottle of poison held out to her to the desperate hope shining in Molly's big doe eyes, and wondered how the heck she was going to get out of this one.

* * *

The last rays of the setting sun still set the sky afire as Jedidiah walked into Pruitt's Bed & Feed.

The place was bustling with supper hour traffic. The dining room on his right was packed to the brim with dusty miners starving from a hard day's work. Waitresses ran back and forth from the kitchen, their arms filled with steaming platters that set Jedidiah's stomach to rumbling.

He'd spent the whole day on a wild goose chase, and it had been a long time since lunch.

He turned to his left and entered the lobby of the boardinghouse. It looked more like a hotel, with a long front desk and a large staircase leading to the upper floor. A young man worked diligently behind the desk, his hair slicked back and his shirt buttoned up so tight it was amazing he could breathe. Jedidiah headed toward him, passing by the guests waiting in line to get their rooms. A few men took one look at Jedidiah and scurried away like mice sighting an owl. Some people—especially those who had once bent a law or two—had a sixth sense when it came to knowing when a man with a badge was in their vicinity.

Jedidiah stepped up to the desk, leaned an elbow on it, and rang the bell. The clerk looked at him in annoyance.

"May I help you, sir?" he said, his manner entirely too supercilious for a kid his age.

"You sure can," Jedidiah replied with a smile that showed all his teeth. "You can find Mr. Hal Pruitt for me and you can do it darn quick, son."

"Mr. Pruitt is a very busy man," the young man said. "Who shall I say is inquiring?"

Jedidiah tugged open his duster so his badge caught the light. "You just tell him there's a U.S. Marshal here to see him."

The clerk's mouth fell open. "Yes, sir!" he stammered. "If you'll just wait here . . . Mr. Pruitt is busy in the dining room. Mrs. Pruitt usually manages the supper hour, but she went out somewhere and hasn't come back yet."

"Is that so?" It was looking more and more like Mrs. Pruitt had indeed been the one to break Susannah out of jail. Was she conspiring with her husband, or acting on her own? There was only one way to find out. "I wouldn't want you to leave the desk unattended," Jedidiah said with a less menacing grin. "Perhaps you could just point him out to me?"

The young clerk heaved a sigh of relief. "You can just ask for him in the dining room," he said. "He's a big man with a mustache, dressed in a very nice suit."

"Thank you, son," Jedidiah said. "I'll be sure

to tell him you were kind enough to point him out to me."

The youngster paled and gasped out a stammering protest as Jedidiah turned and made his way to the dining room.

He spotted Hal Pruitt right away, a big, bellowing fellow in a fancy suit who stood near the doorway just inside the dining room. The man was shorter than Jedidiah but wider in the torso—plump, if the truth be told—balding and red-faced with a large handlebar mustache. He alternately shouted at the waitresses and smiled at the patrons. In between, he furtively kept glancing at the door with a fierce frown on his face, as if watching for someone late for an appointment.

Or, Jedidiah thought, for an errant wife.

He approached Pruitt with a casual grin on his lips. "Evening, sir. Are you Mr. Pruitt?"

Pruitt returned an oily smile of his own. "That's me," he replied heartily. "Are you looking to dine this evening? The house special tonight is steak—from my special private stock of beef."

"That sounds mighty good," Jedidiah replied, "but I'm not here for supper." He opened his duster so Pruitt could see the badge pinned to his vest.

Pruitt paled. "Goodness, imagine that! A U.S. Marshal here in my restaurant."

Jedidiah raised his eyebrows at the reaction. Pruitt glanced around apprehensively, as if assuring himself there was nothing within sight that could get him in trouble, and his hand shook as he nervously smoothed his mustache.

Indications of a guilty man, Jedidiah noted with interest. But guilty of what?

"You know, Mr. Pruitt, I do believe I will have some of that steak," he decided. "We can discuss business after I eat."

"Of course, marshal." Pruitt gestured to a nearby serving girl. "Show the marshal to our best table," he said, "and fetch him the biggest steak in the kitchen."

"Yes, sir, Mr. Pruitt."

Jedidiah gave Pruitt a curt nod. "Much obliged, Pruitt."

"The honor is mine, marshal," the portly man returned with an insincere smile. "Only the finest for officers of the law."

Definitely guilty, Jedidiah thought, as he followed the waitress to his table. Things were getting mighty interesting.

He sat down and ordered some of Pruitt's "private stock" steak, which was priced so high that it ought to have come on a gold plate. The man himself continued to monitor the activity in the dining room, occasionally pulling forth his pocket watch and scowling at it. Jedidiah kept his eye on him, and every time their gazes met, Pruitt gave him that same snake-oil salesman smile.

He didn't trust the man an inch.

Susannah was with Pruitt's wife, and obviously Pruitt was expecting her. So Jedidiah would fill his empty stomach and watch for Mrs. Pruitt to come back. If she wasn't back by the time he'd finished his steak, he and Mr. Pruitt would just have to go fetch her. Together.

The young waitress brought his steak, and he dug in with gusto, doing away with the steak in short order. Pleasantly surprised at the high quality of the food, he started to butter a biscuit when he noticed three men enter the dining room. Cowpokes, from the looks of them, their lack of mining gear was enough to make them stand out in this crowd—at least for Jedidiah. No one else paid them any mind.

No one except Hal Pruitt.

One of them caught Pruitt's eye and jerked his head in an indication to leave the room. Jedidiah kept his head bent over his meal. From the corner of his eye, he saw Pruitt glance at him uncertainly; then the leader of the three cowhands jerked his head again, this time more imperiously. Pruitt slipped out of the dining room.

Pruitt walked through the lobby of the boardinghouse, the trio trailing him in such a way that the casual observer would not make any connection between them. Then the portly businessman climbed the stairs, his cohorts following a few moments behind.

Jedidiah was out of his seat by the time the last man had cleared the top of the staircase. No one paid him any mind as he crossed the lobby, then crept up the stairs after Pruitt and his cronies.

His hand on his Colt, he caught a glimpse of the last of the three cowpokes disappearing into a room. The door shut firmly behind him.

Looked like things were about to get exciting. Darned good thing he'd had supper.

Molly Pruitt dragged Susannah into the dining room, still panting from their mad run from the cellar.

"I can't believe how late I am. Hal must be so angry!" She glanced nervously around the dining room, smoothing her hair with both hands.

"Molly, why don't I just wait here while you find your husband?"

Molly shook her head. "I want you to stay with me," she said. "After I let Hal know I'm here, we'll go into the kitchen to make his dinner . . . and you can do what you need to do."

Susannah glanced down at the bottle of arsenic she still held. How was she going to get out of this one?

"Mrs. Pruitt, there you are!" A well-dressed young clerk hurried over, his adam's apple bobbing with his agitation. "Mr. Pruitt's been looking for you, ma'am. He's mighty angry."

Molly paled. "Where is he?" she whispered.

"Upstairs in his office."

Molly sighed and smoothed down her skirts. "I'd best let him know that I'm here. This way, Susannah."

The young man's mouth fell open in awe as Susannah passed him. And he wasn't the only one. Several of the diners stared at her as well. Jedidiah was right; she *was* too conspicuous. She might as well just sit out in the middle of Main Street and wait for Wayne Caldwell and his lynch mob to come fetch her!

She hurried after Molly as the smaller woman darted through the crowded lobby and headed up the stairs. When they reached the second floor, Molly stopped outside a closed door and took a deep breath before knocking timidly. The rumble of male voices on the other side of the door ceased abruptly.

"Who is it?" a man thundered, his tone short with impatience.

"It's Molly, Hal. I just wanted to let you know I'm back—"

The door jerked open, and Hal Pruitt glared down at his wife. "Where the hell have you been, woman?"

"I—"

"Get in here!" Pruitt grabbed Molly by the arm and dragged her into the room. Molly caught Susannah's hand, pulling her along as Pruitt slammed the door shut.

Susannah glanced uneasily around the room. Two disreputable-looking cowhands sprawled in the only two chairs in the room, and a third man, with dark eyes as mean as she had ever seen, leaned his hip against Pruitt's desk. He looked her up and down, then grinned lewdly.

Susannah stared back coldly. She recognized bandits when she saw them, and she had long ago learned that fear often encouraged such men rather than discouraged them.

"Who the hell is this?" Pruitt demanded, bringing Susannah's attention back to him.

"This is my friend Susannah," Molly said, her voice quavering. "I—I brought her to help in the dining room."

"Who said you could make decisions like that?" Pruitt snarled. Molly ducked her head. "I run this business, woman, and I am the only one who can hire anyone!"

"Yes, Hal," Molly whispered.

"But since she's here, let's see if she's fit to work at Pruitt's." His gaze slid over Susannah's body, lingering on her bosom before coming to rest on her face. He frowned. "Don't I know you from somewhere?"

"I doubt it," Susannah replied, this time not bothering to hide her aversion.

"Don't you talk back to me," Pruitt warned. "If you want this job, you keep a civil tongue in your head!"

"Or somewhere else," the leader of the bandits said. The other two desperados laughed.

"She'd make a hell of a whore," one of them suggested.

Pruitt drew himself up. "This is a respectable boardinghouse, gentlemen, not a brothel."

The three ruffians burst into laughter. "If you say so, Pruitt," the leader said. "Sure is a damn shame, though."

Susannah glanced at Molly. The woman's face was beet red, but she kept her gaze obediently downcast. Pruitt was a loud-mouthed braggart and outweighed Molly by at least a hundred pounds. The idea of him using his greater strength to hurt the sweet woman was enough to tempt Susannah to use the arsenic she still held concealed within her skirts.

"I could swear I've seen you someplace before," Pruitt said, narrowing his eyes in concentration.

Susannah shrugged. "Maybe I look like someone you know."

"I'd remember someone who looks like you." Pruitt glanced once more at her bosom and licked his lips. "If you want the job, it's yours. Maybe that pretty face of yours will bring in extra business."

Before Susannah could respond, he turned to his wife. "Now, where the hell were you, woman? You're over an hour late!"

"I'm sorry, Hal," Molly whispered.

"I don't care how sorry you are! I want to know where the hell you were!"

Molly swallowed hard and glanced up at her husband. "I brought the supper over to the jail like I always do, and—"

"The jail!" Pruitt spun back to Susannah. "That's where I've seen you! You're that whore husband killer!"

"I'm no whore," Susannah snapped back.

Pruitt took a step toward her, rage contorting his features. "What the hell are you doing out of jail?"

"I escaped," Susannah returned defiantly, holding up the bottle of arsenic. "I heard there were some husbands hereabouts that needed killing."

Pruitt's eyes widened, and he glanced from Susannah to the poison in her hand, to his wife. "You ungrateful slut!" he shouted, grabbing Molly by the arm and glaring into her face. "You brought her here? You think she can kill me? I'll teach you to think!" He slapped Molly hard against the face with a loud crack. She crumpled at his feet, curling into a ball and sobbing softly.

"Hey, Pruitt," the outlaw leader said. "Can you take care of your family problems later? We're supposed to be doing business here."

"We'll do business." Pruitt jabbed Molly's sobbing form with his foot. "Get downstairs, you lazy cow. The place won't run itself."

Molly slowly sat up. One side of her face glowed lividly red with the imprint of Pruitt's hand. Susannah started to go to her, but Pruitt grabbed her by the arm.

"Oh no, you don't." He glanced at Molly and cursed. "You stay right here until that mark goes away," he snapped. "I don't want your ugly face to scare off the customers."

Molly crawled to a corner of the room, where she leaned against the wall, her doe eyes blank.

Susannah curled her lip in disgust. "You are a pathetic man," she sneered.

"And you're a man-hating whore," he growled

back. "But I'll fix you good." With a nasty smile, he yanked the bottle of poison from her hand and let it drop to the floor, where it rolled to rest by Molly's foot. Then he dragged Susannah over to the desk and shoved her back against the leader of the bandits. "What do you say, boys? A hundred head of cattle at the price we talked about, and this pretty little slut as an added bonus!"

The outlaw leader curled his arm around Susannah's waist and held her firmly against him despite her struggles. He rubbed his pelvis against her bottom, reaching one hand around to squeeze her breast.

"I think we might have a deal," the outlaw replied.

"The hell you do," Susannah snapped. She jabbed an elbow into his midsection, but he still held on. She could feel him getting aroused and realized that her fighting was exciting him. Abruptly she froze, swallowing her natural revulsion as he pawed her body with greedy hands.

"She sure is a hot piece," the bandit commented.

"She's a man-hater," Pruitt replied with disgust. "She married three men and killed 'em all. Make sure you keep her tied up, 'lessen she do the same to you!"

"I have to agree with Mr. Pruitt," a blessedly familiar voice said. Jedidiah stepped through the window, his revolver pointed straight at the bandit leader's head. "Keeping that gal tied up is about the only way to keep her out of trouble."

Susannah breathed a sigh of relief. She should have known he'd be around somewhere. He'd shed his duster, and his twin revolvers gleamed in the lamplight.

"Who the hell are you?" the outlaw leader demanded.

Jedidiah tapped the badge pinned to his vest. "United States Marshal Jedidiah Brown, at your service."

"A Federal Marshal!" one of the bandits exclaimed.

"Shit, he musta been listenin'!" the other said.

The bandit leader curled his arm around Susannah's neck. "Put it down, marshal, or I'll snap her neck like a twig."

"That wouldn't be very bright of you," Jedidiah returned. "So far I only have you boys on cattle rustling. Adding murder to that is sure to see you hang, instead of just passing some time in prison."

"I don't aim to do any time," the leader replied. "There's four of us and one of you, marshal."

"Nice to see you went to school once upon a

time." Jedidiah looked at Molly's husband. "Well, Pruitt, what do you say?"

"What do you mean, what do I say?" blustered Pruitt.

"Yeah, what are you asking him for?" one of the desperados asked.

"Unless . . ." The bandit leader pulled his gun and pointed it at Pruitt, taking one arm from around Susannah in the process. "Unless he set us up."

"Put the gun down," Jedidiah ordered.

The outlaw ignored him, aiming his weapon Pruitt's heart. "Is that the way it happened, Pruitt? Was this a trap?"

"N-n-no, I swear!" Pruitt protested, slowly raising his hands. "He's trying to trick you!"

"It's all right, Mr. Pruitt," Susannah said with a sweet smile. "You don't have to pretend anymore."

"She was in on it, too!" one of the rustlers cried.

"No! No, she wasn't! I mean, I wasn't . . ." Pruitt glared at Susannah and raised his fist. "Tell the truth, you damned bitch!"

She narrowed her eyes. "Don't you threaten me, you bully. I'm not your wife, and you can't kick me around like a stray dog!"

"Put down the gun!" Jedidiah ordered again, his gaze never leaving the leader of the gang.

"Is she in on it or ain't she?" another of the rustlers questioned.

"She's not! I'm not!" Pruitt rounded on Susannah. "I'll shut your mouth for good!"

Everything erupted. Pruitt swung at Susannah, who threw herself to the floor so that Pruitt slugged the bandit leader instead. Someone fired, and Pruitt staggered. Jedidiah shot the leader's gun hand, then whirled and got a second man in the shoulder before he could draw. Mrs. Pruitt sneaked up behind the third member of the gang and smashed the bottle of arsenic over his head. Stunned, he sank down in his chair.

Susannah scrambled to her feet, looking down at the fallen Pruitt. His eyes stared sightlessly up at the ceiling, his mouth gaped open, and blood flowed freely from a nasty hole in his chest. Unable to take her gaze from the awful sight, Susannah stumbled toward Jedidiah. The marshal pushed her behind him with one arm, keeping his revolver trained on the wounded desperados at the same time.

"Mr. Pruitt's dead," she whispered, swallowing hard.

He glanced at Pruitt's body, then looked at the man's wife. "Mrs. Pruitt, your husband is dead," he said gently.

"I know that, marshal." Molly hung her head

for a long moment, then raised her eyes to his.
"Do you know who shot him?"

"This fellow right here." Jedidiah gestured at
the bandit leader with his revolver. "I tried to get
him first, but I was too slow. I'm sorry, ma'am."

"There was nothing you could do, marshal.
My husband should have expected such a thing
to happen, given the type of men he was deal-
ing with." She let out a sigh and shook her
head. "He always was short-sighted."

"I don't mean to interrupt your grief," Jedidiah said in a gentle tone, "but do you have
anything we can tie these boys up with? I'm
afraid I have only one set of handcuffs."

"I can find something," she responded softly.

"Good." He gave her his most charming
Southern-gentleman smile. "I'd like to thank
you for helping me round up these rustlers,
ma'am. We couldn't have done it without you."

Mrs. Pruitt blushed. "I couldn't let him hurt
you, marshal."

"And I'm obliged, ma'am."

Mrs. Pruitt turned to leave the room, then
faced them again, twisting her fingers together.
"Marshal, there's one more thing. Please don't
blame Susannah for breaking out of jail. I forced
her, and that's the truth." She ducked her head.
"I suppose you'll be wanting to take me into
custody as well."

"Nonsense, ma'am," Jedidiah said. "I don't remember any jail break. You were working with the law to round up these cattle rustlers, and that's a fact."

"But—oh-h-h," she said, understanding dawning. "If that's the way you remember it, marshal—"

"It is, ma'am."

She gave him a shy smile. "Thank you. I'll go fetch that rope now."

Mrs. Pruitt left the room, and Susannah looked up at Jedidiah in wonder. "That was very sweet of you," she said. "You had every right to arrest her for jail breaking."

He shrugged off her compliment. "The woman has been through enough."

"I don't care what you say; it was very compassionate of you." She leaned up and brushed a soft kiss on his cheek.

He gazed down at her, his eyes warm with an emotion that brought pink flooding to her face. A wicked grin curved his lips.

"Hold that thought, princess."

Chapter 8

❦

They left Placerville at dawn the following morning.

Jedidiah had turned the cattle rustlers over to Sheriff Jones and explained that Mr. Pruitt had died accidentally in the scuffle. The sheriff had cast Susannah a dubious glance, but accepted the marshal's story. Molly Pruitt found herself a wealthy widow with a prospering business that would easily allow her to live comfortably and support her child. Jedidiah was considered a hero for capturing the gang.

And Susannah had spent the night locked in jail, wondering what madness gripped her that she had actually gone and kissed Jedidiah.

Yes, she was pleased that he finally believed her innocent of murder and that he would help her locate the witness who would clear her name. And yes, she found him more appealing than any man she had ever met. But he had made it perfectly clear that once his job was done, he would be moving on.

How could she even consider giving in to her feelings for a man who would only leave her broken-hearted?

She had simply been so touched by his gentleness with Molly that she had felt obliged to show it, that was all. There was nothing more to it. Absolutely nothing.

"You're out of your mind if you think this will keep Caldwell off our trail," Susannah said to Jedidiah, as he drove their buckboard wagon away from Placerville.

"People only see what they want to see," Jedidiah replied. "And as long as they don't see that face of yours, at least we have a fighting chance."

"You're not exactly easy to forget yourself," she pointed out.

"Me?" He deepened his Southern accent from a mere trace to nearly overdone. "Heck, ma'am, I'm just a farmer traveling with his wife."

"His *pregnant* wife."

He grinned as if he had indeed been the one to put her in such a state. "Yep."

Susannah snorted and tried to make herself

more comfortable—or at least as comfortable as a pregnant woman could be on the hard wooden seat. She punched at the wadded up pillow stuffed beneath her gown that made her look as if she were ready to whelp at any moment, then shoved yet another stray curl beneath the deep-brimmed sunbonnet that covered her head. No matter which way she turned, she either dislodged her hat or found her way constricted by her false belly. If this was what it felt like to be expecting a child, perhaps she should rethink her dreams of motherhood!

Jedidiah, on the other hand, looked perfectly at ease in his tan britches and suspenders and a soft white cotton shirt. He'd added a straw hat and looked just like any other homesteader as he drove the pair of horses with the ease of long practice. One of the animals pulling the wagon was Susannah's mount, and the other was a plain brown farm horse that had seen better days. Jedidiah's Palomino was tied to the back of the buckboard.

Jedidiah's rifle lay at his feet within easy reach, and his Colts were tucked beneath the seat, hidden behind a coil of rope. He was armed to the teeth and ready for anything.

Which was a good thing for Susannah, considering that she couldn't be of much help with the way her disguise hindered her movements.

Still, she had to give Jedidiah a lot of credit. They had passed two wagons and a few men on horseback, and no one had even looked twice at them. Maybe this crazy plan was actually going to work.

"You never did tell me what you found out about Abigail Hawkins," she said, breaking the silence.

He frowned. "There wasn't much to tell. Mrs. Hawkins only stayed there a day before she picked up a stage to Colorado Springs."

"So she's already gone." Susannah sighed. "Does her friend know why Mrs. Hawkins is headed for Colorado Springs?"

"She wanted to catch the train."

"Where to?"

"I don't know."

Susannah threw up her hands. "Lord Almighty, marshal, if that woman gets on the train at Colorado Springs, we'll never catch her!"

"I've got it under control."

"What do you mean, you've got it under control? How can you have it under control if you're here and she's on her way to Colorado Springs?"

His jaw tightened in annoyance. "I sent a

telegram to an associate of mine who will be watching for her. He'll stop her from getting on the train."

"An associate? You mean, another marshal?"

"Ah . . . not exactly."

Susannah tapped her fingers on her knee. "What do you mean, *not exactly?*"

"Look, you'll just have to trust me. I know what I'm doing."

"Trust you! You're asking a lot, Marshal Brown."

He pulled up on the reins. The buckboard came to a stop and he turned to her, his sherry-colored eyes narrowed with anger. "Listen, you're the one in trouble here, not me. All I was supposed to do was take you to Denver for your trial."

"Well, that's what you're doing, isn't it?"

"Sure, in between keeping your neck out of Wayne Caldwell's noose and trying to track down a witness so I can prove you didn't kill your employer. If I were just doing my job, I would have had you on the train to Denver already!"

"Well, don't let me stop you from doing your job, Marshal Brown!" She glared at him, her heart pounding. Why was she fighting with him? She was grateful for his help, and completely trusted him in the matter of tracking down Abigail Hawkins. But something was eating at her, something that made her want to rile his temper until he lost control.

Jedidiah stared at her for a long, charged moment. He had never met a woman who exasperated him so much, even as she made him want her so badly he could hardly think straight. Her life was on the line, but all he could think of when she put on that snooty attitude was how much he wanted to get her between the sheets and work that sass right out of her.

He was a U.S. Marshal, by God, and he had a job to do. His personal feelings had no place here.

"Don't start something you can't finish, princess," he warned, his voice low and controlled. "I'm putting my job on the line to help you out, but maybe I should just take you to Denver and wash my hands of you once and for all."

"That does seem to be the way you operate," she replied, clearly offended. "Whenever someone gets too close, you hightail it out of town."

"I don't have time for this." He snapped the reins, and the horses moved forward once more.

"My point exactly," she murmured. "You're a coward."

"What?" He pulled the horses to a stop again and rounded on her, his face taut with affronted male pride. "What did you say?"

"I said, you're a coward. Emotionally, anyway."

He leaned toward her, his eyes narrowing. "Are you making this personal, princess? Because if you are—"

"Deny it if you can," she shot back. "You're afraid of your own feelings."

He took her chin in his hand. Her smoky blue eyes sparkled with challenge, and her pulse pounded at the base of her throat. Her skin was so soft, her mouth so ripe. The woman got to him like no other woman ever had.

She was dangerous. Luckily, he was an expert on how to handle dangerous situations.

"I've still got those handcuffs," he warned. "If you don't behave yourself, I'll have to get them out."

She jerked her chin from his hold. "You'd do it, too."

"Bet on it." He picked up the reins and clucked at the horses to start them moving.

She gave him a disgusted look and ignored him until the next town came into sight.

* * *

Chalmers was a large, bustling town right on the cattle trail that boasted a real hotel, several restaurants, and rows of shops.

Susannah caught sight of a dress shop that had her sighing with longing. She loved clothes. Wouldn't that lovely blue-sprigged muslin look wonderful on her? And, oh, that adorable little hat with the flowers on it in the milliner's window . . .

"Forget it," Jedidiah growled.

Susannah put her nose in the air and pointedly ignored him. The man had no idea what was important to a woman.

Jedidiah stopped the buckboard outside the Chalmers Hotel. As he climbed down to tie up the horses, Susannah forgot her pique.

"Are we staying here?" she asked with excitement. "A real hotel? Perhaps I can even have a bath?"

Jedidiah grinned at her. "What kind of husband would I be if I didn't put my wife up in a decent hotel—especially when she's expecting?"

"Why, you'd be the worst kind of cad." Delighted at the prospect of a real bath, Susannah grinned right back at him.

"Exactly." He reached up to help her down out of the wagon, then offered his arm. "I do have a reputation to think of."

Susannah took his arm and waddled proudly into the hotel at his side. She sat in a very comfortable chair in the lobby while Jedidiah spoke with the desk clerk. Then he came over and had to help her out the cushy chair, since her enormous belly kept her from doing so herself.

"If this is what it feels like to really be expecting," she whispered with a laugh as they mounted the stairs, "it's a wonder any woman goes through it at all!"

Jedidiah stopped outside a room and unlocked the door, then turned to look at her with his hand on the knob. "I think you'd look beautiful carrying a child, even if you were as big as a house."

The sincere appreciation in his voice brought a blush to her cheeks, and made her heart pound like never before.

"After you, Mrs. Brown," he said with a grin, pushing open the door.

"Don't get carried away," she retorted, still flushed from his compliment.

The room was small but tidy. A bed with a brass headboard took up most of the space. A small table with a lantern on it stood beside the bed, and a washstand and a wardrobe occupied the far wall. A small mirror hung above the washstand.

Susannah sank down on the bed with a sigh

of relief, swiping the back of her hand across her grimy cheek. "I feel as if I've brought half the road with me."

"We can't take the chance of anyone knowing you're not what you appear to be," Jedidiah said. "So unless you want me to be the one to help you with your bath . . ."

"I see your point." Disappointed, she looked around. "Well, it's a comfortable room, and I can wash up, even if I can't bathe as completely as I'd like." She reached up and pulled off the huge sunbonnet. "How far away is your room?"

"Susannah, this *is* my room."

She hesitated, then smoothed her hair with one hand. "*Your* room?"

He took off his hat and hung it on a peg on the wall. "Maybe I should have said *our* room." He walked to the washstand and poured water into the basin. "The room of Mr. and Mrs. John Brown."

"John Brown?"

He picked up the bar of soap and washed his hands. "Jedidiah is a bit conspicuous. But there are ten John Browns in every town."

"I see." She fingered the ties on her bonnet. "Where are you planning to sleep, Mr. Brown?"

"Right there in that bed." He nonchalantly wiped his hands off on a towel.

"You think so?"

"I know so."

Susannah pressed her lips together. Part of her was outraged that he assumed they were going to share sleeping space for the night. But part of her was excited.

It made sense for them to share a room, since they were masquerading as husband and wife. But there was enough floor space that Jedidiah could certainly stretch out there.

Her flesh tingled at the thought of his lean form resting beside her in the bed.

"Absolutely not," she said, hoping he didn't notice the slight breathlessness in her voice. "What kind of woman do you take me for, marshal?"

"I think after all we've been through—and given the fact that I'm a close friend of the family—you can call me Jedidiah."

"We are mere acquaintances, marshal. And that is precisely the reason you cannot sleep in this bed with me."

He crossed his arms, his brows arching. "We've known each other for over a year, Susannah. And given the circumstances, I think we can safely say that you and I are more than acquaintances."

"What would you call it? Certainly not friends."

"No, not exactly friends." He unfolded his arms and started toward her, his steps slow and measured, as if he expected her to bolt. And if she had any sense, she would, Susannah thought with near panic, as he stopped in front of her.

"There's fire between us," he said. "You can't deny that. I still remember how you tasted when we kissed."

Her cheeks flamed even as her heart started to pound. "I do agree that there's some sort of attraction between us. But acknowledging it is a bad idea."

"Doesn't seem such a bad idea from where I'm standing." Before she could move or even blink, he was there, bending down and kissing her.

A soft sound escaped her as his mouth claimed hers. Dear Lord, his lips were so soft, and so skilled. He cupped the back of her head in his large hand and claimed her mouth with a single-minded purpose that swept the defenses right out from under her.

Something vulnerable had been trapped inside her for so many years, and now it sprang free at the touch of this man. The walls around her heart melted away, and warmth suffused her limbs. She let herself go; she surrendered herself to Jedidiah's care.

His tongue touched hers, and with a hungry

little sound, she dove into the kiss, reaching her hands up to encircle his neck and pull him closer. The floodgates were open, her blood pounded in her ears, and for the first time in a long, long while, she felt what it was to want a man.

All she could think was *yes*. Whatever he wanted of her, whatever he asked, the answer was *yes*.

He groaned and slipped an arm around her, pulling her to her feet. But his intention to draw her into his embrace was foiled by her disguise. With a jolt of surprise, he broke the kiss. Both of them stared down at her swelling belly, which jutted between them like a reminder of possible consequences should they continue in this manner.

Jedidiah broke the silence first.

"We can't do this," he said.

"You're right." But she couldn't move, didn't want to leave his embrace.

"If we give into this thing, we'll never get to Denver, and you'll never clear your name."

"You're right," she said again.

He took a deep, shuddering breath and took one shaky step back from her. "Wash up," he said, avoiding eye contact. "Get yourself comfortable. I'll send someone up with your bag."

"Where are you going?" she asked, as he lifted his hat from the peg on the wall.

"To get a drink. I'll be back in a while. I think it's better if you stay out of sight as much as possible, so I'll have them bring supper up here for you. I'll tell them you're ailing; since you're supposed to be expecting, they'll believe it. And lock the door behind me."

"Wait!" she cried, as he opened the door. "When you come back, how will I know it's you? I don't want to open up the door when someone knocks and find Caldwell out there."

He met her gaze then, his still simmering with a heat that made her ache to be back in his arms. She licked her lips, still able to taste him. His eyes narrowed, and tension settled heavily over the room.

"You'll know it's me," he said, and she knew he was right. She could always sense when Jedidiah was around. No one else stole her reason and sped up her pulse like he did. It was as if there was some invisible connection between them.

"But just in case," he continued, looking away from her, "I'll knock like this." He demonstrated on the doorjamb. "Unless you hear that, don't open up the door. I'll have them leave your supper in the hall."

"All right."

He started to leave, then glanced back at her. "I expect to see you in this room when I get back, Susannah. You have a nasty habit of disappearing on me."

"I'll be here when you get back. I need you, Jedidiah. You're the only hope I have of getting out of this alive."

"I think we'd both better remember that." Then he was gone, closing the door behind him.

Susannah wasted no time. She locked the door as his footsteps faded down the hall, then quickly shed the huge dress and wadding. She hurried to the washstand and squealed with alarm when she caught sight of her grimy face in the mirror.

It was amazing Jedidiah had even noticed she was a woman when she looked like this!

But he had definitely noticed, and had acted on that knowledge with a devastating thoroughness that had her still trembling. His kiss had sapped the strength from her knees until they all but collapsed. What was it about the man that melted her entire body like butter on a hot biscuit?

With trembling fingers, she touched her slightly swollen lips. He made her want to give him everything, but he'd made it clear that once his job was through, he would be moving on. To the next job, the next town—maybe even the next woman.

She refused to be a fool about this; she wasn't going to let this attraction between them get out of hand. When Jedidiah returned, she would inform him that he was sleeping on the floor. And that was that.

Because if he slept in that bed with her, she was afraid she wouldn't be able to keep her distance as she should. And that would be more dangerous than facing Caldwell and a hundred of his lynch mob.

Pushing the disturbing feelings from her mind, she set about repairing her appearance.

Damn that woman. Jedidiah leaned on the bar in the Lucky Lady Saloon and contemplated his glass of whiskey. Kissing Susannah was the dumbest thing he had ever done in his life.

He had made it a life-long policy not to let anyone get too close. He hadn't even been twenty years old when he had fought for the Confederate Army and lost everything he had ever held dear: his home, most of his family, and his intended, Mary Louise. All he had left was his sister Lottie, mercifully spared due to her husband's position as a badly needed physician for the opposing forces when they had come through the area.

His family home had been destroyed. His father had died as a casualty of war, and later, his mother had died of typhoid. His fiancée, Mary Louise, had been killed by a band of renegade

Union soldiers who had been looking for food. Someone had shot her over a loaf of bread.

Jedidiah had come home at the end of the war to nothing.

He had later found Lottie in Charleston, and the reunion had been bittersweet. Even with his profound relief at finding Lottie alive, he still couldn't seem to break through the ice barrier that had formed around his heart. His distant manner had hurt his sister, but he couldn't seem to change it. If he let himself care, he would get hurt—so he'd locked his mind and emotions against anyone getting through.

To spare his sister further pain, he had left Charleston for the West, a place with wide-open spaces where a man could go for days without seeing another soul.

He enjoyed his job. He rode in when an emergency arose, helped people who were in trouble, and then left again before anyone could become attached. The life of a U.S. Marshal was perfect for him—and Susannah did not fit with that kind of life.

Sweet Susannah. The taste of her lingered on his tongue, and he sipped his whiskey to get rid of it. She was an incredible woman: gutsy, smart, compassionate. Most beautiful women were too aware of their good looks, and ended up being vain, envious, and self-serving. Susannah wasn't like that, though she matter-of-factly accepted the effect of her stunning appearance on others.

The attraction he felt for her was stronger than anything he had ever felt for a woman before. But he couldn't afford to let his own hunger get the better of him.

Under the best of circumstances, a woman could muddle a man's mind until all he could think about was getting inside her. In a situation like this, where death awaited at every crossroad, lust could steal a man's concentration, lower his defenses. With Caldwell on their trail, Jedidiah needed to keep sharp. He needed to be ready to defend Susannah with his life, if need be, to see justice done.

There was no way he was going to let her hang.

He tossed back the last of his whiskey and set the empty glass on the bar. His mind was made up; his resolve was firm. He would do his job despite temptation, maintain a professional courtesy that was one step back from friendship, and keep his wits about him at all times.

There was no other choice. If he failed in this, Susannah would be convicted and hanged.

Chapter 9

Susannah awoke to a tantalizing view of Jedidiah, naked from the waist up, shaving his jaw. For a moment she thought he was the figment of a glorious dream.

Morning sunlight streamed in through the fluttering curtains, bathing his muscular form in golden light. Each stroke of the razor was accompanied by the enticing ripple of his sinewy biceps. He had tied back his long hair, and she caught a glimpse of the strong column of his throat and his lathered face as he turned his head this way and that.

No doubt about it—Jedidiah Brown was one beautiful man to behold.

She admired the long, muscular length of his back, the solid breadth of his shoulders, the way his golden hair curled over his nape.

Then her gaze met his in the mirror. He had been watching her admire him, and his dark eyes simmered with quiet intensity. Awareness thrummed between them, and for a moment she wished circumstances were different, that she dared hold out her hand to him in invitation.

Her longing must have shown on her face. His features tightened, and his eyes narrowed to focus on her mouth for a long, breathtaking instant.

Then he closed his eyes, breaking the contact. Sucking in a deep breath, he looked down and rinsed the razor in the basin.

She swallowed and turned away. He was right; if they gave in to this attraction, they'd never get to Denver. And she'd never get her good name back.

Listening for sounds that might indicate he was getting dressed, her gaze slid over the other side of the bed. As she stared at the neatly tucked sheets, it registered suddenly that there was no sign of anyone having slept there. No rumpled covers. No impression of a head on the pillow. She turned back to face Jedidiah again.

"I slept on the floor last night," he said, answering the unspoken question.

"You did?" She glanced over the side of the

mattress and saw his bedding neatly rolled up and waiting to be packed into the wagon. For some reason, the fact that he had resisted the temptation of sharing her bed annoyed her, though she knew she should be grateful. "So you did. I *am* impressed, marshal. Your manners are improving."

He ignored her snide comment and wiped the last of the lather from his cheeks. His neat mustache and clean-shaven jawline made him look as civilized as he always claimed to be, but the heated awareness in his eyes told another story.

He plucked his shirt from the peg on the wall and donned it, turning to face her as he did up the buttons.

"We need supplies," he said. "After you're dressed, we'll head over to the mercantile to pick up a few things. Do you need anything?"

"Yes. Soap," she replied. "At some point I do intend to take a bath."

He shoved his shirttails into his pants and grabbed his hat from the wall. "As soon as it's safe, you'll have your bath, Susannah," he replied. "I'll wait for you downstairs."

"You do that," she muttered, but found herself speaking to a closed door as he quit the room.

Susannah took her time with her morning toilette, entertaining herself with images of an impatient Jedidiah pacing the hotel lobby. An hour after he had left the room, she finally descended the staircase, garbed in her dreaded disguise as a farmer's pregnant wife.

Jedidiah looked up as she leisurely came down the stairs, impatience in every rigid line of his body. But his tone gave away nothing as he said, "I checked on the horses while you were upstairs. One of them threw a shoe, so I need to go see the blacksmith."

"Will that delay our departure?"

"Not if you take this list and go over to the mercantile." He passed her a scrap of paper with the necessary supplies written on it. She noted soap at the very bottom and felt some of her annoyance melt away. He'd remembered.

"How am I to pay for this?"

He handed her some folded bills. "This should cover it. Wait for me there, and I'll come fetch you. Can you handle that?"

Arching her brow, she took the money and tucked it into her drawstring purse. "I can handle anything."

"You don't have to tell me that." With a hand at the small of her back, he guided her out of the hotel.

* * *

The mercantile was owned by a hulking ruddy-faced fellow named Martin Kracke. When Susannah first handed him the list, he was somewhat surly until he saw that she would be paying cash. Then he went about assembling her order with a smile on his thin lips.

While Mr. Kracke put together a box of coffee, beans, and sugar, Susannah wandered over to where two young women were giggling over bolts of fabric. A pretty blue and white dimity caught her eye, and she fingered it wistfully. Less than a week ago, she would have purchased the material and had it made into a stylish day dress designed to turn men's heads. But those days were behind her now, and heaven only knew what lay before her.

She moved away from the piles of cloth and wandered the aisles of the cramped store. If Jedidiah had his way, they would intercept Mrs. Hawkins before she boarded the train in Colorado Springs and convince her to testify to Susannah's innocence at the trial. However, there was every chance that Mrs. Hawkins *was* the murderer, in which case it would be more difficult. But when it came to law and order, Susannah would put her money on Jedidiah Brown every time.

He was as reliable as the sunrise when it came to official matters. But in matters of the heart, he was as capricious as a chinook. One moment passion ran hot between them, and he kissed her as if his life depended on it; the next moment he held himself cool and distant as if she meant nothing more than the completion of another assignment.

And she was no better, she thought with a snort of disgust. One moment she couldn't stand to be around the man, but the next moment she couldn't get close enough to him. She needed to keep her head clear. Falling in love with Jedidiah Brown was out of the question.

She paused before a selection of scented soaps, staring blankly at a jar of small heart-shaped ones. Falling in love with Jedidiah? Where had that come from? She couldn't fall in love with him—*wouldn't* fall in love with him.

She took one of the little soaps from the jar, closing her fingers tightly around it as the scent of roses drifted to her. Loving Jedidiah Brown would be like trying to catch the moon in a bucket, and Susannah was not one to chase the impossible. This was just a case of strong attraction under dangerous circumstances, nothing more. They were sharing an adventure straight out of some dime novel. It was no wonder she was starting to weave these ridiculous fantasies about him.

She pressed her lips together in determination. Susannah Calhoun didn't need to fall off a horse twice to know when she couldn't ride it.

Annoyed by the entire situation, she grabbed another of the small rose-scented hearts and headed toward the front. For some reason, it made her feel better to know she was buying the most expensive kind in the store, and that he was paying for it.

The bell jingled just as she reached the counter, announcing another customer. Mr. Kracke had already boxed up her items, but he rudely left her standing there as he attended to the man who had just entered.

She didn't pay much attention to the exchange at first as she waited impatiently for Mr. Kracke to get back to her. But gradually, something about the new voice registered as vaguely familiar. She glanced over, and her heart stopped beating for one long, agonizing second.

Wayne Caldwell stood two feet down the counter, bargaining with the merchant.

Her first instinct was to run. A furtive glance at the door revealed two of Caldwell's men loitering near the exit, so that way was blocked. Maybe there was a back door . . . ?

"And I need some good strong rope," Caldwell said.

Susannah bit back the whimper that rose to her lips. She kept her gaze forward, grateful for the large hat brim that concealed her features. Caldwell hadn't recognized her yet, and every second that passed was more time to think.

Think, Susannah!

Mr. Kracke passed by her and actually smiled, no doubt thrilled by the affluent customer who patronized his shop. "Be with you in a minute, ma'am," he said.

Caldwell spared her a glance, ran his eyes down her form, and then looked away as if she didn't deserve his notice.

He looked away! She could hardly believe it.

Then she remembered about her disguise and blessed Jedidiah's cleverness. All Caldwell saw when he looked at her was a pregnant woman buying perfectly ordinary staples at the mercantile. As long as he didn't see her face, she might be able to get out of this alive.

Mr. Kracke came back with a stout length of rope. Susannah's throat clogged with terror as Caldwell took it from him with a pleased smile. She had an awful feeling she knew what he intended to do with it.

"That's just the thing, yes, indeed." He examined the rope, then uncoiled a length and tugged hard on it. "I'll take this and a box of cigars." He slapped the hempen coil on the counter.

"Very good, sir!" Mr. Kracke turned to rummage on the shelf and came back with the cigars, which he put down next to the rope. He named an amount, and Caldwell pulled a roll of bills from his pocket.

Pay and go, Susannah begged silently, keeping her head bowed to better hide her features. *Don't look at me, just pay and go.*

"So tell me," Caldwell said as Mr. Kracke handed him his change. "You seen a pretty blond gal come through here recently?"

"I don't remember every woman that comes into town," Mr. Kracke said with a snort.

"You'd remember this one. Looks like an angel, blond hair and blue eyes."

"There are hundreds of blondes around here," Mr. Kracke retorted. "Heck, this nice lady is blond! Maybe she's the one you're looking for."

Susannah stood so still she thought her spine would snap from the pressure. Any moment she expected Caldwell to discover her ruse and drag her to the nearest hanging tree . . . and Jedidiah was too far away to help.

She glanced out the corner of her eye at Caldwell, who considered her bulging belly for a bare second before shaking his head and dismissing her with a wave of his hand. "Nah, the one I'm looking for is a real beauty. And she's traveling with a U.S. Marshal."

"No marshals come through here since last week," the merchant said.

"Maybe I beat him here," Caldwell murmured.

"Sir?" The shopkeeper glanced quizzically at him.

"Never mind," Caldwell said. "How much for this again?"

Mr. Kracke named the amount, and Caldwell paid him.

Susannah squeezed the soap in her hand so hard she thought it would break into pieces. Caldwell's heavy footsteps grew more distant as he reached the door. The bell jingled, and he and his men left the mercantile. Susannah let out a breath she didn't realize she was holding.

Safe.

"Sorry about that, ma'am. Is that everything you need?"

Susannah placed the two heart-shaped soaps in the box. "Yes, that's everything."

"Let me just total the bill, and I'll help you carry this out."

She waited while he counted the money, her racing heartbeat gradually settling down to normal. Caldwell hadn't recognized her, thank

God. He didn't even know she was in town, and the faster she got *out* of town, the better! She just hoped Jedidiah was back with the wagon.

Mr. Kracke hefted the box and led the way to the door. Susannah reached for the knob to pull it open for him, but it suddenly swung open before she could touch it. The tinkle of the bell rang like a death knell as Caldwell's bulky body filled the doorway.

"Forgot my cigars," he said, brushing past Susannah.

Her heart leaped into her throat as Caldwell headed back toward the counter. His two cohorts lingered outside the door. One of them smirked at her bulging belly while the other idly watched traffic roll by.

"Here you go, ma'am," Mr. Kracke said, setting the box down outside the door. Then he hurried back inside to tend his store. Susannah stepped outside just as Jedidiah pulled the wagon to a stop in front of the mercantile. Glancing behind her, she saw Caldwell heading right for her, a box of cigars clutched in one fist and the coiled rope in the other.

Jedidiah hopped down from the wagon, his attention on the box of supplies, and Susannah started toward him. The door to the mercantile opened behind her. Caldwell stepped out and stopped right next to the box of supplies, barely sparing her a glance. He immediately started conversing with the two men who waited for him. Jedidiah continued to approach the box, his path taking him only inches away from Caldwell.

Caldwell would recognize him; she was sure of it. Jedidiah was walking straight into danger, completely unarmed.

She didn't even pause to think. Stepping boldly past Caldwell, she laid a hand on Jedidiah's arm before he reached the box. He glanced at her questioningly, but before he could speak, she stood on tiptoe and pressed a kiss to his lips.

She felt his start of surprise, and she coiled her arms around his neck before he could pull away. Her lips lingered on his, tasting and testing. After a moment, he angled his head to better fit his mouth to hers.

One of the men behind her gave a snort of derision. "Guess we know how she got that way," he remarked, sending his partner into gales of laughter.

"Let's head out," Caldwell said, breaking up the jocularity. "I want to get a room at the hotel and wait that gal out. She and that marshal ought to be along any time now."

Jedidiah's shoulders tensed beneath Susannah's hands, and she realized that he had recognized Caldwell. But it wasn't until the thud of the men's footfalls against the wooden walkway faded into the distance that Jedidiah gently broke the kiss.

"Caldwell," he said in a low voice.

She nodded.

He frowned after the man's retreating back, his expression grim. "Let's get out of here."

They wasted no time in leaving Chalmers behind.

Jedidiah urged the horses on, and the town grew smaller and smaller behind them until Susannah could no longer see it. There was no sign of pursuit, yet she still felt strangely edgy. She couldn't seem to shake the tension that gripped her.

The near confrontation with Caldwell had rattled her badly, as if she had danced a waltz with the angel of death. She owed her life to Jedidiah's clever disguise of her. She just wished he would extend some of that cleverness to himself. Her pounding heart had nearly stopped in her chest when she realized how close he had come to being recognized.

She needed Jedidiah desperately, both for

protection and in other ways that she dared not even admit to herself yet. She feared the power he seemed to hold over her. It wasn't that he would ever make her do anything against her will; he tempted her to give in to her passionate instincts—something she had never done before with any man. He made her long to surrender.

But surrender what? Her body? At the advanced age of twenty-six, she had encountered many men who wanted her body. Some of them had even wanted her heart. But Jedidiah would demand everything: her body, her heart, and her soul. She might start out only giving her body, but in the end he would walk away with everything—and he *would* walk away.

And she'd be left behind with a hole where her heart had been.

Getting involved with Jedidiah Brown could only lead to heartbreak. She had enough trouble trying to stay alive, never mind attempting to manage a romance on top of it.

So, she would follow her head, not her heart. And just maybe she would come out of this heart-healthy, if not heart-whole.

Just as long as she didn't fall in love with him.

Jedidiah managed the speeding horses automatically, his mind locked on the fact that Susannah had barely escaped with her life. His blood ran cold when he thought about how close she had come to being captured by Caldwell.

It was his fault. He wasn't usually so careless, but he had been so busy trying to ignore his desire for Susannah that he'd relaxed his usual vigilance and almost gotten them both killed. His sharp instincts, which in almost twenty years of law enforcement had never failed him, had been completely submerged beneath his fear of getting too close to her.

And fear it was. He'd never encountered a female who had managed to wriggle past his sturdy defenses and wrap herself around his heart like Susannah Calhoun.

Over the years he had faced cannon fire, bullets, raging storms, and a near hanging or two without blinking an eye, but this woman wielded weapons that he feared could destroy him. She was sensual even in her innocence. Fierce even in fear. Invincible even in her vulnerability. The contrasts that made up Susannah fascinated him and drew him toward her, despite his best efforts to remain apart. He wanted to study all her facets, become familiar with her hopes and fears, grow attuned to her slightest emotional shift until he knew what she was thinking even before she did.

He wanted to discover her over the years until they were both old and gray. He wanted to stay with Susannah Calhoun until the day he died—and that scared him more than any murdering desperado ever could.

Chapter 10

⟨◦———∽◯◯∽———◦⟩

Jedidiah seemed to grow more and more distant with every mile. Any question Susannah asked was met with a brief though courteous reply. By the time they stopped and made camp for the night at the edge of a stream, Susannah was spoiling for a fight, if only to jolt Jedidiah out of his exceedingly polite emotional distance.

The setting sun cast a pink glow over the sky as he steered the wagon off the main road and along a barely discernible dirt path through the woods. The horses, scenting water, eagerly trampled fallen leaves and broken branches, jarring the wagon so that Susannah had to hold on to the seat with both hands.

Jedidiah finally pulled the wagon to a stop in

a clearing at the bank of the stream, and Susannah gingerly climbed down, wondering if they had cracked any of the wheels in the horses' mad dash to quench their thirst. Jedidiah unhitched the team and led the animals to the water's edge.

Susannah tried to stretch the kinks from her back, but her ponderous belly would not allow such freedom of movement. As Jedidiah worked with the horses, she tried to think of what she could do to begin to set up camp. Jedidiah had always done all the work, which didn't seem fair. She had never had to live off the land before, but she could certainly learn how. She decided to begin by collecting some of the dry tinder to build a fire, but found her efforts hampered once more by her faux belly. Nevertheless, she attempted to handle the task.

"What do you think you're doing?" Jedidiah's quiet voice echoed across the clearing.

"Collecting firewood."

"I'll do that. You sit here." He came and led her to a large boulder by the water's edge. "I can handle things."

"But I can help!"

"Never you mind about that," he said with a politeness that set her teeth on edge. "Just sit back and let me take care of everything."

"You act like I'm really expecting," she complained with a snort of disgust. "I'm not useless, you know!"

The stubborn man ignored her and set about collecting the tinder himself. She made a rude face at his back, then folded her arms across her chest.

When the fire was burning merrily, he pulled out the coffee pot. Susannah leaped to her feet and came to stand beside his crouched form.

"I can make the coffee," she offered.

"Thank you, but no."

She waited, but he said nothing more. "Why not?"

"It's not necessary." He stood and took her arm, leading her back to her rock again. "Just sit here and stay out of the way. Don't worry about a thing."

Susannah fumed as he turned his back on her and knelt by the fire to measure out the coffee. Of course she shouldn't worry—not as long as big, strong, *capable* Jedidiah Brown was around to take care of everything. He may as well have added a pat on her pretty little head to go with his politely patronizing tone!

Other women might enjoy the role of damsel in distress, but not Susannah. She would not sit idly by, wringing her hands while Caldwell and his lynch mob pursued them. And she certainly had no intention of facing the judge in Denver with tearful eyes and a sob in her voice. She meant to take part in the outcome of her own future, and she'd be darned if she would let Jedidiah Brown sit her on a shelf somewhere.

She got to her feet just as Jedidiah turned toward the stream with the coffee pot in his hand.

"I want to help you, Jedidiah," she challenged. "I am far from helpless, and I refuse to just sit here while you do everything!"

"I don't see why you feel you need to." He didn't even look at her, merely walked toward the stream.

"Well, it doesn't seem fair that you do everything all the time when I'm perfectly capable of helping you," she replied, attempting a reasonable tone.

"And here I thought you enjoyed being waited on, princess," he drawled.

His unexpected sarcasm made her abandon sweetness with all alacrity. "There's no reason to be nasty," she retorted with a glare. "And I've asked you not to call me that ridiculous name."

He didn't even look at her as he knelt by the stream and filled the coffee pot with water, which just made her angrier. No man had ever ignored Susannah Calhoun!

"I'm talking to you, Jedidiah."

"I think the name suits you . . . *princess*." He

rose, water dripping from the stainless steel pot, and gave her a tight smile. "You do like to give orders."

"I am not giving orders," she replied, stung. "I've *tried* to help, but you won't let me."

"I don't need your help, princess. Don't think just because you managed to get us out of trouble today that you're suddenly in charge of this little expedition."

"Is that what's bothering you?" She frowned up into his face. "You're upset because I managed to keep Caldwell from recognizing you?"

His mouth thinned. "He wouldn't have recognized me."

She made a sound of disbelief. "Yes, he would have. Taking off your badge does not constitute a disguise, Jedidiah."

"Now you're the authority on disguises, too?"

"What has gotten into you?" she demanded, exasperated. "You're treating me like a child. I'm an adult, capable woman, and I saved our necks back there. Accept it and get over your little snit."

"Snit?" He drew himself up, every inch the indignant male. "I am not in a *snit*. I thought about it, and I've decided not to let you be so reckless in the future. You shouldn't have put yourself in danger like that."

"You would have done the same thing for me."

"That's different."

"Oh, is it?" She arched her brows. "Because you're the man, so it's all right for you to take chances?"

"I'm the one with experience," he replied stiffly.

"Was it your 'experience' that led you to send me to the mercantile alone?" she demanded.

"That was a mistake," he admitted.

She sighed and closed her eyes, shaking her head. "No, it wasn't, Jedidiah, because if you'd come to the mercantile with me, we would have been discovered for certain."

"Then what are you so mad about?"

She threw her hands up in the air. "You're the one who started this," she snapped. "I was just trying to help. You're the one who feels guilty, not me."

"I do not feel guilty!"

"Then why are you acting so contrary?" she demanded. "If you feel bad because you had to leave me alone for a short time, then don't. No one knew Caldwell would be around."

"*I* should have known!" he snarled, bringing his face close to hers, his eyes fierce. "We were almost killed, and it's my fault."

"Oh, Jedidiah." She laid a hand against his cheek. "It's not your fault. It was just plain bad luck."

He stepped away, leaving her hand to drop to her side. "I have a job to do," he said, stalking back to the fire. "And that job involves getting you to Denver alive."

She curled her fingers into her palm. He couldn't have made his rejection of her more evident if he had shouted the words from a mountain top. Anger and hurt simmered together in her veins, and she suddenly felt the urge to shake him free of his polite defenses.

"Well, at least I know where I stand," she said, noting with satisfaction the way his shoulders tensed at her haughty tone. "I'll just stop worrying about you, *Marshal Brown*. Obviously, you are a man who needs no one in his life. How silly of me to forget."

He turned toward her as if to say something, but she presented him with her back as she marched to the wagon and dug out her heart-shaped soap from the box of supplies. As she turned back toward the water, he looked as if he intended to speak, but her icy glare froze the words on his tongue. He merely watched her with raised eyebrows as she made her way to the edge of the stream.

She crouched down and ran her fingers through the water. She had hoped the sun would warm it, but it retained a chill from the snow-capped mountains that fed it. No doubt the water would be absolutely freezing after nightfall, but for the moment it was adequate for bathing.

"Just what do you think you're doing?" he asked from behind her.

She didn't deign to look at him as she rose. "I am planning on taking a bath, marshal. Please have the decency to act the gentleman you proclaim yourself and turn your back while I do so."

Silence. Then, "You're just gonna strip down and jump in the stream?"

"I haven't had a proper bath in several days, and since you refused to allow me one at the hotel last night . . ." She shrugged. "I do intend to keep my shift on, however."

"You need to keep all of it on. What if someone comes by?"

Her response was to slip off her padding from beneath her voluminous dress and let it fall in a heap to the ground. Ignoring his disapproving scowl, she went to sit on the rock and bent to unfasten her shoes. "Perhaps you could do some of that protecting you're so fond of while I am incapacitated," she drawled. "I wouldn't care for Wayne Caldwell to come upon us while I have soap in my eyes."

A flare of emotion crossed his face, and she hid her smile of satisfaction. Oh, he was so calm about it all. So professional. So aloof from everything but the job at hand. But somewhere inside this polite stranger was the man who had admitted his desire for her just yesterday.

She only had to goad him into showing himself.

"Caldwell is the least of your problems," he said. "You'll probably freeze in that water."

"I'll survive." She didn't mean to look at him, but as she slid off the first shoe, she couldn't help herself. He stood watching her with overt male interest, the coffee pot forgotten in his hand.

"Do you suppose a weapon might be in order?" she asked pointedly. "If you meet Caldwell with a coffee pot, he might take that as an invitation to stay for supper."

His glower satisfied her quite nicely, and she began to hum as she removed her other shoe.

"You think this is funny, don't you?"

She looked up. "No, Jedidiah," she said, slowly peeling off one stocking. "I think *you're* funny."

"Me?"

She couldn't help but chuckle at his sour expression. "Yes, you. That male pride of yours is smarting because I managed to get us out of a nasty situation all by my little female self."

"And your *female* pride is getting carried away with itself." He plunked the coffee pot down on the fire and turned to the wagon to retrieve his guns. "I just don't want you getting cocky and putting yourself in danger."

"I have no intention of doing so," she replied, watching as he efficiently strapped on his guns. "At least, not when I have a big, strong man like you to defend me." She met his suspicious glance with a dulcet smile and a fluttering of her eyelashes.

"Don't waste your wiles on me, princess," he grumbled. "I know you too well for that."

"I wouldn't dream of it," she replied, then proceeded to take off her clothes.

The woman was trying to tempt him.

Jedidiah held on to his control with effort as she stripped the other stocking from her shapely leg. She wouldn't win. Already she had caused him to snap at her; he was damned if she would make him forget himself again.

She dropped the stocking to the ground to join the first one.

She won't do it, he thought, swallowing hard. Always before, she had hidden behind a bush or a rock while she changed her clothes. There was no way she would suddenly strip nearly naked in front of him after taking such pains to protect her modesty. She was trying to get at him, that was all. He recognized the glint of challenge in those gorgeous blue eyes.

He scanned her long, smooth limbs one last time before pasting an impassive expression on his face.

They couldn't become involved on a sexual level. It was too dangerous. He knew that.

But as he watched her slim hands smooth over her bare legs, none of it seemed to matter. He knew those delicate fingers hadn't wielded the knife that had ended Brick Caldwell's life. They would find the witness, clear Susannah's name, and he would move on. That was the way it had to be.

But when she stood and stretched, he found reason staggering beneath the force of his hunger for her. Without the padding, every swell and valley of her full-breasted body was outlined against the ugly brown woolen dress. Her pouty lips curved in a half smile that was both mysterious and female, and made him wonder what wickedness was passing through her mind. With effort, he maintained his stoic expression and crossed his arms over his chest, scanning the horizon as if searching out danger. But he watched her from the corner of his eye.

With a mischievous arching of her brows—as if she knew he was watching—she unfastened the first button of her dress.

Siren.

She opened another one.

Temptress.

Every button she flicked open showed a hint of more flawless skin, another glimpse of creamy bosom. Who was this sensual enchantress? He thought he knew all the faces of Susannah: Susannah the flirt, Susannah the stubborn, Susannah the clever. Never before had he seen this side of her, this incredibly feminine creature who exuded sensuality like a perfume that tickled his senses and tempted him to touch. To taste.

He thought of all the times he had touched her in the course of simple courtesy. Cupping his hands to help her mount, aiding her in dismounting from her horse, taking her arm as they crossed the street together. Small touches. Intimate in a way, but with the easy distance of gallantry standing between them.

But now, watching her slip the brown dress from her shoulders, he wanted to touch her in other ways. Ways that mattered.

The dark wool slid over her generous bosom, down her slender arms, past her flat midriff, then caught at the curve of her hips. She made a small undulation of her pelvis, and the garment slithered down to land in a crumpled heap at her feet. Pure lust streaked through him.

The thin lawn of her shift hid nothing from his hungry gaze—including the fact that she wore nothing beneath it. A soft evening breeze blew loose tendrils of silver blond hair across her face, and pressed the flimsy garment to her body. Her nipples grew hard from the chill, and he thought about warming them with his mouth.

When she reached up to undo her long braid, he clenched his fists and deliberately looked away, studying the trees as if the enemy lurked there.

"Are you shy, marshal?"

"Not a bit," he replied, still not looking at her.

"I think you are. Most men would be staring by now."

He tightened his jaw, knowing she was right, knowing how much he wanted to stare. "I'm not most men."

"That is quite obvious, Jedidiah."

His name murmured in that low, sultry voice of hers drew his attention despite his determination to behave like a gentleman. He looked his fill, knowing full well he shouldn't, but unable to resist.

She padded barefoot to the edge of the stream, her undergarment hiding little from his gaze. Lifting her shift to her knees, she cautiously tested the temperature of the water with one toe. "Oh, it's chilly!"

"I warned you."

She slanted him a look of pure coquetry, then glanced coyly away. "So you did."

"Susannah."

She whipped her head around at his husky growl. Despite himself, he feasted on the sight of her, blond hair flowing down her back, soft breasts swelling temptingly above the embroidered neckline of her shift, long legs exposed to the knee. He indulged himself for a long moment before he raised his eyes to her face.

"This isn't a game."

"I know that." She slowly withdrew her foot from the water and let her shift fall back into place.

"It isn't wise to start something right now. Distraction could get us killed."

"I know that, too." She approached him slowly, her eyes half-closed with the need that pulsed between them. Her skin was flushed, lips parted.

"I think it's best if we both just keep our distance."

"We should." She stepped closer. "But what if I don't want to keep my distance?"

"Then we have a problem."

She took another step toward him. "Then, marshal . . . I'd say we have a problem."

Her throat captivated him. Her palms. The bend of her elbows. The delicate skin at her temple. He wanted to touch everywhere, taste everything.

"We've already agreed that this is a bad idea," he murmured, reaching for her.

"You're right." She came into his embrace and rested her hands on his chest, tilting her face to his with a gleam of expectation in her eyes that he couldn't resist.

"Aw, hell." Bending his head, he kissed her with a thoroughness guaranteed to make her head spin.

She clung to his shirt as he explored her mouth with wild skill, his tongue slipping between her lips like a sleek predator in the night. He caressed the curve of her spine from shoulders to buttocks, and her body pressed against his as if she'd been molded to fit him.

He demanded everything with his kiss, and she gave it without hesitation. An eager moan rose in her throat when his hands cupped her buttocks and urged her closer, and he deepened the kiss.

He nipped at her mouth, then soothed the sting with his tongue. He tilted his head this way and that, trying new angles, exploring the recesses of her mouth from every possible direction.

He felt her curious palms stroking over his chest. Moving his mouth to the smooth column of her throat, he reached up with one hand and tugged at the buttons of his shirt. A second later, her fingers joined his. Together they managed to open his shirt and long underwear.

"Touch me," he murmured, pressing his tongue against the madly beating pulse of her throat. He curled his hands around her shapely bottom and pulled her tighter into his embrace. The first tentative touch of her fingers against the bare flesh of his chest made his heart pound. "That's it," he murmured as her caresses grew more confident. "Stroke me. Like a big old cat."

She gave a breathy laugh and did as he asked, stroking her palms down his chest with just the right amount of firmness, her fingers tangling in the curling hair. He felt just like a cat for a moment; he wanted to stretch out beneath her touch and purr from the pleasure of it.

She tugged open more buttons, continuing to explore him with curiosity. He pressed his mouth to her shoulder, nipping her there. She made a squeak of surprise, then gasped as he bent down and took one of her nipples in his mouth, right through the cloth of her shift.

"Jedidiah." Her body echoed the plea in her voice as she arched her back. He suckled harder, reaching up to cup her other breast in his hand, kneading it rhythmically. "Oh, sweet Lord, what are you doing to me?"

Something in her voice broke through the haze of passion that blinded him. She sounded as if she'd never done this before. Even the mere thought of such a possibility was enough for Jedidiah to regain control of himself.

Reluctantly, he let her nipple slide from his mouth, watching with regret as it beaded instantly in response to the cooler air of the evening. He made himself release her other breast, placing his hands on her hips and easing her a step away from him. She looked at him with the light of discovery in her eyes, her skin flushed with passion. He couldn't resist pressing one last, soft kiss against her sweet lips.

She made a whimpering sound and tried to come back into his arms, but he managed to disentangle himself and step away.

He was hard as a rock from wanting her, but he had to do the right thing. His code of honor demanded that he make sure she was willing before he made love to her.

"Is this what you want?" he asked, his voice rough with passion. "You have to be sure, Susannah. I told you I can't stay. Knowing that, do you still want to share my bedroll tonight?"

Her eyes grew wide, and he saw the answer in her face before she spoke.

"I'm sorry, Jedidiah."

He sucked in a deep breath. "That's what I thought you'd say."

She looked miserable. "I didn't mean for things to go this far."

"I know. But if this isn't what you want, then I suggest you get on with your bath and get yourself dressed."

She reached out a hand, then drew it back before she touched him. "Are you all right?"

He gave her a grimace. "Don't worry about me. I'll be fine in a little while, once I calm down."

She glanced down past his waist, then jerked her gaze back up, color flooding her cheeks like crimson flags. He wondered how many aroused men she had seen. Dozens, maybe.

The thought made him scowl. He had no doubt that a beautiful woman like Susannah had attracted a lot of men over the years. How many of them had touched her? Kissed her?

Even though he knew he had no right to think it, the idea that there may have been someone before him chafed like a burr beneath his blanket.

"Jedidiah?" She watched him with concern in those oh-so-innocent blue eyes. Had she looked at other men like that? Said their names like a caress?

"You still want that bath or not?" he asked. He knew his tone was too harsh when dismay crossed her face, but he couldn't seem to stop from making a jackass of himself.

"Yes, of course I do."

"Good. Let me help you." He scooped her up. Her squeak of protest turned into a shriek as he stepped up to the edge of the bank, and dropped her into the chilly water. Then he turned his back and stalked away, ignoring the outraged shrieks that followed him.

Chapter 11

"**T**his is ruined."

Jedidiah looked across the campfire at Susannah. Freshly bathed, and dressed in her own shirtwaist and skirt, she calmly held up the dripping bundle that used to be her disguise. He tried to ignore the way the firelight made her skin glow like alabaster and the way her drying hair glittered like strands of gold. Calling on every bit of his self-control, he focused his attention on the soaking garments.

"What happened to that?" he asked.

"It got drenched when you . . . when I went into the water."

Her tone was calm, her eyes determined. Obviously, she was going to pretend that the past hour—especially their embrace—had never happened. He wished he could forget as easily.

He wasn't very pleased with the way he had lost control and thrown her in the stream. He was a grown man, not a green boy jealous of his sweetheart making eyes at another. He was a professional, a lawman, and he shouldn't have given into his temper like that.

As for the passionate embrace, although he should feel some chagrin about it, he couldn't. No, it wasn't wise to become physically involved with his charge, but they were both human beings, and these things sometimes happened—though it had never happened to him before. He found it was easier to deal with if he looked at it philosophically; he had made the offer, and she had refused it. There was no reason to feel guilty about it. As long as he didn't dwell on how right she felt in his arms, or on the uncomfortable emotions that sprang to life whenever she came near him, he would be able to treat the whole thing casually.

To prove it to himself, he rose and crossed to her, noting how she tensed when he came near. For a moment, shame made him hesitate. Had his conduct frightened her? That would never do, if she were to trust him enough to get her out of this.

Then her gaze dropped to his mouth, and he

realized from the expression softening her face that she wasn't afraid of him at all. His body responded eagerly to her sweet look of desire, but he ruthlessly quelled his baser instincts.

Simply because of his age, he knew that he had to be the more experienced one; it was up to him to set the tone of their association from now on. She had made it clear that she wasn't interested in a physical relationship. He had to respect that, no matter how many hungry glances she gave him.

"Will it dry out?" He took the dress and padding from her hands. The cotton-stuffed pillow that had made up her false pregnancy was wet clear through. Already he could smell the musty scent of the stream that clung to the cotton, and the seams looked like they would give way at any second.

"The dress might," she responded. "But that thing is ruined."

"What about the bonnet?" he asked, keeping his gaze on the wet material as she moved a step closer. The smell of her rose-scented soap made him wonder if this woman had been born knowing how to drive a man to distraction.

"The bonnet is fine," she was saying. "It was by the fire when the rest of this got wet."

"All right." He shoved the gown back at her. "Wear the bonnet with your regular clothes. I'll think of something else for when we come to the next town."

She took the garments from him, her fingers just brushing his and sending a fresh flood of desire surging through him. He stood stone-still, not daring to move lest he reach for her.

"Jedidiah."

He glanced at her face, seeing the acknowledgment of his own longings reflected in her eyes.

"Thank you," she said. "Thank you for stopping things before they got too . . . complicated."

He gave her a short nod, afraid that if he tried to speak, he would beg. She turned and walked away, the gentle sway of her hips an invitation that he struggled to resist.

She said no, he reminded himself, so it was best that he keep his lusty thoughts to a minimum. He had to get them to Denver alive.

He sat down on his bedroll, his guns within easy reach, and set about eating his supper.

Susannah deposited the sopping mess that used to be her disguise into the back of the wagon, then glanced across the clearing at Jedidiah.

The firelight flickered over him, bathing him in golden light from head to toe. He looked lean and dangerous as he ate a bowl of the stew he'd cooked, his eyes moving restlessly around the perimeter of their camp as if expecting the enemy to burst from the bushes at any moment. His guns rested beside him on the ground, but she knew he could move like the wind when he wanted to. Anyone approaching their camp would be met with a Colt pointed at some vital organ.

Jedidiah would see that she made it to Denver alive, no matter what the personal cost to himself—even though she'd rebuffed him.

Her heart swelled with tenderness toward her gallant protector. She knew she had made the right decision. As heavenly as it had been to have his hands on her, as arousing as his kisses were, she could not give herself to a man who would not stay.

She wanted to. Oh, how she longed to cross the clearing and offer herself to him. Never before had she experienced the heady power of being a woman the way she had when she'd teased him by slowly stripping the clothes from her body. But then, no man had ever caught her attention like Jedidiah.

What would she have done if things had continued to their natural conclusion? If he hadn't asked her to make a choice? Most men wouldn't have asked. Most men would have taken what they could get and then left when the time came without a second glance, leaving the woman with bitter regrets and a sense of betrayal.

But not Jedidiah. He was too honest, too much the gentleman to ever do something like that. She had been angry with him for leaving so abruptly last year, but in hindsight, she realized she had really been angry at herself. She had been so rude to him at every turn simply because she had been disturbed by her own feelings for him. He had owed her nothing, had made no promises nor broken any. All they had shared was a kiss, and even then he had told her that he wasn't staying around. There had been no reason at all for him to give her notice that he was leaving, and perhaps that was why she had been so furious at him. Because she'd wished there *had* been a reason. She'd wished there had been something more between them than just one kiss.

The more she got to know Jedidiah, the more complex he appeared.

With a sigh, she turned back toward the campfire. They were only half a day away from Colorado Springs and Abigail Hawkins. She only hoped Jedidiah's associate had managed to stop the woman from getting on the train, or else they'd never find her.

She needed her life back. She needed to clear her name and return to her career as a singer. However, those goals came with the unfortunate consequence of having to say good-bye to Jedidiah, perhaps for good. And outside factors—like Wayne Caldwell and the murder trial that awaited her—were pushing things along at a swift pace.

Her stomach growled, reminding her that it had been hours since her last meal. Thinking deep thoughts was getting her nowhere fast. She would simply take each day as it came, and set her priorities accordingly.

And right now, her priority was supper, followed by a good night's rest.

They came to the town of Beecham early the next afternoon. The fairly large town sat at the crossroads of two major thoroughfares, one a stage coach route and the other a cattle trail. It was easy to see why the bustling community boasted so many hotels, eating establishments, and boardinghouses.

Susannah sat quietly on the wagon seat next to Jedidiah, her hands folded in her lap and her head dutifully lowered. She knew that he had elected to leave the trail for the sole reason of procuring another disguise for her. Even with the huge sunbonnet shadowing her face, her shapely figure still drew eyes. Jedidiah glared at more than one cowboy who dared to send a hopeful glance her way.

For the first time, the appreciative masculine looks made Susannah self-conscious. She edged closer to Jedidiah on the wagon seat. She didn't want to attract any attention that might give Caldwell a hint as to her whereabouts, and the closer they got to Denver, the more serious her predicament became.

The hoots and hollers of randy cowboys got positively deafening as they neared a large gray building on the corner. It took Susannah only a moment to realize that this time, the ruckus was not directed at her.

The gaudy red and gold sign on the front of the building read "Loralee's Dance Hall." From the second floor veranda a bevy of scantily clad women called out enticements to the men on the street, inciting the riot of whistles and shouts.

Susannah cast a glance at Jedidiah. His dark gaze flicked over the flirting beauties, and a small smile tugged at his lips. Without missing a beat, he turned his attention back to navigating the wagon along the crowded thoroughfare, but that smile lingered.

Susannah's breath froze in her lungs; she felt as if she had taken a punch to the gut. She hadn't realized how much it would hurt to see Jedidiah smile at another woman. Turning her gaze away, she stared blindly at the buildings they passed, twisting her fingers together in her lap and squeezing tightly. She knew she had no right to feel jealous. She had refused Jedidiah's advances for very sound reasons, but at the moment, those reasons seemed paltry in comparison to the emotions that gripped her.

Until now, it hadn't occurred to her that he might seek his pleasure elsewhere. It had been just the two of them alone on the trail these past few days, and she had forgotten that she was not the only woman who might find him attractive. She had no claim on him. And he had every right to take care of his needs with any willing woman he chose.

Jedidiah stopped the wagon in front of the sheriff's office. Determined to act as if nothing was wrong, Susannah sighed as he got down to tie up the team. "Are we going to do *this* again?"

Her spared her a stern glance. "I need to know you're safe while I go rustle up a disguise for you."

"I think you just get some sort of perverse pleasure out of locking me up," she retorted, climbing down from the wagon. She turned, then stumbled back a step as she found herself only inches away from Jedidiah's broad chest.

He grabbed her arm to steady her. "Careful, now."

"Heavens! You move like the wind," she

stammered, more aware than she cared to be of the scent of him, the heat of him.

"You might have noticed me, princess, if you hadn't been so preoccupied." He lowered his head until his mouth brushed her ear, his voice a low rumble. "You want to know about my pleasures, perverse or otherwise, you just say so."

She swallowed hard. "I made my choice, marshal."

He stood staring at her for a long moment, those sherry-dark eyes hot with need in his taut face. Then he gave a jerky nod and stepped back, gliding his hand along her arm before breaking contact. "That you did. I'm just letting you know that you can always change your mind."

She met his gaze steadily, starving for the taste of him. "I'll remember that."

Without another word, he turned and led the way into the sheriff's office.

Ten minutes later, he stormed back out again, Susannah at his heels.

"What a lazy, self-serving son of a bitch!" he snarled, untying the team from the hitching post with one sharp jerk. "That man is a disgrace to the law!"

"I'll say." Susannah climbed into the wagon.

Jedidiah hauled himself into the driver's seat with easy strength, snatching up the reins and setting the horses to a brisk trot down the street.

"What kind of sniveling piece of scum charges another officer of the law for use of his jail?" he went on furiously. "Ten dollars! He should be horse-whipped."

"I didn't like the look of him," Susannah said, shuddering as she remembered the way the portly sheriff's black eyes had speculatively scanned her body. "I have a feeling he wouldn't have stayed on his side of the bars for long."

"I have a feeling you're right. And I have a better place for you to go, one that won't cost me ten dollars." He turned the wagon toward the end of town. Once more they passed Loralee's Dance Hall, but this time Jedidiah didn't even glance at the buxom beauties. Instead, he headed right for the church.

The closer they came to the white clapboard structure, the tighter Susannah's fingers grew on the edge of her seat.

"You'd better not be thinking what I think you are," she warned.

His mouth quirked in a grin. "I need to put you *somewhere* while I go find you a new disguise. Besides, every time I leave you in a cell, you end up in trouble."

"Which seems to indicate you should take me with you," she retorted.

Jedidiah laughed as he stopped the team in front of the church. "If it weren't for that face of yours, princess, I wouldn't even have to go through all this."

"Oh, sure, blame it all on me."

Still chuckling, Jedidiah tied up the team, then offered a hand to help Susannah out of the wagon. She broke the contact the instant her feet touched the ground.

Jedidiah raised his brows at her hasty retreat. "Behave yourself so I can introduce you to the reverend."

Susannah rolled her eyes.

There was a smaller structure of matching white clapboard beside the house of worship, which was the residence of the local minister, the Reverend Mathias. The Reverend and Mrs. Mathias welcomed Susannah warmly and accepted Jedidiah's story about having his "wife" visit with them while he ran an errand in town. As the moon-faced preacher looked on, Jedidiah took Susannah's hand and placed a chaste kiss on her cheek.

"Stay put this time," he whispered, as his lips grazed her cheekbone.

Unable to resist, she placed a hand on his chest and looked up at him with adoring blue eyes. "Don't be long now, darling," she simpered, playing to her audience. "You know how much I miss you when you're gone."

"I'll be back directly." He took her hand from

his chest and squeezed it in warning before he took his leave.

"You two must be newlyweds," Mrs. Mathias said with a knowing smile, as Jedidiah closed the door behind him.

"Why yes, we are. How ever did you guess?" Susannah moved to the window and peered out, watching Jedidiah's retreating form as he headed down the street.

"Oh, I can sense these things," the plump minister's wife said with a smile. "He can't take his eyes off you. Young love," she sighed.

"Oh, he definitely likes to keep me in sight." Jedidiah had crossed the street and was headed in the direction of the mercantile.

"He seems like a good man," Reverend Mathias said. "You're a lucky young woman to have such a devoted husband."

"Yes, very lucky." Susannah's mouth fell open as Jedidiah passed by the mercantile and walked through the swinging doors of Loralee's Dance Hall. Shock was followed quickly by raw fury. It was all she could do not to storm out of the reverend's cottage and drag Jedidiah out of there by his mustache. He was supposed to be keeping her safe from Caldwell, not whiling away the day in the arms of some dance hall tart! What kind of lawman was he, anyway?

An honest one, she remembered suddenly. The thought doused the flames of her anger like a bucket of cold water. Jedidiah Brown would never put aside his duty in favor of his own pleasures, no matter what the provocation. He must have some good reason to be wandering into Loralee's Dance Hall in the middle of the day.

The fact that she was acting like a jealous shrew annoyed her. It was a typical reaction, and Susannah Calhoun prided herself on *never* being typical.

"Come have some tea, dear," Mrs. Mathias said. "Hanging about the window isn't going to bring your husband back any sooner."

Grateful for the distraction, Susannah dropped the curtain and smiled at her hostess. "Thank you, Mrs. Mathias. Tea sounds wonderful."

Chapter 12

❦

Jedidiah stepped through the swinging doors of Loralee's Dance Hall. The saloon was open for business, but since the girls didn't dance until the evening hours, there were only a few men sitting at the bar. In the corner, two rough-looking characters played a silent game of cards.

No doubt the place got pretty lively at night. The red wallpaper and gilt molding attempted to give an element of elegance to the room, but instead it created a gaudy lack of refinement that Jedidiah found oddly comforting.

It was the kind of place where a man could kick back and be a man without worrying about the mud on his boots or cleaning up his language. If he wasn't in such a rush, he wouldn't have minded spending a relaxing evening smoking cigars and drinking whiskey.

But Caldwell was right behind them, and the sooner he got Susannah a disguise, the better. Besides, he had a feeling Susannah might not understand the allure the dance hall had for a man.

He walked over to the barkeep, an elderly man who was polishing glasses at the end of the bar.

"Afternoon," he said with a friendly smile. "I'd like to speak to Loralee."

"Miss Loralee don't come down until after sunset," the barkeep said, turning his back in dismissal.

"I'd still like to see her. I'd make it worth your while if you could tell her that."

The old man peered at Jedidiah with narrowed eyes. "How much worth my while?"

Jedidiah slid some money across the bar. The barkeep looked at it for a moment, then snatched it up and stuffed it into his pocket.

"Who should I tell her is calling?" the old man asked with ill-concealed sarcasm.

"A friend from Charleston."

The fellow snickered as he sidled out from behind the bar. "Yup. Miss Loralee sure does have a lot of 'friends.' "

Jedidiah shook his head and settled down on

a stool to wait. A few minutes later, the bartender was back.

"She says she'll see you, so go on up," he said, not bothering to disguise his surprise. "Last door on your right."

"Much obliged." Jedidiah ignored the stares of the other patrons as he headed up the stairs and down the hall. When he came to the last door on the right, he knocked softly.

The door opened immediately to reveal a tall, spectacular redhead dressed in a lacy dressing gown of deep green silk. In her hand she held a derringer pointed straight at his heart.

Jedidiah slowly put up his hands. "I surrender," he said.

The redhead blinked her dark brown eyes, then burst out laughing and lowered the gun. "The day you surrender to anyone, Jedidiah Brown, is the day I join the church choir!"

Chuckling, he lowered his hands. "Aren't you going to ask me in?"

"Sugar, I've been asking you in for years." The husky purr in her voice gave the ordinary comment a seductive twist as she turned and walked into the room, leaving him to follow.

Jedidiah stepped inside and closed the door. "It's been a while, Loralee."

"Too long, handsome." She placed the derringer in a jewelry box on top of the bureau, then leaned back against the piece of furniture, unconsciously taking a pose that made the most of her curvaceous figure. Surprisingly, he didn't feel the rush of arousal normally brought on by such a sight.

"I saw you come into town before," she said. "Where's your friend?"

"It's a long story, but she's why I'm here." He gave her his most charming grin. "I need your help."

A slow, sexy smile curved Loralee's lush mouth. "Anything you need, sugar." She straightened and came toward him, the silk and lace accenting every bountiful curve. She stopped in front of him, then reached out to glide a teasing finger down his chest. "Anything at all."

Jedidiah grinned. A man always knew where he stood with a woman like Loralee. She used to make him hotter than a branding iron with little more than a smile. Now he felt only the fondness of an old friend, despite the fact that she was trying to seduce him. Puzzled over his own lack of response, he still played the game as was expected. "Darlin', I need your clothes."

"Why, Marshal Brown," she purred. "I thought you'd never ask."

"And a wig if you have one," he continued. "Dark hair would be best."

Loralee raised her perfect eyebrows, her lips curving in delight. "My, my, Jedidiah, I never suspected you had such diverse tastes. Is there anything else I can get you?"

"No, that ought to do it."

"Are you sure?" She slanted him a seductive glance. "I have all sorts of interesting toys."

Jedidiah raised his brows in feigned confusion. "I'm talking about a disguise for my friend, Loralee. What are you talking about?"

"I'm talking about getting friendly," she said with a wink.

He laughed. "As much as I'm tempted, I have to resist. I'm here on business."

Loralee pouted. "You can't blame me for trying."

"No, I can't. Now, behave yourself, and tell me if you can help me out."

"I can certainly get you some clothes and a wig. So they're for your friend?"

"They're surely not for me," he replied with a chuckle.

"No, you're not the type." Laughing, she went over to throw open the wardrobe. "She looked about my size."

Jedidiah studied the woman's ample curves and compared them to his mental image of Susannah's shapely body. "She's a little smaller than you," he said, "but not much."

"Huh. Young, too, I'll bet."

"Not too young."

"Good, then I won't have to hate her." Loralee pulled out a gray gown with a demure lace collar. "This ought to do. I use it for funerals. Add a dark wig and give your lady a Bible to hold, and no one will recognize her."

"She's not my lady," he felt compelled to point out. "I told you, this is business."

"Uh huh." Loralee looked him up and down. "Jedidiah, you and I have known each other for a lot of years."

"Going on ten," he agreed.

"And never before have you come to see me and left again without at least being tempted by what I can offer."

"Loralee, I told you—"

"I know what you told me, Jedidiah. You've said all the right things and smiled in all the right places, but this time you're all talk." She paused, studying him with her head tilted to the side. "She must be someone very special."

"She is." Uncomfortable with the whole conversation, Jedidiah took the dress from her. "I'm sorry if I hurt your feelings."

"Not at all. It does my heart good to see how the mighty have fallen," she said with a grin.

"I haven't fallen," he muttered. "Do you have the wig?"

Loralee pulled several boxes out of the wardrobe and rummaged around until she came up with a wig made of straight black hair. "Here you go, sugar. I used to wear this for a fella who liked to pretend I was a squaw. It braids real nice."

"It'll do." Jedidiah rolled the wig up in the dress. Then he took Loralee's hand and pressed a kiss to the palm. "I can't tell you how much this means to me, Loralee. As soon as I saw your name on the sign for this place, I knew I could depend on you."

"Don't mention it." Loralee sauntered to the door and opened it for him. "I'm just glad I got to see the day that Jedidiah Brown finally surrendered."

"This is *business*."

"If you say so." Laughing, Loralee shut the door behind him. He scowled at the closed door before setting off to recover Susannah.

Jedidiah came to collect her from the reverend's care, refused an invitation to dinner, and then whisked her off to the wagon so quickly that Susannah barely had time to draw breath. Then they were headed down the main street at a fast clip.

As they passed the dance hall, a stunning redhead stepped out onto the second floor terrace. Clad only in a deep green dressing gown, she folded her arms across her chest and met Susannah's interested stare with raised eyebrows.

Was this magnificent creature the person Jedidiah had gone to see? Susannah lifted her chin proudly and nodded once in acknowledgment. Surprise crossed the woman's face, followed swiftly by amusement. She nodded in return, then went back into the building.

Susannah faced forward just in time to catch Jedidiah's scowl. "What's wrong?" she asked.

"What was all that about just now?" he demanded.

"What?" Feigning confusion, she widened her eyes at him.

He only looked disgusted. "Don't try that innocent look on me, princess. I saw that little exchange just now. What do you think you're doing?"

"What's wrong with giving a nod of greeting to someone?" she challenged. "I assume that was the person you went to see when you went to the dance hall. I also assume that she provided you with that gray dress in the back of the wagon, correct?"

"It's not what you think—" he began.

She smiled. "I think it was a brilliant idea to go to the dance hall looking for a disguise. These women are entertainers. Naturally they would have costumes and wigs and all manner of things that could be used for disguises."

"Well, that's what I thought." He glanced at her, clearly confused. "I just didn't want you to get the wrong idea. Loralee is an old friend of mine."

"Did you think I would be jealous?" Susannah gave a trilling laugh that made such a conclusion seem ridiculous. "I made my choice by the stream, Jedidiah. And I would be the worst sort of hypocrite to hold it against you if you went elsewhere to . . . ah . . . take care of your manly needs."

"You're not jealous?" he asked skeptically.

"Of course not." It wasn't a lie—not exactly. She certainly wasn't jealous *now*. And she only had felt murderous for a few minutes before she remembered Jedidiah's dedication to the law.

"Good," he replied. "Because if you were jealous, I was just going to remind you that you could always change your mind about your decision."

It was getting harder and harder for Susannah to maintain her casual tone. "I think we're both wise to keep things the way they are."

"If that's the way you want it."

She glanced at his handsome profile. "That's the way it has to be," she said quietly.

"All right, then. I'll find a secluded place at the side of the road, and you can put on your new clothes. There's a wig with the dress. I plan on stopping in a town before nightfall so I can send a wire."

"You seem to have everything taken care of," she said with admiration.

He sent her a glance that was only half teasing. "Except my 'manly needs.'"

She rolled her eyes, and he laughed, the sound echoing over the wide-open road.

"Susannah," he said with a grin. "I know you were jealous."

Her only reply was a haughty sniff.

Proctor's Corners was a rough and ready mining town.

Susannah took comfort in the fact that Jedidiah had taken to wearing his guns again, though his badge remained absent. This town looked like a man could get shot in the street and no one would even notice. She was dressed in the prim gray gown and dark wig with her deep-brimmed bonnet. The Bible in her hand served to turn unwanted male attention away from her.

Jedidiah pulled the wagon to a stop in front of the mercantile. As he leaped out to tie up the horses, Susannah climbed down her side of the wagon. Jedidiah met her there and took her arm.

"Stay close and keep your head down," he murmured, leading her to the wooden walkway. "I want to work our way down to the telegraph office without seeming too obvious about it."

She nodded and played the part of obedient wife as they made their way down the street.

The crowd was full of rough-looking miners who strode along without consideration for others, jostling people and shoving them out of their way. Children clung to their mothers' skirts to avoid being trampled by the rowdy crowd, and women walked quickly along with their eyes down so as not to draw unwanted attention to themselves.

Susannah stayed close to Jedidiah, his lean, warm length lending a sense of security that was welcome in this very uncertain crowd. The rowdies took one look at Jedidiah's face and turned away; people moved out of his path rather than attempt to jostle him or block his way. They arrived at the telegraph office in short order, and Jedidiah quickly hustled her inside.

The office was empty except for the gangly young man who operated the telegraph.

"Stay here," Jedidiah murmured, then stepped up to the counter to handle his business.

Susannah stayed where he had left her, just to the left of a window overlooking the street. Jedidiah spoke in a low voice to the telegraph operator, then took a pencil and a scrap of paper and began to write. Bored, Susannah turned to glance out the window.

A man stood just across the street, scowling at the door to the telegraph office.

Susannah stiffened. The fellow was tall and broad, bigger than Jedidiah, and he wore tan pants and a blue shirt that made his blond coloring all the more striking. But despite his boyish good looks, there was an element of danger about him, a watchfulness that claimed every muscle of his body as he casually leaned against a post, his gaze fixed steadily on the doorway. She couldn't help but notice that he wore his guns as if they were a part of him.

Fear rippled down her spine. She looked around the office, but she and Jedidiah were the only ones present, aside from the clerk. She glanced back at the blond man. He hadn't moved.

Did he work for Caldwell? Or perhaps she was simply imagining things.

Jedidiah crossed to her. "Let's go," he said, taking her arm.

"Wait. There's someone out there." She resisted his efforts to pull her along and gestured toward the window.

He peered out at the street over her shoulder. "Who are you talking about?"

"He's right there . . ." Her words died unspoken as she looked back where the man had been standing. He was gone.

"Where?"

"Never mind." Feeling like an idiot, she refused to look at him. "I thought someone was watching us. I guess I was wrong."

He squeezed her hand. "Don't you worry about it," he said softly. "Being on the trail this long tends to make people jumpy. But we'll be in Denver in a couple of days, and then you can relax."

"Oh, sure I can," she retorted as they stepped out into the sunshine. "I find being tried for murder so relaxing!"

He chuckled, and the sound warmed her heart. The tension between them lately had done away with most of their easy banter, and she had missed his dry sense of humor.

She smiled up at him, then noticed a flash of

blue out of the corner of her eye. She turned her head and met the gaze of the blond man who had been watching the telegraph office. This time there was no mistake. He was definitely staring at them.

"Jedidiah," she whispered. She didn't dare break eye contact, lest the fellow slip away again.

"What is it?" Jedidiah stopped and pulled her to the side of the walkway.

"He's back. The man who was watching us."

She felt him tense beside her. "Where?" he asked, following her gaze.

"Right there. The blond man with the blue shirt who's standing by the sheriff's office."

She knew the moment he spotted the man, because he jerked with surprise. Then a slow smile crossed his face.

"I'll be damned," he said.

The man in the blue shirt lifted a brow at Jedidiah, then turned and entered the sheriff's office. Jedidiah took her hand and started after him.

"I take it you know him?" Susannah asked.

"Yup."

That one word was all the answer she got. The rest of her questions remained unanswered as Jedidiah led her into the sheriff's office.

The blond man was hanging his hat on a peg

on the wall when they entered. He turned to face Jedidiah, slowly crossing his arms across his chest.

"Afternoon, Jedidiah," he said.

"Nate." Jedidiah gave a nod of acknowledgment. "So, where's the real law in this town?"

"You're looking at him."

Jedidiah looked Nate up and down. "Like I said . . ."

Nate scowled. "I ought to put a hole in you for that."

"You'd best learn to shoot, then."

"You first."

Jedidiah narrowed his eyes at Nate, and Nate did not look away. Silence reigned for a long, charged moment. After a minute or so, Susannah shook her head in amazement; it took a man of fortitude to hold Jedidiah Brown's gaze.

Suddenly Jedidiah grinned and broke the eye contact. He held out a hand. "You always were more reckless than smart."

Nate laughed, reaching out to firmly shake Jedidiah's hand. "I learned everything I know from you, you sorry son-of-a-gun."

"Don't be blaming me for your bad habits." Still smiling, Jedidiah turned to Susannah. "This is Nate Stillman, an old friend of mine. Nate, Susannah Calhoun."

"Pleased to meet you, ma'am." Nate took the

hand Susannah extended and only held it a moment longer than necessary when he got a good look at her face. A flicker of appreciation lit his very blue eyes for a brief instant, then he released her hand and turned to Jedidiah. "Loralee sent me a wire, said you might be coming through. What are you doing in this neck of the woods?"

"Escorting Miss Calhoun to Denver."

"Most people take the stage." Nate's teasing remark held a question.

"It's a long story," Jedidiah replied, and Susannah breathed a sigh of relief. She had a feeling that Nate's gentlemanly demeanor towards her might undergo a change should he discover she was accused of murder.

"Aren't they all," Nate drawled. "Can you stay a spell, or do you have to move on?"

"What do you have in mind?" Jedidiah asked.

Nate grinned. "Things have changed since I last saw you," he said proudly. "I got myself a bride."

"You got married?" Jedidiah stared. "By all that's holy, who would have you for a husband?"

"The orneriest female in Colorado, that's who. Her name's Darcy. We got married last autumn." Nate kept a straight face, but his eyes sparkled with mischief. "I was planning to ask you to stay to supper, but I don't know how the wife would feel about a no-good saddle bum like yourself setting his feet beneath my table."

Jedidiah gave a bark of laughter. "You're just worried I might steal her from you."

Nate arched his brows. "My Darcy knows a real man when she sees one—which is why she'd never look twice at you."

"We'd be pleased to stay for supper," Jedidiah said with a grin, "if only to meet this brave woman who took you on."

"Just don't get her mad," Nate said with an exaggerated shudder. "She'd make mincemeat out of both of us."

Jedidiah burst out laughing, and Susannah watched him with a fond smile tugging at her lips. Never before had she seen Jedidiah so open and relaxed. The next few hours promised to be very interesting indeed.

Chapter 13

Darcy Stillman was not at all what Susannah expected.

Nate had led them down the main street to a pretty white house that stood at the edge of town. Flowers lined a stone walkway, and a white picket fence surrounded the front yard and disappeared around the corner of the house.

Jedidiah glanced at Nate. "This is your place?" he asked with disbelief.

"Yup." Proudly, Nate surveyed his home. "It used to be the mayor's house, but he built a bigger place farther out, so I bought it from him. Makes it convenient in case I need to get to town in a hurry. Come on in."

They followed Nate into the house. He hung

his hat on a peg in the foyer. Directly in front of them was a staircase leading to the second floor. To their right was a hallway with a shiny wood floor and the doorway to what seemed to be a parlor. Susannah caught a glimpse of pretty white and blue china sparkling on the shelf of a china cabinet and comfortable rugs spread out before a large fireplace. A rocker and a sturdy cushioned chair faced the fire.

"Nate, is that you?" a feminine voice called from somewhere in the house.

"It's me, darlin'," Nate called back. "I brought some company for supper."

"Who is it?" A woman came down the hallway. She couldn't be more than five feet tall, yet had a buxom figure any woman would envy. Her red-brown hair caught the sunlight as she came into the foyer, a friendly smile curving her cupid's-bow mouth. Her dark eyes warmed as she looked at her husband. "Nate, aren't you going to introduce me?"

"Of course I am. This here is Marshal Jedidiah Brown—I've told you about him. And this is Miss Calhoun."

"So this is the famous Marshal Brown." Darcy held out her hand with a pleased smile. "Nate has talked about you often. I'm so glad you came by."

Jedidiah's lips curved in that charming smile that always made Susannah's heart skip a beat. Bending over Darcy's hand, he brushed his lips gallantly across her knuckles. "Had I known Nate had married so delightful a lady, I would have come to visit sooner."

"Oh, my." Darcy gently tugged her hand away. "Mr. Brown, you'll turn my head with such compliments."

"I'm just telling the truth." Jedidiah stood, continuing to smile. "If Nate doesn't treat you right, you let me know about it, and I'll knock some sense into his head."

"That will be the day," Nate retorted.

"Behave, Nathaniel," Darcy said mildly, "or I might just take Marshal Brown up on his offer." She turned toward Susannah. "Hello, Miss Calhoun. I'm Darcy Stillman."

"Please, call me Susannah."

"Susannah it is. And you can call me Darcy."

"Jedidiah and Miss Calhoun are on their way to Denver," Nate said. "I asked them to stay to supper."

"That's a wonderful idea." Darcy looked at Jedidiah. "Will you be staying the night with us, Marshal Brown?"

"Jedidiah. And I hadn't thought about it . . ."

"Do stay," Darcy entreated.

Jedidiah frowned. "I don't know if that would be the wisest thing, ma'am."

Darcy pursed her lips and put her hands on her hips. "Jedidiah, please excuse me if I speak plainly. Since Susannah is obviously wearing a disguise—your wig is crooked, dear—I am assuming that you are trying to avoid attention. How better to do that than to stay in a private home? How long has it been since you've had a proper bath? Or slept in a real bed?"

"Ah . . ." Jedidiah glanced at Nate, who raised his hands in a position of surrender.

"You're on your own, friend."

"If you can't remember, marshal, then it has obviously been too long," Darcy said sharply. "Come, Susannah. I'll show you to a room where you can wash up. And let's do get rid of that awful wig. It really doesn't suit your complexion. I hope you have something to change into, for I fear my gowns won't suit. You're so delightfully tall."

"I do have something in the wagon," Susannah replied, bemused at the smaller woman's commanding presence.

"Excellent. Nate, please fetch our guests' things from their wagon, and then show the marshal to the guest room so he can wash up. I'll take care of Susannah."

"Yes, ma'am," Nate replied.

Darcy sent him a dark look, obviously sensing something in his tone that rankled. "Don't you start with me, Nate Stillman. This poor woman is worn out, and I intend to see that she gets a bath, a good meal, and a decent night's sleep before Jedidiah drags her back out on the road. It's the Christian thing to do. Now you go fetch that wagon, or there will be no supper in this house tonight."

Turning her back on her husband, Darcy took Susannah's arm. "This way, Susannah. I expect you'd love a nice hot bath about now."

"It sounds like heaven," Susannah agreed. She glanced at Jedidiah.

"Far be it for me to disagree with our hostess," he said. "You go on up. I'll go with Nate to fetch our things and be back shortly."

"Now you're talking sense," Darcy said approvingly. "Nate will show you where to wash up when you get back. Come on, Susannah."

With a last glance backward, Susannah allowed Darcy to lead her up the stairs. Nate's voice drifted up to them as the two men left the house.

"Didn't I tell you not to make her mad?" Nate was saying as he passed through the door. "We had a lucky escape, my friend."

Jedidiah's reply was lost as the door swung shut.

* * *

"So, can you tell me what's going on?" Nate asked later.

Having retrieved the gear, they had ascended to the second floor of Nate's house, where Jedidiah relinquished Susannah's change of clothing to Darcy. Then Nate had shown him to a tiny yet elegant guest room, where Jedidiah proceeded the strip the dusty shirt from his back and make use of the soap and water on top of the bureau. In a corner of the room, Nate lounged in a chair that looked more ornamental than functional, and seemed as if it might break under his weight at any moment.

Jedidiah sponged off his upper body, gladly ridding himself of the scents of mud and sweat.

"If you can't tell me," Nate said in reply to Jedidiah's silence, "it's all right. I just wanted to know if you needed any help."

"You are helping." Soaping his face, Jedidiah picked up his razor and started to scrape the day's growth of beard from his jaw.

"I owe you, Jedidiah. If there's anything else I can do . . ."

Jedidiah paused and met his friend's gaze in the mirror. "Son, you're doing more than you know. I'm just worried that we might bring trouble on you by accepting your hospitality."

Nate sat up straight in his chair. "That's what I was afraid of—you *are* in trouble."

Jedidiah chuckled and resumed shaving. "When am I not?"

"I'm the sheriff of this town, Jedidiah. If there's trouble headed my way, don't you think I should know about it?"

Jedidiah humphed in grudging acknowledgment. "You're an uppity youngster, you know that?"

"I'm twenty-nine years old—hardly a youngster." Nate grinned mischievously. "Of course, everyone must seem like a youngster to an old man like you."

"Like I said—uppity." Jedidiah wiped the last of the lather off his face and reached for his clean shirt. "Still, you do have a point. And you know how to keep your mouth shut when it's warranted."

"This has something to do with Miss Calhoun, doesn't it?"

"Yes." Jedidiah tucked the tails of his shirt into his trousers. "She's been accused of murder, and it's my job to escort her to her trial in Denver."

"Murder!" Nate exclaimed. "But—"

"She says she didn't do it, and I believe her." Jedidiah stared steadily at Nate. "If you have a problem with this, just say so, and we'll leave."

"No problem." Nate leaned back in his chair. "You just caught me by surprise, is all. You haven't been treating her like a prisoner, so I thought maybe she was some rich man's daughter, and you were escorting her to Denver or something like that. Murder was the last thing I expected to hear."

"Susannah said there's a witness who can prove her innocence: the victim's housekeeper. Unfortunately, Mrs. Hawkins left town in a bit of a hurry. The woman knows something all right, and she's running. The only question is why."

"Wasn't there an investigation?" Nate asked. "Seems to me someone should have asked this Mrs. Hawkins if she'd seen anything."

"Someone did—the sheriff. But the fellow who was killed is Senator Caldwell's nephew, so things got rushed along a little bit."

Nate's lip curled in disgust. "Politics."

"My sentiments exactly. Anyhow, Caldwell's brother has decided he doesn't want to wait for the trial. He's after us with a lynch mob. We had a close call with him a day or so ago in Chalmers." Jedidiah ran a comb through his hair, then glanced at Nate. "He's a nasty one."

"Well, if you say she didn't do it, then I believe you. Your instincts about people have always been right on target." Nate stood. "If you give me a description of Caldwell, I'll have my men look out for him. In the meantime, you and Miss Calhoun can have yourselves a nice supper and spend a peaceful night here with us."

"You don't know how good that sounds, Nate."

Something in his voice must have given him away, because Nate frowned. "Is there something you haven't told me, Jedidiah? You look like you have something on your mind. Something more than business."

"Of course not." Jedidiah swept his things back into his saddlebag and buckled the bag securely.

"Something to do with Miss Calhoun, perhaps?"

Jedidiah's head came up, and he glared. Nate held up his hands in a gesture of surrender.

"Hey, I was just asking. She's a beautiful woman, and you've been out on the trail together for a few days. I just thought you might want to talk about it. If there was something, I mean."

"There's nothing."

Nate went on as if Jedidiah hadn't answered. "When I was courting Darcy, there were times when I felt like I didn't know myself at all. She was the mayor's daughter, you know, which is how we got this house. And her father sure as heck had better plans for her than me. But Darcy wanted me, and in then end, she got me."

"That's different, Nate. You intended to marry her right from the start. I have no plans to get married. Ever." Jedidiah tossed his saddlebag into a corner. "My relationship with Susannah is just business. I intend to help her clear her name; then I'm going to leave, just like I always do." Even to his own ears, his protests sounded insincere.

"Just as long as you're sure," Nate drawled.

"Of course I am."

"All right, then." Nate opened the door and gestured for Jedidiah to precede him. "Shall we join the ladies? My Darcy is a heck of a cook, if I do say so myself."

Jedidiah paused before exiting and extended his hand. "Thanks for helping out, Nate."

Nate shook it. "Well, you trained me when I was a U.S. Marshal, and you also saved my life a couple of years back. I'm happy to return the favor."

"A night's sleep in a place where I don't have to watch my back is going to go a long way, Nate."

Nate clapped him on the shoulder as they left the room. "You don't have to tell me, old friend. I've been there myself."

* * *

Susannah stood in the kitchen and watched as her hostess expertly basted the ham she had baking, then slid the meat back into the oven. The sunny kitchen was painted a pale ivory and seemed the perfect backdrop for the petite brunette. Honey-colored shelving and cabinets set off the soft blue gingham curtains that fluttered at the open window, and a vase of daisies stood on the windowsill. The image was one of functional comfort, and it suddenly reminded Susannah painfully of her mother's kitchen back home.

"The potatoes are cooking and the corn is just about done," Darcy said cheerfully. "All I need to do is to make the biscuits. Nate adores biscuits."

"May I help?" Susannah asked. "It's been so long since I made biscuits."

"How long?" Darcy asked, setting out the ingredients.

"Years. I left home about four years ago, and the way I traveled around, it never seemed practical to cook for just myself. I ate at restaurants or in whatever boardinghouse I was staying in at the time."

"It's nice to eat in a restaurant once in a while," Darcy said, cracking eggs open on the side of the bowl with a practiced motion. "But after a while, I start thinking about how I would have prepared the food and what I would have done differently, and it just takes the fun right out of the whole experience."

"I never thought about it," Susannah replied. "I'm a good cook, and I can sew anything—my mother is a seamstress—but I always end up eating at restaurants and buying store-bought clothes."

"Oh, are you handy with a needle?" Darcy energetically kneaded the dough, casting Susannah a hopeful glance. "I've been working on this new dress, but I haven't had anyone to help me get the hem right. Perhaps you could give me a hand after we finish the biscuits?"

Susannah smiled with real delight. "I'd be happy to."

Jedidiah followed the sound of voices into the parlor, then stopped dead in the doorway. And stared.

Darcy stood up on a stool, wearing a half-finished dress of some white material that had little violets on it. Susannah knelt on the floor, a pin cushion at her elbow, chattering and laughing as she pinned up the trailing hem of the gown. He watched the quick, adept movements of her fingers, the way she barely had to look where to set the pin, and realized that Susannah Calhoun had made more than one dress in her life.

For some reason, the knowledge stunned him. He had always thought that Susannah was a woman who preferred town life to the cozy comforts of home. A woman who preferred to have a dressmaker create her garments. A woman who would never soil her fingers by cooking her own food.

But the Susannah he saw before him now, laughing as she conversed with Nate's bubbly little bride, seemed to be a completely different woman. How many sides were there to her?

"Something smells wonderful," Nate said from behind him, drawing the attention of the two women.

"Don't you dare steal a bite, Nathaniel Stillman!" Darcy warned. "Supper will be ready soon enough."

"Just one little piece?" Nate wheedled.

"Don't even bother," Darcy said firmly. "We have guests. Save your begging for another time."

"I don't *beg*," Nate said, clearly insulted.

Darcy ignored him. "Oh, dear, I forgot to check the biscuits!"

"Stay right there," Susannah said, rising. "I'll run in and take care of it, otherwise we'll have to start all over again."

"Thank you, Susannah," Darcy said with a smile.

As Susannah approached, Jedidiah knew he should clear the doorway. But for some reason he stayed where he was, meeting her hesitant gaze as her steps slowed. She wore the pink dress she had been wearing the first day he had seen her in the jailhouse, the one that set off her smoky eyes and made her complexion glow. A few strands of hair had escaped the knot on top of her head, and the silvery blond locks brushed her cheeks and temple in a way that looked nothing like untidy and everything like desirable.

Attuned to her as he was, he saw the way she caught her breath and the way the pulse at the base of her neck started to pound. She wasn't indifferent to him. But she had made her choice clear back by the stream, and he had to respect it.

But damn it all, something about the way she looked as she was hemming that gown for Darcy made him think about promises of forever. And for the first time, he thought that maybe forever might not be such a bad deal.

"Excuse me, Jedidiah," Susannah said softly.

Ever the gentleman, Jedidiah moved aside that she might pass. And then he watched the sweet sway of her delectable bottom as she walked down the hall to the kitchen.

If only he hadn't lost his idealism years ago, he might have followed her into the other room and made a promise or two. Even though he had learned his lesson the hardest way possible, he still felt the longing for a home, for someone to be waiting for him when he came through the door in the evenings.

He wanted that someone to be Susannah.

Jedidiah raked a hand through his hair as the realization hit home and dug in deep. Behind him, Nate and Darcy started to bicker good-naturedly with one another. He glanced over and couldn't help but notice the contentment in Nate's smile and how Darcy's eyes sparkled as she answered his teasing. Darcy leaned slightly toward her husband, as if drawn to him, and Nate couldn't seem to resist taking her hand or touching her hair. The intimacy between them was almost painful to watch, and Jedidiah found that he was jealous of what his friend had found with his new wife.

He wished he could be more like Nate, but he had lived this way for so long that he was certainly too old to change. But though it was too late for him, it wasn't for Susannah. She was so vibrant and young that she would certainly find herself a handsome husband to settle down with.

The thought brought an ache to his chest. If only things were different, he might consider asking Susannah to share his life. But he was old enough to recognize when something wasn't meant to be. No matter how much he wanted to make love to her, in the end, she was better off without him. Susannah deserved someone who could love her fully and completely, not a road-weary, set-in-his-ways cynic like him.

It was best to leave things as they were. He would help Susannah clear her name, and then he would let her go.

Because he cared for her too much to break her heart.

Supper was delicious, and while Nate and Darcy laughingly washed the supper dishes, Susannah stepped outside onto the back porch for a breath of fresh air.

Laughter and music drifted to her from the saloon at the other end of town. In a way, the Stillmans' house reminded her of where she had grown up in Wyoming Territory. Burr was also a small town, and the house where she had lived with her parents stood back to back with Main Street, so she was used to hearing the sounds of the town as she went to sleep at night. But there was also a certain comfort to Darcy's house that reminded her sharply of home. Once upon a time she had longed for a house of her own, much like this one.

She sat on the porch rail and looked up at the

stars. It always amazed her that in the face of the immensity of the night sky, a body could feel positively insignificant. Whenever she stared up at the constellations above her, she always felt as if her own problems were miniscule, like a drop of rain in the vastness of a mountain lake. In the face of the star-studded beauty above her, her difficulties faded to mere annoyances, like the nip of a gnat on a warm summer night.

All that remained huge were her confusing feelings for Jedidiah.

As if her thoughts had conjured him, he stepped out of the shadows near the side of the house. A pinpoint of red light drew her attention, and she realized that Jedidiah was smoking a cigar. He came toward her, his steps measured and easy, then took the cigar from between his lips and blew a stream of smoke into the air.

"I didn't know you could cook," he said by way of greeting.

She raised her brows. "I didn't know you smoked."

"On occasion I enjoy a good cigar."

"On occasion I get tired of eating other people's cooking."

He didn't reply, merely puffed on his cigar for a moment or two. Finally he said, "Where'd you learn to sew?"

"My mother is a seamstress; you know that. She taught Sarah and me. She also taught us how to cook and keep house."

"So why aren't you married with a passel of kids?"

She was surprised at the vehemence in his tone. "Until now I have never met a man who might tempt me to use my domestic skills, marshal."

"Until now?"

Her eyes widened, and she hurried to clarify. "I meant I have not *yet* met a man who made me long to become domesticated."

"Just so we're clear." He took the cigar from his mouth and eyed it for a moment, as if it were a rare piece of artwork. "Some men weren't made to be husbands, Susannah."

"And some women weren't meant to be wives."

He glanced at her, surprise clear on his face. "If you don't plan on marrying a man, that doesn't leave much in the way of defining a relationship."

She sensed a question in the statement, but she couldn't tell what he was trying to ask. "I never said anything about getting married—or getting involved with a man at all. I find men to be a nuisance."

He chuckled. "A lot of men find a woman to be a nuisance."

"I don't doubt it." She stared up at the sky once more.

"You have a lot to offer a man, Susannah," he said quietly. "Don't doubt yourself."

"I don't doubt myself; I doubt men." She looked at him, so impossibly attractive in the half light of the moon. There was something very appealing about the way his face was shadowed, the way she couldn't read his expressions, yet she knew she had his complete attention. "Do you know, I used to enter my peach pie in the Founder's Day pie contest every year? And every year—I won."

"You must make a heck of a pie."

She gave a bitter laugh. "Hardly. I won every year because the judge was interested in courting me. Finally I gave up entering." She sighed. "Just once I wanted to win because my pie was the best, not because the judge wanted to come sit on my front porch on Saturday night."

"Some women wouldn't have cared."

She slid off the railing. "I'm not 'some women,' Jedidiah."

"I can see that." He blew another stream of smoke into the air. "Seems to me the men you've met so far were fools."

"I have to agree with you there."

"Hold fast to your dreams, Susannah," he said quietly. "Someday there will be a man who will fully appreciate you. Don't give up looking for him. You'll find him someday."

Puffing on his cigar, he turned and walked away. Susannah leaned on the rail, clenching her fingers around it, and wished she could tell him that she already had.

Chapter 14

For the first time, Susannah wished she could stop the day from dawning.

She had awakened early and been unable to go back to sleep. She knew that Jedidiah planned to leave today, and she was reluctant to relinquish the peace and safety of the Stillmans' house. As long as they stayed here, it seemed like there was no murder charge, no Mrs. Hawkins, no Wayne Caldwell.

But as much as she wanted to pretend the outside world didn't exist, she also knew that if they did stay, eventually the danger would find them here, and the serene refuge they had enjoyed would be destroyed.

She rose from her bed and set about getting dressed.

* * *

Jedidiah decided Susannah should change her disguise again, just to be on the safe side. It took most of the morning, but eventually Nate and Jedidiah came up with something. It wasn't as clever as the pregnant farmer's wife disguise, but it would do.

Jedidiah had first thought about dressing Susannah up as a boy, but one glance at her very womanly, very curvy figure had changed his mind. The purpose of a disguise was to keep people from noticing Susannah—and her sweet bottom encased in form-fitting britches assured the opposite would be true.

So they settled for making her look much older. She wore the huge sunbonnet to hide her face, put soot in her hair to make it look more gray than gilt, and bundled herself up in a large shawl. She hunched over and walked much more slowly, giving the impression that she was indeed an older woman.

Other than making a face when Darcy had dusted her hair with soot, Susannah had suffered the transformation without complaint. She had come a long way from the snooty and vain princess she had appeared to be a few days ago.

Susannah hugged Darcy good-bye and agreed to the woman's request to stay in touch. Nate offered to walk beside the wagon as they headed toward town, just to make sure they made it out of Procter's Corners without incident.

Susannah stayed huddled in her shawl as the two men conversed casually, both on the lookout for danger as the wagon creaked through town. They had almost made it to the end of the street when a body smashed through the window of the saloon and landed in a heap in the street, blocking Jedidiah's way.

Women screamed and clutched their children to their skirts. Jedidiah pulled the wagon to the side of the street and hopped down as Nate hurried forward to kneel beside the fallen man.

"He's alive," the sheriff announced, just as another man came flying out of the saloon, this time smashing the swinging doors in his passing. He rolled off the sidewalk and landed flat on his back, groaning. Gunshots sounded from inside the saloon, and then all hell seemed to break loose.

Jedidiah stayed close to Susannah as the brawl exploded into the street. A skinny silver-haired oldster appeared in the doorway of the saloon after the last man had stumbled out, his shotgun clenched in his bony hands.

"You're not busting up my place again!" the

old man shouted in a raspy voice. "I just got it fixed up from the last time!"

None of the combatants wanted to argue with a shotgun, so the brawlers continued their fisticuffs in the middle of the street. The smack of fists hitting flesh sounded above the shouts of the fighting miners. Horses screeched and shied away from the fray, and it was all Jedidiah could do to keep his team calm. Nearby, a burly fellow knocked a smaller, filthier one into the horse trough with a left hook, then turned to take on the next challenger.

Jedidiah could see his friend's blond head in the crowd of scruffy miners as Nate tried to get the riot under control. As much as he wished he could help his friend, his first duty was to stay by Susannah and keep her safe.

A tall, skinny scarecrow of a man flew backward and hit the wagon with a thud, surprising a squeak out of Susannah. The man gripped the sturdy wood with desperate fingers, shook his head to clear it, then peered with interest at the bounty of supplies piled in the back of the wagon.

Jedidiah pulled his Colt. "I don't think so," he said softly.

Obviously reconsidering, the fellow backed off, then turned back into the fracas.

Jedidiah continued to hold his revolver in

case anyone else got any ideas about bothering the wagon or its contents. Two of Nate's deputies had entered the fray, trying and failing to subdue some of the main combatants. One deputy ended up face down in the mud, and Jedidiah was hard-pressed to keep from laughing out loud at the expression on the young man's face.

"Oh, my God, Jedidiah!" Susannah grabbed his arm with one hand and pointed with the other. "There's Mrs. Hawkins!"

"What? Where?" Stunned, he followed her direction, but could only make out a mass of ladies huddled against the wall of the mercantile. "Which one?"

"See that dark-haired lady with the valise? The one with the dark blue traveling dress and the straw bonnet with the bow on it?"

"The one talking to the taller woman holding the baby?"

"Yes! That's her, Jedidiah!"

"She was supposed to be on her way to Colorado Springs," he said almost to himself.

"It must have been a false trail. You've got to get to her," she urged, shoving at him with both hands.

"I don't want to leave you alone," he said with a frown. "And the only way to get to her is through *that*." He indicated the commotion.

"Leave me your gun. I'll be fine. What can happen to me here?" She grabbed hold of his arm with both hands, her eyes wide and beseeching. "Please, Jedidiah. She's my only hope!"

"All right." Reluctantly, he handed her the Colt. "Do you know how to use one of these things?"

"Of course." She held the gun on her thigh, hiding it beneath her shawl. "My father taught me how to defend myself at an early age."

Imagining how he would feel if he were Susannah's father, Jedidiah could well believe it.

"You're wasting valuable time, Jedidiah." She smiled at him and patted his arm. "Don't worry about me. I'll be here when you get back."

Still he hesitated. "Every time you say that, something happens that makes you *not* here when I come back."

"Jedidiah, *go!*"

"All right, I'm going." He pointed a finger at her. "Just stay put and keep that gun hidden unless you need to use it."

"Yes, Papa, I'll be good." Her cheeky smile didn't sit well with him at all.

"I'm not *that* much older," he growled, heading into the fray with a surly scowl.

Jedidiah fought his way through the churning bodies, his frustration fueling each jab and punch. About halfway through the crowd, he thought he heard Susannah cry out. He looked back to see a mangy-looking fellow trying to climb into the wagon. Susannah shoved him to the ground with a well-placed kick to the chest. Jedidiah started back, but when the miner tried the same maneuver a second time, Susannah greeted him with the Colt in his face. The fellow put up his hands and backed away, then disappeared into the crowd. Susannah glanced over the brawling bodies, saw Jedidiah watching her, and waved with a sunny smile.

Don't worry, her smile seemed to say, *I can take care of myself.*

Jedidiah hesitated for a moment, and that hesitation cost him a blow to the face that made him see stars. He shook his head to clear it, and his vision aligned just in time for him to duck the meaty fist making a return trip. He grabbed his assailant's arm, twisted it painfully behind him, then gave him a hard kick in the pants that sent the fellow stumbling into the crowd.

With effort, he put Susannah out of his mind. His priority was making it through the brawlers to the other side, before Mrs. Hawkins got away once more.

He was almost to the edge of the roughhousing when Mrs. Hawkins started to move. She slipped past the other women gathered near the door to the mercantile and slowly made her way to the edge of the sidewalk. Her gaze was fixed on something in the distance.

Jedidiah followed her stare and saw a cloud of dust at the end of the street. It was the morning stage.

The woman was about to slip from his grasp if he didn't stop her.

"Mrs. Hawkins!" he called out, shoving his way past the wrestling brawlers. "Mrs. Hawkins, I'm a U.S. Marshal! Wait!"

The woman glanced back at him, her eyes wide with fear. She turned her back on him and quickened her pace. At the end of the street, the stagecoach thundered into town.

Jedidiah spat a curse and jammed a man in the ribs who was blocking his path. He shoved past another one and ducked a flying fist, slipping around and between the fighters as quickly as he could. Finally he broke free of the crowd.

The door was already closing on the stagecoach. He raced down the sidewalk, ignoring the squeals of the ladies as they pressed themselves against the walls to get out of his way. The stage driver snapped the reins; the stage started to pull away.

"Stop! U.S. Marshal!" Jedidiah shouted, but a roar of outrage from the brawlers drowned out his shout. The stage driver, obviously of a mind to keep his schedule, sent the horses galloping right for the knot of fighters in the middle of the road. They scattered like insects, calling their displeasure as the departing stage rumbled past them, neatly breaking up the fight.

Jedidiah tore after the stage, but after only seconds it was obvious he would never catch it. He stopped in the middle of the road, panting hard, and watched his witness disappear out of his reach.

Nate and his deputies used the disruption of the stage to their advantage, clearing out the lingering fighters. Slowly traffic settled into its normal pattern.

Jedidiah swiped the sweat from his forehead, then turned back toward Susannah.

She was gone.

When the two men had attempted to steal the wagon out from under her, Susannah had naturally put up a fight. But one man had managed to get the Colt from her, and the other had grabbed her about the waist in an attempt to throw her from the buckboard. Susannah objected to this plan of action and let her assailants know it by using every dirty fighting trick she had ever learned. In the struggle, her sunbonnet had been ripped off, and her hair had fallen around her shoulders, shining like silver and gold in the sunlight.

The element of surprise had served her well. Instead of an old lady, the bandits found themselves confronted with a young woman—a young woman who took advantage of their amazement by kicking one and hitting the other over the head with the coil of rope Jedidiah kept under the seat of the buckboard.

When she scooped up the revolver from where it had fallen on the floor, both would-be thieves decided the goods in the wagon weren't worth taking on the irate young woman. They had disappeared into the crowd.

That was when she had seen Caldwell.

He stood outside the nearby barber shop, his cohorts cheering on the fighters. Dressed like a city lawyer in a dark blue suit with an embroidered vest of cream-colored silk, he had no interest in the brawl going on only yards away. He raised his cigar to his lips, his gold pinky ring glittering in the sunlight. But when he recognized her, his eyes widened; then his malevolent stare washed over her, leaving her feeling as if insects were crawling over her skin.

Even as he had shouted to his men, she leaped out of the buckboard and ran toward the fighters, screaming Jedidiah's name at the top of her lungs. But the roar of the fighting was too loud, swallowing up her cry for help.

Cruel hands grabbed her arms and yanked her back from the fray before she could lose herself in the twisting bodies. The revolver fell to the ground, swallowed up in the jumble of moving feet. She struggled and screamed, but this time Caldwell's men were ready for her. One of them held each arm, and they quickly hustled her back toward the buckboard. Anyone watching them would think they were only trying to keep a lady from getting hurt in the fight. But once out of sight, one of them stuffed a rag in her mouth and bound it in place with a filthy bandana. The other one wrapped a cord around her wrists, pinning them behind her back.

Susannah kicked out and jerked her body this way and that, but they had apparently learned from their last encounter with her. To her horror, once her wrists were tied, they pushed her to the ground and tied her ankles together, then pulled the rope tight, bending her legs back so that she was hog-tied like a prize calf. Even as the tears of fury started, they shoved a sack over her head and hefted her between them and set off. The sounds of the town faded, and she knew they were taking her away from the main street.

They had put her into some sort of wagon. Caldwell's cruel chuckle reached her ears, and the sound incited her to struggle in earnest. But no matter what she did, she wasn't able to get loose. In fact, the rope grew tighter each time she struggled.

Now she lay helplessly in the back of the wagon with her eyes closed, heart pounding, praying that somehow Jedidiah had seen what had happened. That he would come after her. At this point, hope was the only thing keeping her sane.

After what seemed like hours but was probably only about twenty minutes, the wagon lurched to a stop.

"This looks like a good place," she heard Caldwell say.

Rough hands closed around her arms and legs, and she was unceremoniously hauled from the back of the wagon and shoved to the hard ground. Someone sliced the rope that bound her ankles, but left her wrists bound behind her. Hands jerked her up to her knees, and the sack was swept from her head.

Caldwell stood before her, his lips curling in a grim smile. Everything about the man was pudgy: his fingers, his body, even his lips. And his brain, Susannah thought. Grief had obviously driven the man mad.

"Well, well, how the mighty have fallen," he sneered. "You've cost me a lot of time and trouble, missy."

Still gagged, she glared at him.

He laughed. "If looks could kill, I do believe I'd be a dead man," he said to his companions. "Take the gag off. Let's give the little lady a chance to beg for her life."

His henchmen stood on either side of her. One was a tall, skinny fellow with stringy black hair and breath that smelled like last night's whiskey, and the other was a shorter, ruddy-faced cowhand with huge biceps and straw-colored hair. The tall one reached down to jerk the bandana down around her neck. She spit out the nasty-tasting rag. It landed near the toe of Caldwell's expensive shoe.

"Now, beg for your life," he commanded, a smile playing about his lips. "Maybe I'll be merciful."

"I'm not going to beg," she replied, her voice raspy and her mouth dry from the gag. "And I didn't kill your brother, Mr. Caldwell."

"Give the gal a chance, and she chooses to lie." Caldwell shook his head and made a tsk-ing sound. He took a step closer and grabbed a handful of her hair, jerking her face back with an abruptness that made her gasp. "Now, you do what I tell you, and never mind the lies.

Everyone knows there was only one woman there that night, and that was you."

Everyone knows there was only one woman there that night? A strange way to put it, Susannah thought.

"I didn't do it," she insisted, knowing it was no use.

"String the lying bitch up," Caldwell ordered, releasing her with a careless shove. "Maybe she'll be in a begging mood with a rope around her neck."

"No!" Susannah cried out, digging in her heels when the two accomplices started to drag her toward a nearby tree. "Don't do this! Let the jury decide!"

"Out here we make our own justice," Caldwell said, folding his arms across his chest as one of his men tossed a rope over the sturdy branch of the tree he had chosen. "An eye for an eye, Miss Calhoun."

The rope flipped over the branch, dropping the knotted noose to hang suspended before her eyes. Her stomach lurched.

Where was Jedidiah?

The taller of Caldwell's cohorts came to stand before her. He took the noose and slipped it over her head as his partner held her arms.

The stout rope fell across her collarbone. Her heart was pounding, her head growing light from fear. This couldn't be happening, she thought frantically, as the tall one scooped her hair out of the noose. Her life couldn't end here in the middle of nowhere at the whim of an unyielding, mad-with-grief lunatic.

The noose tightened around her neck, the roughness of the rope scraping the vulnerable flesh of her throat.

"Fetch that wagon," Caldwell ordered. "She can stand on it."

The dark-haired man jogged over to the wagon, a decrepit old thing made of faded wood and rusted wheels that read "D. Kane, Blacksmith" on the side. He hopped aboard and clucked to the tired-looking mule that was hitched to it. Slowly the animal ambled forward, the wagon wheels crunching over the dirt and grass like a funeral dirge.

These were her last moments on Earth.

Susannah's heart thundered in her chest, and her pulse pounded in her ears as she took in the world around her for the last time. A breeze caressed her face and brought the scent of wildflowers to her nose. The trees and the grass looked so green, and puffy white clouds drifted lazily by against a sky of startling blue. The sun flickered through the leaves to warm her face as the wagon rolled to a stop in front of her. The shorter fellow gave a rough jerk at his end of the rope, which she took as a hint to climb into the back of the wagon.

The world was too beautiful a place to be marred by such ugliness, she thought, as the taller man helped her clamber up with a jerk to her bound arm. She would never have the chance to grow old, never have the opportunity to watch her children grow. She'd never again watch the seasons change or enjoy the scent of fresh-baked bread.

"Sure you don't want to beg a little, missy?" Caldwell taunted, interrupting her bittersweet thoughts. "My brother didn't get that chance."

"How do you know?" She stared down at him, the breeze stirring her long hair, her spine schoolmarm-straight. "I bet your brother's murderer laughed at his pleas for mercy before killing him, just like you intend to do to me."

Caldwell's face flushed red. "That was murder, Miss Calhoun. This here is justice. There's a big difference."

"It's still the taking of a life, Mr. Caldwell, no matter how you look at it."

Caldwell took out a cigar and lit it. "You got any last words that aren't preachy?"

She wrinkled her nose. "Do you have any cigars that don't stink?"

"You're pretty uppity for a gal who's gonna die."

She shrugged. "I have no regrets."

"Tell it to your maker. Do it!" he snapped, clamping his teeth down on the stogie.

She braced herself, but she refused to give in to the urge to shut her eyes. She would not leave this world like a coward.

The wagon creaked as the black-haired one got up into the driver's seat.

She *did* have regrets—and one that stood out from all the rest.

She had never told Jedidiah that she loved him.

How ironic that she should admit the truth to herself now, when she would never have the chance to enjoy it. Never again would she look upon his face, see that crooked smile or the way his brows peaked when he was amused. Never again could she indulge in the banter they enjoyed, that verbal courtship that went so far beyond mere words. She would never have the chance feel what it was like to make love with him.

She wished she could turn back time, go back to that day by the river, and show Jedidiah Brown just how much she loved him.

"Heyah!" the tall man called, snapping the reins. The mule took off. The rope tightened around her neck, and she gasped for breath.

She had expected death to be quick, but the

mule didn't cooperate. Instead of taking off at a gallop, the stubborn beast ambled forward at a slow walk, despite the driver's cursing. Susannah walked backward in the bed of the wagon, managing to steal another few moments of life, despite Caldwell's plans.

The back of the wagon bumped her calves.

She thought of her pregnant sister, and the niece or nephew she would never see. Of her mother. She remembered the way Jedidiah made her feel as if she were more than she had ever thought she was, more than she ever thought she could be.

She managed to get her feet up on the back end of the wagon. The rope tightened around her neck, and breathing grew difficult. In another second she would have nothing to stand on, and Caldwell's associate would hold the rope taut until she died.

If she could only do it all again, she thought desperately, as dark spots floated before her eyes, she would cherish the gift of love instead of running from it.

Then her feet slipped off the edge and into nothingness.

Chapter 15

Jedidiah's heart raced, and the chill of true fear kept his jaw tight and his eyes cold. He galloped hell for leather toward the copse of trees in the distance, Nate and a couple of his deputies following along behind.

The silver-haired barkeep had seen what had happened to Susannah during the fight. The old man had been looking out his window and witnessed her abduction by two rough-looking men. He also remembered seeing those same men the night before in his saloon, in the company of a rich fellow who answered Caldwell's description. It hadn't taken much deduction to realize that Caldwell intended to finish what he had started back in Silver Flats.

The mere thought made Jedidiah want to tear the town apart in his search for Caldwell, but all he had found was his own revolver lying in the dust where Susannah had dropped it. Damn it, he should never have left her alone. However important it was to find Mrs. Hawkins, Susannah's safety was paramount.

He didn't even try to pretend it was just duty anymore; somehow she had gotten under his skin. He cared, much more than he ought to.

And the thought of losing Susannah forever scared him more than anything he'd ever known.

He galloped over the rise and pulled his mount up sharply. His heart seemed to stop in his chest.

Susannah, silver-blond hair gleaming in the sunlight, with a rope around her neck, stepped into nothingness as the wagon that had been her foothold suddenly pulled away.

"*No!*" he roared. He kicked his horse into a gallop, pulling his gun from its holster.

His gunshot echoed off the mountains around them.

Surprise twisted the features of the man holding the rope as a burst of crimson bloomed on his chest. The rope slipped from his fingers, and Susannah landed on the ground with a thud and lay still.

Caldwell turned, his cigar dropping from his mouth as he saw Jedidiah thundering toward him. He ran to his horse and mounted faster than Jedidiah would have given him credit for, then spurred the horse to flight.

Nate and one of his deputies headed after the fleeing Caldwell. The other deputy raced to intercept the tall, skinny man who was running for the trees. Jedidiah pulled his horse to a skidding stop and dismounted to kneel beside Susannah's limp body.

She had only been hanging for a second, but if her neck had broken . . .

Gently, he slipped his fingers between the rope and her throat. Her pulse fluttered against his knuckles. He sagged with relief, then took a deep breath and loosened the noose. An angry red welt encircled her throat where the rope had rubbed the delicate skin raw.

"Susannah," he whispered, following the mark with trembling fingers, pressing cautiously to test for anything broken. "Susannah, can you hear me?"

Slowly she opened her eyes. She took a deep breath, then winced. "I feel like I fell off a horse," she whispered.

The utter joy and relief that flooded through him brought the sting of tears. Manfully, he blinked them back. "I thought you were dead," he said, his voice rough with the emotion he couldn't hide. "I thought we were too late."

She brought a hand to her throat, her fingers shaking as she traced the rope still encircling her neck. "Try not to cut it so close next time," she said, her voice raspy.

"I'm not leaving you alone again," he vowed. "Didn't I tell you what would happen?"

She gave a laugh, then winced.

"Don't try to talk," Jedidiah advised. "Can you sit up?"

He placed his hand behind her head and helped her into a sitting position. Then he gently lifted the noose from around her neck and tossed the rope aside.

"Where's Caldwell?" Susannah asked, gingerly turning her head to look around at the deserted countryside.

"He skedaddled out of here like the skunk he is," Jedidiah replied. "Nate went after him."

"He's not right in the head, Jedidiah," she said, feeling her bruised throat.

"I know it." Getting to his feet, he bent forward and scooped her into his arms.

She let out a surprised squeak and flung her arms around his neck. "Where are you taking me?"

He grinned, rather liking the way she clung to him. "Back to Nate's house. We're going to stay there tonight, and you're going to see a doctor."

"I blacked out from lack of air, but it was only for a minute. I am capable of walking," she pointed out.

He tightened his arms around her. "Maybe I just need to hold you, Suzie," he said, using her family nickname.

She gave him a startled glance, but what she saw in his eyes apparently reassured her. Her mouth curved. "All right, then."

Nothing more needed to be said as Jedidiah carried her toward his horse.

Death had a way of changing one's outlook on life.

Susannah stood at the window in the guest room of the Stillman house. Garbed in just a white cotton nightgown—which fell only to mid-calf because it was Darcy's—she stared out at the night and thought about her brush with death.

Now she knew, truly and intimately, what awaited her should the trial in Denver go badly. If they didn't find Mrs. Hawkins, there was every possibility that she could be found guilty of murder, no matter how circumstantial the evidence. Then she would once more feel the tightening of a noose around her neck.

In that split second after the wagon had

pulled away and before she lost consciousness, she had realized how short life could be. It seemed so silly to worry about the rules of society, when what was important was being with the people you loved while you were still alive to do so.

She had let the fear of a broken heart hold her back from taking that last step into Jedidiah's arms. Honestly, what would happen if she gave herself to him as she longed to do, and then he left her? She could now truthfully say that though she would be unhappy, she would certainly survive. And down the line, when the pain faded, she would have beautiful memories to treasure for the rest of her life.

Now that she was no longer afraid, she found that she also had the courage to look at the other side of it. What if she gave herself to Jedidiah and he came to love her as much as she loved him? What if she missed out on years of happiness with him by her side because she hadn't dared to take that risk?

Life was short, and her life could be even shorter if she were found guilty of murder. So why not take advantage of what little time they had together to discover each other as man and woman? What was stopping her from going to him right now and asking him to make love to her?

Not a thing.

She turned away from the window and headed toward the door. This time if she died, she truly would have no regrets.

Jedidiah sprawled in the chair in the corner of his room and nursed his second glass of whiskey. Things had definitely not turned out as he'd planned.

Caldwell had gotten away. Nate was working on getting a warrant for the man's arrest, but Jedidiah still felt restless. For the first time in his life, he wanted to bypass the law and deal with Caldwell himself.

He wasn't proud of how he felt, but he didn't deny it, either. He was done lying to himself. Susannah was *his* woman, and Caldwell had tried to harm her. Therefore, Jedidiah wanted to rip Caldwell apart with his bare hands. A perfectly logical reaction, under the circumstances.

He tossed back a swallow of whiskey. The image of Susannah dangling from that rope—even for those few seconds—would live in his nightmares for the rest of his life.

He had wanted to stay with her. After the doctor had pronounced her shaken but not badly hurt, Jedidiah had longed to take her in his arms and hold her tight. But he didn't dare. It was his fault Caldwell had gotten ahold of her, and he wouldn't blame her if she was just as angry with him as he was with himself.

Caring definitely confused things, he thought sourly, taking another swallow of whiskey.

He heard a sound at the door and turned to look, just as Susannah slipped into the room.

She wore a white nightdress that showed off a distracting amount of slender ankles and calves. Her blond hair fell over her shoulders in loose waves, and when she closed the door and turned to face him, he realized that he could see the shadow of her nipples through the thin cotton.

He closed his eyes. Two glasses of whiskey in him, and now this temptation?

"Jedidiah?" Her soft voice stroked over him like silk, stirring his blood and his body. Opening his eyes again, he took in the sight of her, silently promising that all he would do was look.

Later, he would take a long, cold bath.

"What can I do for you, Susannah?"

She tilted her head to look at him, her gray-blue eyes so serious, and her hair falling forward like silken moonbeams. "I came to thank you for saving my life."

"No thanks necessary."

"Oh, I think it's very necessary." She came toward him, her nightgown billowing and settling over every tempting curve. "If not for you, I'd be dead."

"If I hadn't left you alone, it would never have happened."

Her eyes widened, and he pressed his lips tightly together, realizing how harsh his words had sounded.

"Surely you don't blame yourself?" She came closer, reaching out one slender hand to touch his shoulder. "It couldn't be helped, Jedidiah. We needed to find Mrs. Hawkins, and you were doing what you were supposed to do."

"Mrs. Hawkins got away, so it didn't do a damned bit of good to leave you like that."

"Lordy, I don't think I've ever heard you swear before," she teased, obviously trying to cajole him out of his foul mood. "Isn't that against the rules of a gentleman?"

He wasn't in the mood to be cajoled. "I'm just a man, Susannah. Once who almost cost you your life today."

"Then I suppose you would be in my debt, wouldn't you?"

"What?" He frowned at her, puzzled by her casual tone.

"Since you almost got me killed, you're in my debt," she clarified.

He shifted restlessly. "I wouldn't put it that way."

"Then how would you put it?"

"I almost got you killed, and I'm sorry for it!" He didn't realized he was shouting until she winced and glanced at the door.

"I'm sorry, too," she said, turning back to him. "But it's done now. And I'm still alive, thanks to you."

"You're welcome." Tossing back the last of his whiskey, he brushed past her and fetched the bottle from the top of the bureau with shaking fingers. Another moment with her standing so close, and he would go insane.

"I know you're upset, Jedidiah, but you don't have to drink away the pain." She came up behind him and stroked her hands over his shoulders. He froze, clenching the whiskey bottle in his hand. Didn't she realize what she was doing to him?

Of course she did. She was Susannah Calhoun, irresistible flirt and accomplished seductress. He turned his head to look at her, arching his brows as he drawled, "Do you have another suggestion?"

"You could make love to me."

He stared. He hadn't expected her to accept his challenge, but the steady blue eyes that met his showed no nervousness, no hesitancy as a virgin might display. Obviously Susannah Calhoun had been down this road before.

The thought pricked him, but he wanted her anyway. He put down the whiskey bottle. "Is that an offer, princess?"

"As a matter of fact, it is." She lifted her chin, straightened her spine. "If you don't want me, Jedidiah, just say so. I can handle it."

"Can you?" He turned to face her, cupping her cheek and spearing his fingers into her hair. "Be very sure, Susannah, because I'm in no mood to stop. I want you very badly."

She swallowed hard, but her eyes never left his. "I want you, too."

"All right then." Smooth as water, he dipped his head and pressed his mouth to hers.

He was so demanding, Susannah thought with a thrill, parting her lips for his seeking tongue. Demanding, but gentle. She followed the urging of his hand on her back and stepped into his embrace, pressing her body to his. It was heaven the way their bodies met and matched, fitting together as if made for one another. Eager for more of him, she wound her arms around his neck and kissed him back with all the love and hunger she'd bottled up for so long.

He groaned, slanting his mouth across hers, showing no signs of the gentleman she had always known him to be—and she loved it. His hands caressed her back and held her trapped against him. She felt his fingers tangling in her hair, his thigh pressing between hers, his heart pounding hard and furious in his chest.

He broke the kiss finally, gasping for air like a drowning man, then held her face in her hands and looked deeply into her eyes. "I asked you once before, Susannah. Are you sure this is what you want?"

"Yes." Boldly, she took his hand and kissed the palm, then laid it on her breast. "I want this. I want you."

"No turning back."

"No turning back," she echoed.

When they reached the bed, he sat down on it, pulling her to stand between his legs.

"You are so beautiful," he said with quiet reverence. "Not just your eyes and your hair, but your smile and your wit and your laughter. And I feel like the luckiest man alive tonight."

She smiled slowly, pleasure blooming like a rose inside her. "I am the luckiest woman."

He took her hand and guided it to his shirt. "Here. Unbutton it."

As she did so with fingers that trembled, he reached out and cupped one of her breasts in his palm. She gave a soft gasp as he tested the weight of it, squeezing it gently and rubbing his thumb across her hardening nipple. No man had ever touched her like this before, and even if one had, she doubted it would have felt this good.

"You like that." Laughing softly, he caressed the other one as well. "I want to see you. To taste you."

Her knees almost buckled. Heat smoldered in his sherry-colored eyes as he continued to fondle her breasts. She managed to get four buttons undone on his shirt, but the touch of his hands was making her light-headed.

"Touch me," she begged, rubbing her palms against the hair-roughened expanse of his chest. "I want to feel everything."

"Come here." He edged her closer. Then he slipped his hands beneath the hem of the nightgown and glided them up the backs of her thighs to cup her rear end.

She gasped with surprise, then groaned as he leaned up to take one nipple in his mouth through the material. Her knees felt watery, and she thought she would pass out from the pleasure of his hands and his mouth. A flush stained her cheeks as his strong hands began to knead her bottom. No one had ever touched her there, either. Jedidiah would be her first lover, and she was glad she had waited for him.

"Take this off," he murmured, bunching the nightgown in his hands. "I want to see all of you."

She hesitated, shyness taking over. But Jedidiah impatiently tugged at the nightdress, finally drawing it over her head and tossing it into the far corner.

"Sweet Lord." He studied every inch of her, from the top of her head to the tips of her toes. Almost reverently he stroked her breast, smiling as the nipple beaded beneath his fingers. Then he touched her slender waist, teased her navel, and finally, with a soft sound of triumph, tangled his fingers in the nest of blond curls at the juncture of her thighs.

She grabbed his shoulders as her legs collapsed, and he laughed, falling backwards on the bed with her straddling him. Instantly he cupped her breasts in both hands, kneading the sensitive mounds with gentle skill.

"Open my shirt, sweetheart," he urged. "I want you to touch me, too."

Susannah reached for his remaining buttons, but the sensations his hands were bringing forth staggered her all over again. She managed to get his shirt open, and by the time he leaned up to suckle one pale pink nipple, she realized that they had only just begun.

The tugging of his mouth at her breast combined with the tickle of his mustache against the delicate skin was an incredible sensation—one she wanted to feel everywhere. Suddenly she got greedy for his kisses and his knowing hands. Tugging his face to hers, she kissed him with all the sweet passion streaking through her veins. She fell forward, still kissing him, and he held her as he gently rolled them over.

Now she lay on her back, naked beneath him even while he was still mostly clothed. He pressed his mouth to her neck, his mustache sending streaks of excitement shooting to her center. He strung kisses down her throat, then paused, coming to the mark the noose had left around her neck. Very gently, he brushed slow, tender kisses along the welt.

Her heart swelled and all but burst from the love that overflowed from it. She knew he didn't want her love, but she gave it to him anyway with her hands and her mouth, showing him without words how she felt about him.

He shuddered under her touch, this tall, strong man who had the strength of a cougar but now purred like a kitten. He traced her thighs with first his fingers, then his mouth. She opened to him like a flower in the sun, and shivered with reaction as he stroked her delicate woman's flesh, his caresses soft and sure.

She was burning with a hunger she had never known but had waited for all her life. She lifted her hips off the bed, her body longing for a completion she didn't fully understand. She knew what happened between men and women; she had been raised working with farm animals, after all. But somehow she had never suspected the force of the need that went with the physical act. This demanding fire that stoked desire and burned away all vestiges of reason.

"Jedidiah," she whispered, stroking his hair, arching beneath his hands.

"I've got you, sweetheart."

"I want . . ."

"I know." He pressed his thumb over a sensitive spot that made her gasp and open wider, offering herself to him.

"Please, Jedidiah!"

"Yes," he murmured, kneeling up to shed the rest of his clothing. "Here, help me." He took her hand and placed it at the front of his trousers.

"Oh!" Blushing furiously, she jerked her hand back from the strange male hardness.

"Susannah?" With a puzzled frown he took her hand and put it back where he wanted it. "Don't you want to touch me?"

"Of course I do." Tentatively she stroked. "I'm just not used to it."

It took a moment, but she knew when the meaning of her words struck home. He stopped her wandering hand by putting his over it. "Are you telling me you've never done this before?"

"That does appear to be the case."

"Never mind that sharp tongue." He leaned forward and took her chin in his hand, making her look at him. "Susannah, are you a virgin?"

"Not if it means you intend to stop."

"You are." He sat back again, closed his eyes.

"Jedidiah?" She reached for him, her fingers brushing his belly before he grabbed her hand and held it fast.

"Wait a minute; I'm trying to get some control here."

"I don't want you to get control!" She sent a questing hand sliding up his thigh. "I want you as wild as I feel."

"I am," he said with a shaky laugh. Then he stood and stripped off the rest of his clothes. "That's the problem. This is your first time. I want it to be good for you."

"It already is." She couldn't help staring as he climbed back on the bed. His thrusting manhood fascinated her. She touched it curiously, surprising a strangled groan from Jedidiah.

"Am I hurting you?"

"In the best possible way." He lay back on the bed, then tugged her hand until she took the hint and straddled him.

"I like this." She stroked her hands over him, caressing him as she would a big cat, as he had once instructed her. His body was so different than hers, so furry and hard where hers was soft and smooth. Except for his sex. She tentatively traced her fingers along the hard, silken flesh. He made a sound as if he were being tortured; then suddenly he had his hands on her bottom, urging her up on her knees.

"This way is better for you," he muttered. "You have control. Take your time."

She knew what was supposed to happen, but she allowed him to guide her hips as he positioned her over his hardness. Leaning her hands on his chest, she moved with him as he tentatively probed the slick folds. She let out a soft sound of surprise as he penetrated slowly.

Jedidiah shut his eyes tightly and concentrated on control. Dear God, let it be easy for her. He didn't think he could last very long.

She seemed to know how to move instinctively, undulating her hips in rhythm with his shallow thrusts. Her breasts bobbed with each shift of her sinuous body. She was getting used to him, but he wanted more. He slid a hand behind her neck to pull her into his kiss.

He was losing it, he could feel it. Releasing her mouth, he kneaded her thighs and held her gaze. "Do it, Susannah," he whispered hoarsely. "Before I go mad."

She lowered herself an inch more, then

stopped and looked at him helplessly. "Help me. I don't know how."

He smiled tenderly. "Come here." He tugged her down to meet his kiss, then gave one strong thrust of his hips.

Her body stiffened for a moment as he breached her virginity. Murmuring soothingly, he stroked her back and pressed small, nibbling kisses to her mouth as he held still inside of her.

It took a few moments for her body to adjust to the penetration. Her inner walls rippled deliciously against his rod, making it even harder to maintain control. But he managed it. And soon he felt it, that first, hesitant movement as she experimented with having him inside her.

"Yes-s-s." Wordlessly, he showed her how to move, slow, then fast, making circles with her hips until she caught the rhythm on her own. Then she set out to drive him crazy by indulging her sensual side with reckless abandon.

He should have known it would be like this with her. Though he'd bedded dozens of women, it had never been like this.

He filled his hands with her breasts, then leaned up to suckle one hardened nipple. She gave a soft gasp, and her body tightened around him. Smiling, he turned his attention to the other breast, licking and sucking, until her pleading whimpers had them both in a frenzy. Holding her hips so he wouldn't become dislodged, he rolled them over until she was beneath him.

Susannah found herself on her back, surrounded above and around and inside with Jedidiah. He was everywhere, kissing here, touching there, murmuring soft words of praise and desire against her flesh. He coaxed her thighs wider, lifting her legs around his hips in what suddenly seemed to her a natural position as it urged him deeper inside of her.

Experimentally, she lifted her hips, seating him yet deeper, and was rewarded with a strangled groan. Power surged through her, the power of a woman who knows that she can pleasure her man. She raked her nails down his back and gave a little squeeze with her inner muscles—muscles she had never before known existed. He muttered a curse and shut his eyes and picked up the pace of his movements.

Yes, this was what she wanted. She met his increasingly deepening thrusts with abandon, glorying in the way he filled her and wild with the emotions that flooded her. Something was building, and she wiggled against him, trying to get him to move just like *that* and touch *this* place. He reached between them, slowing his pace, and pressed his thumb in a circular motion against one particular spot. And it hit her. Whatever had been building snapped. Her heart stopped, and her breath left her lungs as her entire body sang with the joy of release. A soft keening noise escaped her throat as she shuddered with a pleasure she had never known before.

"Yes, damn it," he muttered. And even before she could stop trembling, he began thrusting deep and fast inside her, stretching out her pleasure as he worked for his own.

She realized what he was after. She boldly met his thrusts, stroking his shoulders and nibbling at his neck and ears, whatever she could reach.

Suddenly he stiffened, then gave one, two jerks of his hips. With a low groan, he shuddered in her arms as his own release took him.

Susannah held him as he trembled, stroking his hair, his shoulder, his arm. A soft smile curved her lips.

Yes, indeed, she was glad to be alive.

Chapter 16

They slept.

When Jedidiah awoke in the dark hours just before dawn, he thought at first that it had just been another dream. Yet here was Susannah in his arms, her naked body snuggled to his as if they were longtime lovers.

Surprisingly, he felt none of the urgency to send her back to her own bed that he had felt with other women. In fact, his sated body stirred to life again, and he couldn't resist stroking a hand over her smooth hip.

He was in love with her. The lock on his heart had grown rusty, and his feelings had burst free. For the first time, he fully acknowledged that this was not something that would just go away. If he were a marrying kind of man, he would want to spend the rest of his life with this woman.

But he wasn't a marrying man. He traveled too much, and he didn't have it in him to make that sort of commitment. It wasn't fair to Susannah to ask her to sacrifice her happiness with someone like him, someone who couldn't give her the future she deserved.

All they had was now. She seemed to accept that, though he wouldn't blame her if she didn't. Women wanted a wedding ring and a house and a couple of kids. And even though it pained him that Susannah would no doubt find that life with some other man, he knew he would have to let her go. He wasn't cut out for that.

In two days, they would be in Denver. He would do everything in his power to make sure she was cleared of all charges, and once the trial was over, they would have to say good-bye. He knew it, and she knew it. So they would have to get all their loving in over the next two days.

Moved by emotions he was reluctant to name, he touched her again, teasing her soft nipple, and smiling a little as it slowly hardened. Her eyelids flickered, then opened, and she gave him a sleepy smile.

"Hi, there."

Her voice, husky with sleep and satisfaction,

rippled over him like an electric shock. His heart pounded so hard he thought it would burst out of his chest. He leaned forward to kiss her, gathering her into his arms, suddenly so hungry for her, for the closeness they shared, that he couldn't wait another minute to be inside her.

He wanted to see all of her, wanted to watch as she came apart for him.

He parted her legs and slipped inside her, swallowing her soft gasp of surprise in his kiss. He stayed there, barely moving, glorying in the feeling of her surrounding him. But gradually their kiss grew hotter, and the gentle clenching of her inner muscles around his sex was making him wild. He rolled on to his back, sliding even deeper inside her. Her low, husky groan of pleasure at the new position echoed his own.

"Ride me, Suzie," he urged.

Her eyes grew wide with feminine power, and she smiled slowly. She rose above him, her naked body glowing white in the shadowed room, her thighs a subtle invitation as she shifted to better straddle him. He reached up to caress her lush breasts, groaning as the satiny combination of soft skin and hard nipples filled his hands. She gave a sweet cry of arousal and arched her back to press herself more completely into his hands, pushing him deeper inside her as she did so.

He clenched his teeth against the pleasure and teased her breasts, each pleading undulation of her hips bringing both of them closer to the edge. He strained to hold back, silently demanding with sheer will that she go first over the precipice. But she was woman and therefore capricious; he saw the knowledge in her smoky eyes that she intended to hang on as long as he did.

It became a battle of wills. Each of them worked with eager hands and hungry mouths to drive the other mad. Finally he pulled her head down for a hot, open-mouthed kiss that sent both of them shuddering to completion.

The pleasure rolled over him, more intense than anything he ever felt in his life. She sank down on him with a hoarse cry, her face buried in his neck, the utter limpness of her body testifying to the strength of her own climax. As he stroked her sweat-dampened back, she murmured his name into the flesh of his throat.

I love you, he thought, nuzzling her hair. But he didn't dare say the words aloud. For he knew if he did, he'd never be able to let her go.

* * *

Susannah awoke to a tickling sensation on her fingers. She swatted at it, but it came back again, this time accompanied by a masculine chuckle. She came fully awake with a start and stared at Jedidiah, who continued to nibble her fingers. The tickling sensation was his mustache brushing across her knuckles.

"Good morning," he said with a smile. He was fully dressed. She, on the other hand . . .

With a squeak of dismay, she jerked the covers to her chin. He roared with laughter.

"Sweetheart, unless something's changed since the sun came up, I've already seen everything that you're hiding."

Heat flooded her cheeks. "You'll have to excuse me if I am unfamiliar with the etiquette, marshal. This was my first time, as you recall."

"I do recall." Still grinning, he tucked a lock of hair behind her ear. "And there is no 'etiquette.' What happens in the morning depends on the people who spent the night together."

"And we certainly did that." Never a reticent person, Susannah was surprised at her own shyness this morning. But then, she'd never spent the night making love with a man, either. "I don't know what to say. Or how to act."

"Say 'good morning.' And kiss me." He tilted

her face to his with a finger beneath her chin
and pressed a soft kiss to her lips.

She closed her eyes and responded as her
body warmed with echoes of the night's pleasure. A smile curved her lips as he broke the kiss,
and she opened her eyes. "Good morning."

"It's a wonderful morning." He touched her
shoulder, her cheek. "Are you all right? No
soreness or anything?"

She shook her head. "Not really. A twinge or
two."

"Good. I hated to hurt you."

"You didn't. You made me feel incredible."
She leaned forward of her own volition this
time and brushed her lips over his. "Thank you,
Jedidiah."

"My pleasure." He reluctantly rose from the
bed. "As much as I wouldn't mind staying here
with you, we do have to get going today. We'll
be in Denver in a couple of days."

She sighed. "Why did you have to remind
me?"

"I'll do everything I can to help you out of
this, sweetheart. You have my word on that."

"I know you will." She started to get out of
the bed, then paused. "Umm ... could you
please hand me my nightgown?"

He looked as if he wanted to say something,
but then he simply went and fetched her night-

gown from where it had gotten tossed the night before. She could feel that her cheeks were still burning with an uncharacteristic blush, but tried to ignore it.

Jedidiah handed her the nightgown. "I'll be downstairs with Nate. You come on down when you're ready."

"All right."

He left the room without looking back. For an instant she felt a stab of dismay as she watched his retreating back. In a few days' time he would leave her for good.

She refused to think about it.

She slid from the bed and slipped the nightdress over her head. The night had held fascinating discoveries about both herself and about Jedidiah. She felt like a different person altogether and found herself grinning at the hint of an ache that lingered between her thighs. It was as if she had gone through some initiation, passed into a new phase of life, and become a woman grown. She was still smiling as she stepped out into the hallway.

Darcy was just coming up the stairs as Susannah stepped from Jedidiah's room. They both paused and looked at each other.

Darcy bore a tray of eggs, toast, and coffee. Susannah shifted her bare feet guiltily as she realized the woman was bringing breakfast to the sickroom—*her* sickroom. Darcy tilted her head to the side and glanced from Jedidiah's door and back to Susannah.

"Lost?" she teased.

Susannah let out the breath she had been holding. "No, actually, I think I've found myself."

Darcy grinned. "That's the way you should feel. Why don't you come to your room and eat while I find you something to wear?"

Her stomach growled, and Susannah suddenly realized she was ravenous. "That sounds like a wonderful idea."

"And we can talk, if you like."

"I think I'd like that, too." Giving in to the inevitable, Susannah followed Darcy into the bedroom.

Jedidiah packed the last of his supplies in his saddle bags and firmly fastened the bags to the back of his Palomino. Nate brought out Susannah's paint, saddled and ready.

"I'll have wanted posters made up and distributed by tomorrow," Nate said. "But are you sure you want to take the chance by riding?"

"Caldwell's a wanted man now," Jedidiah replied. "At this point, it's probably better to ride for speed than to amble along in a wagon."

"Maybe so." Nate eyed him thoughtfully.

"Funny, I thought you might want to delay your trip a little, take it slow."

"Oh?" Jedidiah checked the cinch on the paint's saddle, though he knew perfectly well that Nate would have been careful to buckle it right.

"I just thought you and Susannah might want to spend a little more time together. You seem to have gotten . . . closer."

Nate knew. Jedidiah scowled at his friend. "Don't you start with one of your lectures, Nate. For a kid, you sure are preachy."

"I haven't been a kid for a long time, Jedidiah."

"You'll always be a kid to me."

Nate continued as if he hadn't heard him. "When I met Darcy, I wanted her like I never wanted a woman before in my life."

"Nate, do we really have to—"

"But when I realized I loved her," Nate continued, cutting off Jedidiah's words, "I was scared like I've never been scared before in my life."

Jedidiah stiffened. "I'm not scared."

The hell he wasn't, but he wasn't about to admit that to the younger man.

"I never said you were, Jedidiah. I said I was." Nate paused. "Loving a woman can mean a lot of changes in a man's life. But most of the time, they're good changes. And once you get used to them, you realize you never want to go back to the way you were."

"I don't want to change. I can't change." Hating the edge of panic in his voice, he scowled at Nate. "Look, I appreciate what you're trying to do, but some men aren't meant to get married."

"Like you?"

"Like me," Jedidiah confirmed.

"Does Susannah know that?"

"Of course she knows. I've always been honest with her. I told her straight out that I'm going to be moving on after this job is done." He frowned as he said the words. For some reason, the prospect didn't seem as appealing as it once had.

"I'm glad to hear it, because I certainly wouldn't want to see that girl get hurt." Nate sighed and clapped his friend on the back. "Just be careful, Jedidiah. And if you can't be careful, at least be kind."

They left later that morning. Darcy had somehow found Susannah a plain brown skirt and a shirtwaist that fit, and also a man's flat-brimmed hat to shade her fair skin from the sun. Jedidiah wore his customary duster and battered hat, and the two rode for about an hour without exchanging a word.

Susannah stared at Jedidiah's back. He

hadn't said much once she had come downstairs, dressed and ready to go. Except for a murmured question about whether or not she was too sore to ride, he hadn't spoken since they'd left Proctor's Corners. She wondered if he regretted what had happened last night.

She had thought she might have some regrets of her own, but her uncertain future made it all inconsequential.

Right now they were on their way to the next town where the stage stopped, to see if they could pick up the trail of Abigail Hawkins. But when time ran out, she knew that Jedidiah would do his duty and bring her to Denver.

She only hoped they had a chance to be together again. She didn't want to die without knowing all there was to know about loving. She didn't intend to leave this life without taking every bit of happiness she could from being with Jedidiah.

And if a miracle happened and she was not convicted, she promised herself she would smile when he had to leave her. She would remember only the good things, and she would cherish this precious time they had had together for the rest of her days.

Jedidiah rode silently, his eyes on the road ahead of him. He couldn't think about Susannah now, about what had happened last night, about the fact that he wanted it to happen again . . . *intended* for it to happen again. His emotions were all churned up, and if he let his feelings distract him, they could both end up dead.

Just because there was a price on Caldwell's head now didn't mean the bastard had gone away. No, he was out there, watching and waiting like a snake in the grass, ready to strike at the first opportunity. He would be angry as all hell that Susannah had slipped away from him once again. And he would not be too pleased with Jedidiah either—the man who had stolen her away from him twice now.

Part of him, some soft, romantic part of him that had been locked behind the rusty door of his heart for decades, wanted to sit on a grassy hill with Susannah and watch the clouds drift by and make slow, sweet love for hours. He wanted to linger over the softness of her skin, the scent of her hair, and lose himself in the pleasure of holding her. The other part of him, the hard-hearted and practical side, knew that he had to ignore his own longings and do the job. If he didn't, he could lose the very thing he was trying to preserve.

The stage they were following stopped at several towns. They would go through each one and see if anyone fitting the description of Abigail Hawkins had gotten off there. Luckily, the route the stage followed also headed in the general direction of Denver.

His chest tightened dangerously at the thought of surrendering Susannah to the authorities in Denver. He desperately wanted to find this witness who could save the life of the woman who meant so much to him, but he had to face the possibility that things might not happen that way. There was every chance they would not find Abigail Hawkins, and Susannah would have to go on trial for murder—alone, with no one to stand up for her.

Not quite alone, he corrected himself. After all, she had him. He would do everything in his power, invoke every friendship he had, call in every favor and marker to get her the best representation possible. But even so, he didn't hold much hope that anything he could do would help. This whole situation was driven by politics, and political pressure was a powerful weapon. Judges could be bought. Lawmen could be bribed. The jury could be filled with people loyal to Senator Caldwell.

The best possible outcome would be if Mrs. Hawkins were to testify to Susannah's innocence.

He had some thoughts on that. It was clear as day that Abigail Hawkins knew something, but what? Perhaps she was the killer, in which case it would be difficult—but not impossible—to convince her to testify. But at least he could take her into custody and give the jury something else to chew on. The other possibility was that Mrs. Hawkins had seen the real murderer and fled for her life.

Either way, the woman knew what had really happened that night at Brick Caldwell's house.

But if they couldn't find her, would he be able to remain objective as Susannah went through the justice process? What if all his efforts and connections failed and Susannah was sentenced to die? He would never be able to simply stand by and watch her be hanged. Should the worst happen, there was a very good chance he would betray his dedication to the law and help Susannah escape to some foreign land where she was safe from American law.

He hoped it didn't come to that, but he knew that if he had to choose between Susannah's life and his career, he would make any sacrifice necessary so she could live.

The force of his emotions for her shook him as no danger ever had. The criminals he'd pursued and the wars he'd fought had only threatened his life. Losing Susannah threatened his mind, his heart, and his soul.

He wasn't afraid to die; in his line of work,

dying was always a possibility, and he had long ago made his peace with himself.

But Susannah dying—that was something else entirely. It would be like losing a limb yet continuing to live, constantly in pain, constantly bleeding, constantly grieving for that missing part of him. He would rather catch a bullet than know she was no longer in this world.

And he would take a bullet, if it meant that Susannah would live.

Love was a funny thing. He had lived most of his life avoiding it, but now that it had a grip on him, he knew he would never be the same.

No matter what happened, he would love Susannah completely—and forever. And he didn't mind a bit.

Chapter 17

They rode through two towns, but no one remembered a woman fitting Mrs. Hawkins's description getting off the stage. Jedidiah pressed on, his face grim with determination.

Susannah assumed that he had decided to forget last night. It saddened her, as she had looked forward to being in his arms again. She hadn't expected an emotional withdrawal so soon.

As dusk fell, they set up camp in a clearing not far from the road. Jedidiah built a fire and then went off to get some water from the stream for coffee. Susannah busied herself getting together the ingredients for their dinner.

She had just pulled out the frying pan when

she heard a step behind her. Holding the iron skillet as a weapon, she whirled around. Jedidiah stopped at the edge of the clearing, water dripping from the coffee pot in his hand. He raised his brows in amusement. "Problem, sweetheart?"

Her heart pounding like a locomotive, she slowly lowered the skillet. "I didn't know who it was."

His face sobered as he approached her. "I should have thought of that and left you the rifle."

"That wouldn't help any," she said, as he knelt down to place the coffee pot on the ground beside the kindling she had gathered.

"You can't shoot?"

"Not worth a nickel."

He stared at her in disbelief. "What about all the times I gave you my Colt? You always said you could shoot."

She shrugged and avoided his gaze. "Most of the time the sight of a woman with a gun is all it takes to scare a man off. Besides, anyone can hit a target at point-blank range."

"You took a hell of a chance." He stared at her broodingly, irritation warring with concern on his face. "Have you *ever* shot a gun?"

"Of course," she retorted. "My father figured

it might encourage the young men to stay honorable. I just don't tend to hit what I aim at."

Jedidiah stood. "I can't believe there's something Susannah Calhoun can't do."

"No one can do everything."

He gave her a roguish grin that made her pulse skip. "Please, you're spoiling my image of you."

He'd clearly meant the remark in jest, but she took it seriously. "I've heard that from a lot of men," she said with a dismissive shrug. "Most of the time the image is too perfect anyway. No real woman could live up to it."

"Don't lump me in with those mooncalves who chased after you," he shot back. "I know exactly how you are, Susannah Calhoun: every sensual, clever, stubborn inch of you."

The growl in his voice surprised her. "I wouldn't dream of it," she said softly, watching him with wide eyes.

"All damned day I've been trying not to think of you," he continued. "It's my job to protect you, by God, and I can't watch for danger if I'm looking into those blue eyes of yours."

"Is that what's been going on?" she asked with relief. "I thought you regretted last night."

"Not hardly." He reached for her, the heat in his dark eyes making her step forward. Her pulse skidded through her veins, and her breath hitched as he caught her wrist.

"What's gotten into you?" she breathed, thrilling at the way he pulled her feminine form hard against his masculine one.

"You have. You've crawled into my mind until I can't think about anything but you. All I want to do is to make love to you again."

"Here?" She looked around the clearing.

"Right here." He wrapped his arms around her, easing her closer. "Right now."

"Goodness . . ." Her sentence trailed off as he stopped her words with his kiss.

His mouth conveyed hunger and need and other wild emotions she couldn't name. She wrapped her arms around his neck and hung on as he took her on a turbulent ride of passion and desire that fogged her brain and weakened her limbs.

He couldn't seem to help himself from wanting her. He knew he should probably let her rest; after the long ride following a night of hard loving, she was probably not up to taking him again. But he wanted to touch her. He wanted to see everything and taste every part of her, experience every nuance of Susannah before time ran out and he would have to step out of her life.

He pulled the ribbon from her hair, letting it fall about her shoulders in a pale gold waterfall.

He gathered it in his hands, silky and curling, as he slanted his mouth over hers and pretended that tomorrow would never come.

All that existed right now was this time, this place.

He broke the kiss to look into her eyes. Slowly he lifted his hands to the buttons on her shirtwaist, forcing himself to go slowly, though his fingers shook with the effort it took to do so. "Tell me if I hurt you," he murmured. "I have no business doing this so soon after last night."

"You should have done it sooner." She stood on tiptoe to kiss his lips as he parted the shirtwaist to reveal her plain white cotton shift.

"You might be sore." He cupped her breasts through the shift, tracing the budding nipples with his thumbs.

"I'm not." Arching her back, she pressed herself into his hands. "Make love to me, Jedidiah."

Leaning forward to nibble her ear, he whispered, "I try never to disappoint a lady."

A shiver of excitement rippled down her spine, prickling her flesh and hardening her nipples even more. He followed the column of her neck with teeth and tongue, his mustache adding a delightful tingle that made her tremble.

"I can't believe how much I want you," he murmured, pressing his mouth to the base of her throat. "This is crazy."

"I like being crazy." She clung to his shoulders, her eyes half-closed in passion.

"I've got to be inside you." He tugged at her shirtwaist, pulling it from the waistband of her skirt.

She helped him, slipping her arms free and letting the garment drift to the ground. He made a low sound of approval in his throat, gathering her into his arms to press hot, ardent kisses along her collarbone. Her breasts swelled enticingly above the neckline of her shift. He pressed his palm hard against the right one, plumping the soft flesh and gently squeezing the nipple. A long, deep breath shuddered out of her.

"Easy, sweetheart," he whispered, then tugged down the edge of her shift and dipped his head to take her nipple in his mouth.

She moaned. He sucked strongly at her breast as she clung to his neck, tangling her fingers in his long hair. His other hand cupped her bottom, squeezing the soft globes gently as he pressed her belly into his erection. Slowly he moved his hips, rubbing this way and that, going in a circle, then stopping all together, leaving her moaning and rubbing against him.

"I know what you want," he murmured, releasing her breast to kiss her lips. He took her hand in his and pressed it against his hardness. "Touch me, Susannah. Feel what you do to me."

She stroked him with curious fingers, tracing his rigidity and watching his eyes drift half-closed with pleasure. He kept one hand on her breast, kneading the firm, sensitive mound.

"This seems like a miracle," she said softly. "The changes that occur in a man's body."

"The miracle is that I've managed to hold myself back. I want you so badly it hurts."

"Does this hurt?" She caressed him gently.

"It feels too good," he said through gritted teeth. "I'm trying not to shock you."

"Shock me?" Her graceful fingers fluttered over him again. "You don't shock me, Jedidiah."

"I will if you don't stop that." He covered her wandering hand with his and flattened it hard against the front of his pants. "See what you do to me?"

She smiled. "I like doing that to you."

He groaned. "I'm not going to survive this."

"Don't hold back on my account." She stood on tip toe and took his lower lip between her teeth, then released it. "Shock me, Jedidiah," she whispered against his mouth.

He answered her with a hot, open-mouthed kiss that left both of them trembling.

Breaking the kiss, he yanked off his duster and tossed it on the ground. "Be sure you want this, Susannah, because I don't know if I can stop."

"Don't stop." She slipped into his arms, pressing her mouth to his, parting her lips the way he'd taught her and touching her tongue to his.

With a low groan, he pulled her hard against him, cupping her bottom in his big hands and kneading her buttocks with an almost frantic rhythm as the kiss went on and on. He was only a breath away from taking her hard and fast as they stood, but that wouldn't be good for her since she was still tender from the night before.

He broke the kiss. "Tell me to stop, Suzie," he groaned, unable to resist nuzzling the soft, fragrant flesh of her neck. "Tell me to slow down, before I bend you over and take you like a beast."

A small sound escaped her throat as his rough whisper sent a new flood of heat rushing through her. "Sounds like fun," she breathed.

He jerked his head up to meet her gaze, his face tight with desire barely under control. His eyes blazed with a hunger that thrilled her.

"Teach me, Jedidiah." She deliberately rubbed herself against him, her thigh pressing hard against his erection. "I want you to show me everything you like. *Everything*."

He closed his eyes, sucking in a sharp breath. "Susannah . . ."

"Everything," she repeated in a sultry whisper.

His control snapped. Taking her by the shoulders, he turned her around so she stood with her back to him. Then he pulled her back against him, tugged the straps of her shift down her arms, and cupped both breasts in his hands. She gasped and arched her spine as he slowly kneaded the full, soft mounds.

"You're so wonderful," he whispered at her ear, his voice ragged with need. "You don't hold anything back."

She squirmed closer to him, her curvy bottom snuggling against his erection in a way that made the breath hiss from between his teeth.

"I can't see you," she complained softly.

"You wanted to see what I like. Don't you like this?" He rocked with her, driving himself crazy as he rubbed himself against her lush derrière, his hands full of her breasts, her hair tangling against his chest.

"I do, but . . . it's different." She arched into him.

"There are lots of ways to make love." He nipped her ear, her neck. "This is one of them."

With an arm around her waist, he urged her down until they both knelt on the duster, her back against his chest. Following the guidance of his hands, she bent forward to brace herself on her hands and knees.

"Jedidiah?" Her voice held a quaver of excitement.

He slid his hands up under her skirts, stroking over her cotton-clad thighs. "You sure do wear a lot of clothes. Maybe you should think about leaving some off when you're getting dressed in the morning."

"Jedidiah!"

He chuckled. "It's only practical," he teased. Then he flipped up her skirt and tugged off her drawers.

Susannah squealed as the cool night air hit her bare behind. She tried to look back and see what he was doing, but then his big, warm hands slid over her buttocks, and she could only close her eyes in ecstasy as warm pleasure seeped through her.

She knew she should be embarrassed. But the way he stroked her flesh, squeezing her bottom, trailing his fingers along her thighs, made her so hot that she had trouble thinking straight. Then his hand was between her legs, coaxing her thighs apart, and he found the core of her. She moaned despite herself as his clever fingers teased the sensitive flesh, caressing that part of her that felt as if it were going to break apart. She arched her back, pressing against his hand, and his pleased chuckle reached her ears. She no longer cared that her bottom was exposed to the setting sun; she wanted Jedidiah inside her, and she wanted it now.

"Please," she begged, her voice husky with arousal.

"What do you want?" he asked softly.

"I want you." Her breath hitched as he found a particularly sensitive spot. "Inside me. Now."

"Me too."

He kept one hand on her bottom while he opened his pants. Then she felt the hot, blunt tip of him probing before he slid easily into her damp sheath.

She let out a gasp as he filled her. It felt different this way, deeper. He grasped her hips with his hands and set an easy rhythm, the globes of her bottom bouncing against his flat, hair-roughened belly.

Her own lust stunned her. There had been a twinge of discomfort at first, but now the pleasure built with alarming speed, and she found herself rocking with his thrusts and making pleading noises in the back of her throat. Then suddenly she exploded, the pleasure shattering and complete, and she cried out in surprise and satisfaction as her body shuddered.

Sated, her limbs grew almost too weak to hold her. Only Jedidiah's hands on her hips held her in place as he raced toward his own finish.

Jedidiah closed his eyes as his climax built, gripping her tightly as his body stiffened and his seed shot free in shuddering release. How was it that no other woman had ever made him feel this way? This was more than just a physical act, more than just simple release.

It was simply . . . Susannah.

Afterward there was a companionable silence, punctuated by tender smiles and small touches. Jedidiah made a show of shoving Susannah's drawers in his saddlebags, then laughed as her face flamed. She left her hair loose, and as they ate their supper of bacon and beans, he found himself reaching out to touch the pale blond curls, stroking one back from her face, mesmerized by the glints of silver and gold that danced through them in the light of the fire.

She watched him constantly, her eyes growing dark with new arousal, her caresses hesitant whenever she chanced to touch him. When they finished their supper, Susannah knelt beside the fire to gather up the plates to wash them in the stream. Jedidiah reached out, tangling his hand in her hair, then brought her mouth to his for a tender, unhurried kiss that stoked the already building fire between them.

Later, as they bedded down for the night, Jedidiah wrapped her in his blankets and made slow, sweet love to her until they both drifted off to sleep, smiles of contentment on their faces.

"Well, well, isn't this a pretty picture?"

The sneering voice jerked Jedidiah from a sound sleep. Sitting up, he reached for the revolver that he always kept nearby, but his fingers grasped only dirt. He jerked his gaze to the man standing at the foot of his bedroll. His own Colt stared back at him.

Wayne Caldwell laughed. "Looking for something, marshal?"

"You're in a lot of trouble, Caldwell," Jedidiah replied, his tone ringing with authority. Holding Caldwell's gaze, he slowly brought his hand back. "Do you know what the penalty is for assaulting a United States Marshal?"

"Probably not as serious as the penalty for killing a United States Marshal."

Caldwell obviously had no fear of the law; no doubt he figured his high-powered uncle would get him out of any inconvenient legal tangles.

"What do you want, Caldwell?" Jedidiah demanded.

"The same thing I've wanted all along. To hang that bitch for killing my brother."

"I can't let you do that."

Caldwell laughed and aimed the revolver at

Jedidiah's forehead. "I can't see how you're going to stop me."

Jedidiah didn't either, but he'd think of something if he could just buy them some time. He was disgusted with himself for getting caught naked as a babe and completely off guard.

Susannah stirred beside him.

"Sleeping beauty awakes," Caldwell observed.

Susannah's eyes fluttered open. Her gaze settled on Jedidiah immediately, and she gave him a soft, intimate smile. He didn't smile back.

"Must have been a hell of a ride, eh, marshal?" Caldwell taunted. "Wonder what your superiors would think about you taking advantage of your prisoner like that?"

Susannah's gaze jerked to Caldwell. She stared at the gun in his hand.

"You don't know what you're talking about, Caldwell," Jedidiah said in a bored tone.

"Looks pretty obvious to me. She sure is a looker, marshal. For a murderer, that is."

"I didn't kill Brick," Susannah said, sitting up and holding the blanket to cover her nakedness. "How many times do I have to tell you that?"

Caldwell swung the gun around to Susannah. "You and I both know you were the only woman there that night, missy. So you keep your lies to yourself!"

"So what are you going to do with us now, Caldwell?" Jedidiah said, trying to redirect the man's attention on to himself. "Shoot us and leave us at the side of the road?"

"It sure is a tempting thought, marshal. Lord knows you've caused me no amount of trouble. But I want justice, not murder."

"Justice would be letting a jury decide, not taking it upon yourself," Jedidiah pointed out.

Caldwell shrugged. "I'm sorry, marshal, but I have to do this. For my family."

"You'll have to go through me," Jedidiah warned. "I'm not going to just let you take Susannah."

"I'm real sorry to hear you say that, marshal. *Real* sorry."

"You don't look sorry," Susannah snapped. "You know, your brother told me all about you, Wayne. He said that you're the family failure. Gambling debts, illegitimate children, drunken brawls. You're an embarrassment to the Caldwell name."

"Shut up, missy, or it'll be a bullet in the head for you!"

"Is that what this is all about, Wayne?" Jedidiah asked. "Are you trying to prove you're worth something to your family? Maybe make them forget about those gambling debts?"

"That's not what this is about!" He glared at

them, his pudgy finger trembling on the trigger. "She's supposed to hang for killing my brother, and nothing is going to stop me from seeing that happen!"

"Nothing but me," Jedidiah said. He lunged at Caldwell.

Susannah cried out in alarm as Jedidiah tackled Caldwell around the legs. Both men went down, and the Colt flew out of Caldwell's hand. Grasping the blanket around her body, Susannah scrambled for it.

Caldwell was big, but Jedidiah was more fit and more furious. Caldwell tried to get to his feet, kicking out at Jedidiah, who grabbed his leg and twisted it hard. Caldwell yelled in pain and then Jedidiah was on him, flattening the bigger man to the ground. He straddled Caldwell's stomach before the man could get up and pummelled his face.

He only got in one or two good hits before Caldwell screamed and flung up his arms to protect his face. Jedidiah let out a snort of disgust and stood, looking down at his foe.

"Jedidiah!"

A gunshot sounded as Susannah yelled the warning, and pain seared through his arm. He jerked around to see a tall, dark-haired man coming out of the woods, the one who'd helped Caldwell try and hang Susannah. The man aimed his still-smoking pistol again, sighting on the middle of Jedidiah's bare chest.

A second gunshot exploded and the tall man went down like a felled tree, a look of surprise on his face.

Jedidiah looked at Susannah, who lowered the revolver as she exhaled with relief.

"I thought you said you couldn't shoot."

"I can't. I was aiming for the tree to his right." A scowl crossed her face as she looked beyond him, and she pointed the gun at Caldwell, who was attempting to crawl away. "Of course, I can't possibly miss at this range."

Jedidiah frowned and stalked over to Caldwell, grabbing the burly fellow by the collar of his fine blue coat with his good hand. "I'd listen to her if I were you," he advised. "She might aim for your leg and hit your head."

"Jedidiah, you're hurt!" Susannah exclaimed, as she caught sight of his bleeding arm.

"I've had worse. Get the handcuffs out of my saddlebags." Susannah put down the Colt and rummaged in the bags, coming up with the handcuffs. She handed them to Jedidiah, who snapped the metal bracelets on Caldwell, wincing as the movement hurt his arm. Then he gave Caldwell's arm a jerk that sent the man stumbling. "Let's break camp and get this fellow to the sheriff."

"What about the other one?" Susannah cast a glance at the motionless body of the tall man.

"We can drag the body with us on a litter. Or we can send someone back out for him."

"All right."

Jedidiah went over to his horse and took down a length of rope, which he tied to Caldwell's handcuffs. The big blowhard was bleeding from his nose and looked as if he had a split lip.

"You'll regret this, marshal," Caldwell hissed as Jedidiah knotted the other end of the rope to his saddlehorn. "I'll have your badge for this."

"More likely you'll have a nice long stay in the jail." Jedidiah jerked the rope too quickly and winced.

"Jedidiah Brown, you sit down right now and let me tend to that!" Susannah ordered.

He sent her an exasperated look. "I can handle it. It's nothing."

Offended, Susannah made a sound of disgust. "Fine. Be the big, strong man. But Jedidiah?"

"What?"

"Before you ride into town, you might want to put your pants on." Still clad in the blanket, she sailed past him, scooped up her own clothes, and disappeared into the bushes to change.

Jedidiah glanced down at his naked body. "Aw, hell."

With a scowl toward the bushes, he stalked to the saddlebags. His arm was still bleeding, and he had just thought of a good use for those pesky drawers of hers.

Chapter 18

"**I** can't believe you used my underwear for a bandage!"

"I couldn't think of a better use for it." His arm in a sling, Jedidiah stepped out of Doc Benson's clinic in the small, lively town of Benediction.

"You claim to be a gentleman, Jedidiah Brown, but if you ask me, I think you're the worst kind of rogue."

He flashed her a quick grin. "Now, Susannah, my mama would roll over in her grave if she heard you say that."

She sniffed with disdain as they headed down the street. "Your mama is probably hale and hearty back there in Charleston."

His expression sobered. "Actually, she died some years ago. In the war."

Immediately, Susannah felt contrite. "I'm so sorry, Jedidiah. I didn't know."

"It's all right. It was a long time ago."

The tone of his voice indicated that it *wasn't* all right, but Susannah didn't want to probe farther. Though she did want to know more about him and his past, this was their last evening together, and she didn't want to waste the precious time on unhappy memories.

"What do you say we get a room in the hotel," Jedidiah suggested, changing the subject. "You can take one of those baths you're so fond of. I heard there's a social over at the church tonight, and I thought you might like to go."

She smiled up at him, pushing away the feelings of dread that tomorrow would bring. "That sounds wonderful."

It had been a long time since Susannah had been dancing.

They had eaten supper at the hotel, where the dining room lived up to its excellent reputation. For the first time in days, Susannah felt more like her old self, dressed in her pink dimity dress with ribbons in her freshly washed hair. Jedidiah had bathed and shaved and dressed in a clean white shirt, black tie, and brown pants, looking dashing despite—or perhaps because of—the sling on his arm. The twin Colt army revolvers he wore only enhanced the image.

The people of Benediction were friendly and a bit curious, reminding her of her hometown of Burr in Wyoming Territory. There were the usual stares from the men, but for once Susannah had no wish to play to the crowd. She only had eyes for Jedidiah.

It was delightful to attend a function with a man and not have to worry about him stealing a kiss or staring at her bosom during a conversation. She could smile at people and not think about that smile being misinterpreted as an invitation. For the first time, she didn't have to play the charming diplomat to keep men from coming to blows over her.

She could simply be with Jedidiah, smile at Jedidiah, and bask in the love she felt for Jedidiah, without the onerous task of being the belle of the ball.

Jedidiah was doing enough glaring for both of them, she thought with a giggle as he sent a warning glance to a young pup who was staring open-mouthed at her. Her admirer was so startled that he jerked backwards and ended up with his elbow in the punch bowl. One of the matrons started scolding him and swatted him away.

"Would you dance with me, Susannah?" Jedidiah asked.

She smiled up at him, so in love she felt as if she could dance on air if he asked it. "I'd love to."

The musicians were playing a waltz. Jedidiah led her out onto the floor and guided her hands to his shoulders. He placed his good hand at her waist, and despite his wounded arm, swept her into a skillful step that surprised a delighted laugh from her.

If only they could stay this way forever, she thought wistfully.

Jedidiah gazed down into Susannah's eyes and felt something stirring inside him that had been asleep for a very long time. He couldn't believe this beautiful woman was his, if only for tonight. Masculine pride rose up, fierce and strong. Every other man at the social had been staring at her, but she was there with *him*, Jedidiah Brown. He didn't even think she had noticed the two fellows who had gotten into a fistfight over what shade of blond her hair was. Her eyes had never left him, and her smile spoke of intimate secrets only the two of them shared.

An elderly couple danced past them, the silver-haired lady smiling adoringly into the face of the wizened, balding man who held her in his frail arms. Their steps matched perfectly, no doubt from years of dancing together, of anticipating each other's moods and thoughts. Of finishing each other's sentences.

Susannah matched his moves as if she were a part of him, as if she had been created to fit into his arms and into his life. He could so easily envision the two of them fifty years from now, whitehaired and feeble, partners in love and in life.

He should marry her.

The thought stunned him. *Marry her?* Where had that come from?

Anything could happen once Susannah arrived in Denver. How could he possibly ask her to marry him when her future was so uncertain?

How could he not?

The notion left him dazed, and he missed a step. Susannah gave him an inquiring glance, but he just smiled reassuringly—although his insides were tied up in knots—and stepped back into the rhythm. His heart was pounding so hard he was amazed she couldn't hear it.

How could he ask her to marry him? How could he promise her forever, when forever might only be a day?

This was their last night together. Tomorrow he would have to turn Susannah over to the officials and then watch as she went through the ordeal of a murder trial.

Tonight was all they had, and he had no intention of wasting it.

"Let's go," he murmured.

The night had taken on a magical quality, as if time stood still and anything could happen. Susannah hummed a waltz as she preceded Jedidiah into their hotel room, then with a laugh, did a little twirl and dropped into a chair.

"What a wonderful idea it was to go to the social! Thank you for thinking of it."

"I thought you might enjoy it." He closed the door and locked it, then turned to face her, a half-smile on his lips. "You looked wonderful. I was the envy of every man there."

"It was so nice to attend something like that without having to fight off a bunch of suitors." She sent him a flirtatious smile. "All of them were too afraid of my dangerous-looking escort."

"It's my job to protect you." He shed his guns, then tugged at the tie he had donned for the occasion.

Her smile faded. "Is that all it was, Jedidiah? Your job?"

He swore softly, startling her. "I didn't mean it like that."

"What did you mean?"

"Don't push me, Susannah," he warned with a scowl, tossing his tie onto the bureau.

Slowly she rose to her feet. "Actually, Jedidiah, I would really like to know. I would *really* like to know," she repeated more loudly, "if the man I chose to give myself to considers me nothing more than just another job!"

"Will you keep your voice down?" he snapped. "I told you that wasn't what I meant. Damn it, can't you see I'm no good with words?"

Both his uncharacteristic cursing and the frustration in his voice cut through her anger, and she took a deep, calming breath. "I've never known you not to say exactly what you mean, Jedidiah. Now, please answer my question. Has this meant *nothing* to you?"

"Of course it's meant something!" He jerked open the buttons of his shirt, emotion darkening his sherry-brown eyes. "You got to me, Susannah. Is that what you wanted to hear? Well, there it is. You got to me. Are you happy now?"

His voice cut like a lash across her heart. "I never asked you for anything, Jedidiah. I knew you couldn't make any promises when we started this."

"Every woman wants promises."

"I'm not 'every woman'!" She took a deep breath that just barely avoided being a sob. "I can't make any promises, either. How can a woman accused of murder even think of having a future?"

"You didn't do it."

"I know that, and you know that. Will the jury believe me? We've had no luck at all tracking down Mrs. Hawkins. What was I thinking, starting a love affair with you? What do I possibly have to offer besides a few moments of shared pleasure?"

"Don't talk like that." He came across the room and took her by the shoulder. "You have so much to offer. Don't berate yourself because I'm too much of a bastard to take a chance on us."

Tears welled in her eyes as she looked up at his beloved face. "Don't you see, Jedidiah? There is no 'us.' We've been fooling ourselves all this time."

"This is real." He shook her once, gently. "What we feel, what we have together—it's real, Susannah. I've never felt this way before about anyone. I don't think I've been feeling anything for years. Not until you came into my life."

"Oh, my God." She raised a trembling hand to her mouth, tears overflowing down her cheeks. "Not now, Jedidiah. Please don't make me feel these things now."

"You do the same thing to me." He cupped her cheek in his good hand and brushed the teardrops away with his thumb. "You make me feel things I never thought I would ever feel again, Susannah. You make me long for things I had packed away in the back of my mind and labeled 'impossible.' You make me think about taking a chance again."

"A fine pair we are," she said, trying to smile.

"Susannah." He rested his forehead against hers. "A long time ago, I lost everything dear to me in the War Between the States. My parents died, my sister had disappeared, and my fiancée was killed by Union soldiers. I had nothing left, and I decided that I would continue to have nothing so that nothing could ever be taken away from me again."

She pulled back to look at him. "Oh, Jedidiah, I'm so sorry. That must have been awful. How old were you?"

"I was nineteen. Eventually I found my sister again, but the damage had been done. For years I've traveled around, able to help people with my skills, but with the advantage of leaving them after the deed was done."

"That explains why you left so abruptly last year," she realized.

"You were getting too close," he admitted, stroking her hair. "And Donovan. And Sarah. For the first time in a long time, I wanted to stay someplace. I got scared, so I left. But I'm not leaving now."

"No, you're still here," she said with a faint smile.

"I don't want to leave you, Susannah. But to-morrow, in Denver, I may not have a choice."

"I know that."

"All we have is tonight, and I want to spend it with you. I care about you, Susannah, more than I've ever cared about anyone in the past twenty years."

"I care about you, too. In fact," she continued with a deep breath for courage, "I'm in love with you."

He opened his mouth to speak, but she placed two fingers against his lips. "I'm not ask-ing for words or for feelings back. It's enough for me that you wouldn't leave me if you had a choice. But I didn't want to go through tomor-row without you knowing how I feel."

"You're so brave," he said with quiet admira-tion. "You aren't afraid to feel, to face the un-known of tomorrow. In a lot of ways, you're much more courageous than I am."

"It's not easy to admit how you feel to a per-son," Susannah said tenderly. "Even if you hadn't been hurt, there's always the chance of rejection. I admire you, Jedidiah, for having the courage to tell me that you care. It means a lot to me."

He pulled her into a one-armed embrace,

burying his face in her fragrant hair. "I wish we had more time."

"We've got tonight. And I want to spend it with you, Jedidiah."

"I want to show you how I feel," he said. "When you're standing up in front of that courtroom, I want you to remember tonight and to know that I love you."

A sob escaped her. "Oh, my God."

He smiled, his eyes uncertain. "Hell. I said it, didn't I?"

"You certainly did." She hugged him hard, burying her face in his neck. "And I can face anything, knowing that you love me."

He stroked a hand over her hair. "Letting you go tomorrow will be the hardest thing I've ever done," he whispered.

"No regrets," she said, tilting her head back to look at him. "Let's make this night perfect."

"Yes," he agreed, then took her mouth in a sweet, lingering kiss.

Everything seemed to slow to the steady rhythm of a heartbeat. Every touch meant something more than a means to arouse, every kiss spoke of words of love and a longing that tomorrow would never come.

He pulled the ribbons from her hair so it fell like spun moonlight over her shoulders. She opened his shirt one button at a time, following the path of her fingers with her mouth. His heart pounded against her lips as she pressed soft, loving kisses to his chest.

They touched as if they had never touched before, lingering over caresses designed to stimulate the senses. When he discarded his sling, she peeled the shirt from his body, marveling at his strength, making a soft noise of dismay at the bandage wrapped around his upper arm.

"It's nothing," he said, leaning down to kiss her. "What hurts more is my need to be inside you. I love you, Susannah." He gave her a lopsided grin. "Maybe if I say it enough times, I'll get used to it."

"You can say it a hundred times, and I'll never get used to how you make me feel," she replied. "Let me show you."

He inhaled sharply as she pressed a soft kiss to the bandage, one delicate hand tracing his sensitive nipple.

"I want to make love to you tonight," she whispered against his skin, pressing her tongue to the pulse that thundered at the base of his throat. "Let me love you, Jedidiah."

"Anything," was his husky response.

She took his hand and led him to the bed, pushing against his bare chest until he sat on the edge. Then she knelt at his feet to tug off his boots.

It was an erotic sight. As she bent forward, her breasts plumped forward above the neckline of her pink dress, and her long hair spilled over his legs as she struggled with his boot.

"As much as I'm enjoying the view," he drawled as she struggled with his boot, "it might be easier if you turned around. Straddle my leg and pull the boot with both hands."

"All right." Smiling gamely, she lifted her skirts, exposing a pretty length of shapely calves, then stepped over his outstretched leg so that she straddled it. She bent forward to grab the boot. Her new position offered him an arousing view of her shapely backside that sent a sharp dart of lust through him as he remembered their lovemaking that morning. Slowly, he lifted his other leg, braced it against that firm bottom, and gently pushed. She stumbled forward, taking his boot with her. Cheeks flushed with victory, she grinned at him and tossed his boot aside, then got into position to repeat the action for the other boot.

By the time she stripped his socks off his feet, he was hard and desperate to be inside her.

But Susannah was having none of it. When he reached for her, she smiled like a siren and shoved him backwards on the bed. He would have protested, except she reached for the fastenings of his pants. The feel of her fingers against his belly made him groan with need, and he let her have her way with him.

Susannah smiled as she tugged the rest of the clothes from his body. He was such a beautiful man. His body was as long, lean, and muscled as a man ten years younger. Broad shoulders, a slim waist, slender hips. His legs were long, his thighs roped with muscle from sitting astride a horse for long hours. And his feet were long and narrow. Kneeling between his legs, she traced a finger along the bottom of his foot, surprised to find the skin there so soft. He jerked and she giggled.

"Ticklish, Jedidiah?" she teased.

"You want to tickle something, sweetheart? I'll give you one guess at a better place than that."

She knew what he meant, and she reached out to stroke her hand down the hard length of his erect shaft. It twitched as she touched it, startling her. But then she became fascinated with the hardness beneath the velvety texture of his skin, the delicate drop of moisture that beaded at the tip, the rough-skinned pouch that tightened at her tentative touch. From the way his fists clenched on the bed, she knew he was sensitive here. She leaned forward and pressed a soft kiss to his belly.

"Jesus, Susannah," he hissed with an indrawn breath.

Heady with power, overflowing with love, she drew her hands slowly up his thighs to cup his manhood between her fingers. He jerked and arched his hips as she explored this new territory.

"Tell me what you like," she whispered.

The words all but made his eyes roll back in his head. He knew what he wanted her to do, but she was inexperienced, and he didn't want to shock her. Instead, he leaned up on his elbows. The sight of her kneeling between his thighs with his erection cupped in her pale, delicate fingers almost sent him over the edge right there and then.

"Take off your clothes," he said instead. "I want to see you."

Her eyes grew dark with emotion. Slowly she stood and reached for the buttons of her dress. Her gaze never left his as she removed each article of clothing, drawing out every movement until he was surprised he wasn't foaming at the mouth. When she was naked, he reached for her, guiding her down to the bed with him so they lay skin to skin, nothing hidden.

Facing each other, their mouths met in a leisurely kiss, hands gliding over each other's flesh, seeking to tease, to stimulate, to glory in simply being together.

He cupped her breasts one at a time with his good hand, kneading the soft globes as he tenderly suckled at one, and then the other. She fisted her hands in his hair and made sweet soft sounds in the back of her throat. Her thighs slid over his, tucking his aching manhood between them as they sought to linger over the pleasure of exciting each other.

When his shoulder started to ache, he rolled onto his back, tugging her with him so that she straddled him. Then he shocked her by wrapping his arm around her hips and placing an intimate kiss on the soft folds between her thighs. She grabbed at the headboard of the bed as he pleasured her with lips and tongue, and when the orgasm exploded through her, she cried out his name.

As the ripples faded, he shifted her sated body over his and sank into her, his penetration rekindling the echoes of her satisfaction, and when he took her nipple in his mouth, she climaxed all over again.

They couldn't get enough of each other. Throughout the night, they made love, then dozed, then woke to make love again. There were no limits, no inhibitions. They learned each other through soft words and deeds, curious touches, and experimental kisses. Toward dawn, they lay in each other's arms, longing to make love yet again, but their bodies were exhausted. In the end, they simply lay in contented silence, communicating through tender caresses that meant "I love you" as the first rays of dawn crept over the horizon.

Chapter 19

$\sim\!\!\infty\!\!\sim$

Morning came, though it was late morning by the time Jedidiah awoke.

Memories of the night had not yet faded, and he leaned on his good elbow, watching Susannah sleep beside him. It seemed right that he should wake up beside her. Like something that should happen every day.

But today was the day they had to leave for Denver. Their time had run out.

Suddenly furious, he sat up, wincing as the abrupt movement jostled his wounded arm. It wasn't fair. Had he dared to love again, only to lose her so soon?

Twenty years ago, fate had ripped away almost all he held dear, and here he was, in the same situation all over again. Was he going to calmly sit on the sidelines and wait for fate to snatch away the first woman he had ever truly loved?

To hell with that.

He had to face down destiny and steal what time there was. He would not let fate have the upper hand this time.

But how could he keep her safe? Once they arrived in Denver the authorities would take her away, and he would have no more rights to her. In their eyes, his job would be done.

Unless he married her.

Impossible! The practical side of him rejected the idea immediately. It was a clear conflict of interest. He would be putting his job on the line—perhaps he would even lose his badge. He couldn't step so far over the boundary.

But could he stand back and let Susannah face what was coming all alone?

If he married her, he would have all the rights of a husband. He could continue to be with her through the ordeal ahead and all the years afterward.

He needed time to think.

Slipping from the bed, he gathered his clothes. He would take a walk, go see how Caldwell had spent the night, perhaps telegram his superiors and feel out the situation.

There had to be a way he could have Susannah and keep his job as well. And he would find it.

It was nearly noon when Jedidiah walked into the office of Sheriff Ransom MacElroy.

And into a battle zone.

"I demand you release my nephew to my custody immediately!" The commanding bellow shook the tiny structure. A cluster of well-dressed gentlemen crowded around the sheriff's desk, the most vocal of whom was a tall, older man with a mane of flowing silver hair. None of them had noticed Jedidiah's entrance, so he leaned in the doorway and listened.

"Now, Senator, you know I can't do that," MacElroy replied. "Not with a warrant out on him."

"Warrant, indeed! I'll have your job for this, young man!"

"Senator." Jedidiah's brows rose as Nate's voice came from somewhere within the crowd. "You're not doing anyone any good. If you would kindly wait until I can contact the proper authorities—"

"Authorities?" the Senator roared. "I am a United States Senator, Sheriff Stillman. And you have *some nerve* attempting to calm me down when it was you yourself who put out that abominable wanted poster for my nephew!"

"Your nephew attempted to hang a woman who was under the protection of the law, Senator Caldwell. Around these parts, we call that murder."

"That woman," the Senator snarled, "murdered my nephew, Brick. She deserved to die!"

"That," Jedidiah said, "is a decision for a jury."

Everyone turned to face him. He gave Nate a nod of greeting, then looked at MacElroy. "I take it this is Senator Caldwell?"

"I am," the Senator answered, before the sheriff could reply. "And you are . . . ?"

"United States Marshal Jedidiah Brown."

"Ah." The Senator had striking blue eyes and aristocratic bone structure to go with his thick head of hair, and those eyes narrowed on Jedidiah in speculation. "Marshal Brown. I understand you are responsible for this outrage?"

"Depends." Shrugging away from the door jamb, Jedidiah strolled into the room. "Which outrage would that be?"

"The incarceration of my nephew."

"Oh, that." Jedidiah stroked his mustache. "Yes, I am responsible for that particular outrage. But Wayne was trying to kill someone, so I really did have to stop him."

"Marshal, I'm sure you comprehend the circumstances here." The Senator gave him a winning smile. "The boy was stricken with grief over the senseless murder of his brother. I'm sure you understand."

Jedidiah didn't return the smile. "What I understand is that he tried to hang Susannah Calhoun—twice—and that he conspired to murder me as well."

"Conspired?" The Senator laughed indulgently. "Certainly you exaggerate, marshal."

"Certainly I don't, Senator. Wayne Caldwell held my own gun on me and informed me that he intended to kill me so that he could hang Miss Calhoun. It's hard to exaggerate a gun in the face, Senator."

"Your own gun, marshal?" the Senator repeated, a calculating gleam lighting his very blue eyes. "How ever did poor Wayne manage that?"

"He stole it."

"I see. And you were where when he stole it?"

Jedidiah stared at the Senator, careful to keep his expression neutral. "I was asleep."

"Asleep? Are you such a sound sleeper that a man the size of my nephew can manage to steal a weapon from a skilled professional such as yourself?"

Jedidiah never looked away from Caldwell. "Apparently this time I was, Senator."

"Well, I think it's clear to all of us what really

happened here." The Senator looked around with a knowing smile, as if including everyone present in the secret. His gaze came back to Jedidiah, as sharp as a well-honed knife. "I understand Miss Calhoun is a very attractive woman, Marshal Brown. I would certainly hate to discover that you used your position of authority to take advantage of the young lady."

"Now, there's a leap of logic," Jedidiah said, with a disgusted snort. "I was asleep, and from that you deduce that I must have taken advantage of a young woman in my care? You'll have to do better than that, Senator."

"You have ties to this woman," Caldwell said, surprising him. "I have it on good authority that you requested this assignment for personal reasons."

Everyone looked at Jedidiah.

"That's hardly a secret, Senator. I'm acquainted with Miss Calhoun's family. They asked me to help if I could."

"So you admit that you are involved with this woman?"

"What I *admit*, Senator, is that I am acquainted with this woman's family and that I agreed to escort her safely to Denver."

"Something which you have yet to do!" the politician pointed out triumphantly.

"Because your nephew kept getting in the

way." Jedidiah turned away from the Senator and looked at the sheriff. "I just stopped by to check up on the prisoner, make sure everything was all right."

"Looks like it from my end," MacElroy replied.

"Don't you turn away from me, marshal!" the Senator thundered. "I'm not finished with you!"

Jedidiah turned his head and looked the older man in the eye. "But I'm finished with you, Senator. You put pressure on the sheriff of Silver Flats to railroad Susannah Calhoun into a murder charge. I was assigned to escort her to Denver for trial. And that is what I intend to do, despite you and your nephew!"

The Senator drew himself up. "Your superiors will hear about your impertinence, Marshal Brown. I will have your badge for this!"

"You may get my badge," Jedidiah shot back, "but your nephew still broke the law, and he's still going to jail for it. I suggest you content yourself with the way things are, and get on back to Washington or Denver or wherever you were before all this happened." He turned his back on the senator and headed for the door.

"You get back here, Marshal Brown! I am a United States Senator, by God, and you will listen to what I have to say!"

"Save it for your constituents," Jedidiah

replied. He slammed the door behind him, ignoring the raised voices that followed him.

When Susannah awoke, Jedidiah was gone.
For a moment, she panicked. Then she saw
his saddlebags in the corner and his shaving
things on top of the bureau, and she breathed a
sigh of relief. But it didn't last long.

Today was the day they would reach Denver.

She sat up in bed and buried her face in her
hands. Dear Lord, she'd thought she would be
strong enough to handle it. But now that the
moment was at hand, she was scared down to
her toes.

Murder—at first it had seemed like an amusing joke. But after feeling that noose around her
neck and almost losing her life, she realized that
it was all very real.

She wouldn't be able to charm a jury into believing her innocent, the way she often cajoled
men into carrying her bags or opening doors for
her. She wouldn't be able to simply leave the
room when things became uncomfortable, and
she wouldn't be able to find comfort in Jedidiah's
arms, because Jedidiah wouldn't be there.

He would try; of that she had no doubt.
Though no promises had been made, he had
declared his feelings for her, then followed that
declaration up with a night of loving that

would convince the most hard-hearted and cynical woman that she was loved. But his authority had its limits, and once he handed her over he wouldn't be able to do much more than sit in the courtroom after the trial started.

She would be alone—completely and utterly on her own.

She didn't even know her hands were shaking until she raised one to brush back a straggling lock of hair. She stared at her trembling fingers, then slipped from the bed and walked to the mirror hanging on the wall. What she saw appalled her.

She was pale, and her eyes were anxious and huge in her face. Her hair was a mad tangle of loose curls, and her lips were pressed together in a hard line that promised wrinkles later on. And her hands shook like those of the guilty.

Unacceptable.

She was Susannah Calhoun, and darn it, she was innocent! She would not go to this trial like a lamb to the slaughter, but like a lioness who would feed off the carcasses of those who stood in her way. And by God, she thought, grabbing her hairbrush from atop the bureau, she would look good doing it!

The door to the room opened, and Jedidiah stalked in. He glanced at the empty bed and stopped, then turned around until he saw her.

She realized all of a sudden that she was naked, but she didn't care. She lifted her chin in challenge.

"Susannah?" he questioned.

"I need a new dress," she told him. "I also need a hat, and some talcum powder. I do not intend to go on trial looking like a washerwoman!"

He grinned. "I rather like the washerwoman look—if that's the look you've got on right now, that is."

She sniffed with disdain. "Typical man."

"Sweetheart, there's no need to insult me." He closed and locked the door. "If you want a new dress for the trial, then we'll get you one."

"Thank you." As haughty as a queen, she walked across the room and scooped her clothing from the floor.

"Have I ever told you that you're magnificent?"

She paused and looked back at him where he leaned against the door. He smiled at her with such pride and such love that she softened.

"Thank you," she whispered.

"Nothing gets to you. Nothing stands in your way. I love that about you," he said, stepping away from the door. "The way you sort out all the unimportant nonsense and cut right to what matters."

"It's the only thing that will get me through

this." She cleared her throat as she started to feel dangerously misty.

"Marry me, Susannah."

At first she thought she had misheard him. "*What* did you say?" she asked, staring.

"I said marry me." For once the unflappable Jedidiah Brown looked positively nervous. "Now. Today."

"We can't," she replied. "What about your job? Wouldn't that be a problem?"

"I don't care. I'm tired of politics anyway. Just say you'll marry me. Let me be there for you."

"Oh, Jedidiah." She closed her eyes as her heart clenched with love, and with regret. He had given her no words of love, no promises, no reassurances. And she was standing there stark naked. But it was still the most romantic proposal she had ever gotten.

"Don't say no." He came to her and took the clothing from her hands. "I want to stay with you, Susannah. For the first time in twenty years, I'm willing to take a chance on love. I want to grow old with you. I want to give you children."

"But what if things don't work out that way?" She laid a hand over his pounding heart. "I am honored and thrilled that you want me to be your wife. If things were different, I would say yes without hesitation."

"But—"

"Let me finish," she said, placing a finger on his parted lips. "If we get through this, if I can prove my innocence to that jury, then I will gladly marry you. But if I can't, I would never forgive myself if you sacrificed your career for a marriage that lasted only days. I couldn't die knowing that you had been left with nothing."

"You're not going to die." He pulled her into his embrace. "I won't let you die, do you hear me?"

"I hear you." She sniffed back the tears and held on tighter.

"I'll get you out of this," he vowed. "And then you'll be my wife."

"Yes, Jedidiah." Burying her face in his chest, she squeezed her eyes tightly closed to hold back the tears. "If I get out of this, I'll be your wife. That's a promise."

Chapter 20

Jedidiah left Susannah at the mercantile, dickering over fabrics and ribbons, while he went over to the stage depot. In the excitement of arresting Wayne Caldwell and getting his arm tended, he had forgotten to ask around about Mrs. Hawkins. He needed to do that before they left for Denver. If there was a chance to find the woman, they had to take it.

He bumped into Nate right outside the door to the mercantile.

"I had a feeling you'd be coming this way," Nate said, falling into step with him.

"Aren't you supposed to be following the senator around?" Jedidiah asked.

"Hey, I didn't bring him here," Nate protested, throwing up his hands in a sign of surrender.

"He came to me because I was the one who sent out the wanted posters. Then I got word that Caldwell was in custody, and he insisted on coming here. I figured I'd better come along in case you were still in the area. I thought you might appreciate a friendly face."

"I do, actually." They arrived at the depot, and Jedidiah walked inside with Nate on his heels.

"You going to hop a stage to Denver? Probably a smart thing to do with Senator Caldwell hanging around."

"Not exactly." Jedidiah walked up to the ticket window. "Excuse me—"

"Can't help you," the pointy-faced clerk said without looking up from his paperwork. "The stage ain't running today."

"We're not interested in the stage today—" Nate started, but Jedidiah jabbed him in the ribs and leaned forward.

"What's wrong with the stage?" he asked conversationally.

"Driver's sick. Came in two days ago and started tossing up his dinner. He ain't been able to lift his head from the pillow, so the stage ain't going nowhere."

"What about other drivers?" Nate asked.

The clerk finally looked up, annoyance

pinching his ratlike features. "Three other drivers in the same area all got the same thing. Got us an epidemic. Only one stage running through here, and that's tomorrow. Anything else you want to know?"

"As a matter of fact, there is." Jedidiah casually tucked his duster aside so the clerk could see his badge—and his revolver. "So the people from Tuesday's stage had no way of continuing on their way?" he asked politely.

"That's right." The clerk glanced at the revolver and swallowed. "A couple of 'em ended up sick like the driver. The doc set them up at his place."

"Here in town?" Excitement shot through him.

"Yup."

"Thank you for your time," Jedidiah said, then grabbed Nate's arm and dragged him out of the depot.

"Do you think your witness is over at the doc's?" Nate asked.

"We'll see."

Susannah left the mercantile with a smile on her lips and several wrapped parcels. With the money Jedidiah had given her, she had bought a new dress of blue-sprigged muslin that made her look fresh and innocent, and the most adorable bonnet adorned with blue ribbons.

If she had to go on trial for murder, at least she would look good standing in front of the jury.

When she got back to the hotel, she immediately unpacked her purchases and held the dress up against her, standing on tiptoe to see how it looked in the mirror over the bureau. Then she tried the garment on. It fit perfectly, and she grinned, twirling in a circle.

A knock sounded at the door. Still smiling, she went to answer it. "Who is it?" she called.

"Sheriff MacElroy, ma'am."

"One moment, sheriff." She unfastened the locks on the door and peeked out. Sure enough, Ransom MacElroy stood in the hall, hat in hand. He was accompanied by a silver-haired gentleman.

"Sorry to disturb you, ma'am." MacElroy looked distinctly ill at ease. "You see—"

"Why don't you let me explain, sheriff?" The tall, well-dressed gentleman pushed his way past the sheriff and into the room. "Miss Calhoun, I take it?"

"Yes." Uncertain, she glanced at Sheriff MacElroy. "What is this about?"

"Where is Marshal Brown, Miss Calhoun?"

"He's out."

"Out, is it?" The silver-haired gentleman sent Sheriff MacElroy a smug look. "Do you know where he went?"

"Would you care to explain who you are and why you care to know?" she replied in the same snooty tone he had used.

His eyes narrowed. "Who am I, you ask? I will tell you who I am, Miss Calhoun. I am Senator Morris Caldwell, and you murdered my nephew."

"Senator Caldwell." Instead of being frightened, Susannah shook with fury. This was the man who had rushed the murder investigation. This was the man who had ruined her life! "I hate to disappoint you, but I did *not* kill your nephew. Though your other nephew, Wayne, tried to kill *me*."

The Senator looked chagrined. "Yes, so I am told. Poor Wayne was driven mad with grief, it seems."

"I see." She looked from one man to the other. "Was there something else, gentlemen?"

"Are you staying in this room with Marshal Brown?" The Senator began to stroll about the room without so much as a by-your-leave. He fingered Jedidiah's shaving cup, then picked up her hairbrush and turned it around in his hand.

"I have to. I'm in his custody."

"Are you?" With a charming smile, the Senator replaced her hairbrush. "I find that hard to believe. After all, the marshal is not here, yet you are. If you were in the man's custody, would it not be more customary for you to stay in the jail rather than in the hotel room with him?"

"I used to do just that," she replied stiffly. "But there were problems—most notably, your nephew—so Marshal Brown took to keeping me with him."

"But my nephew was arrested yesterday. One would think the jail would be a safe place for you now." The Senator smiled in a blatantly patronizing way. "Yet I understand you stayed the night here."

"I don't like your implication, Senator," Susannah said.

"I haven't implied anything, Miss Calhoun, simply stated facts. You did stay the night here with Marshal Brown, did you not?"

"Yes, but—"

"Is he your lover, Miss Calhoun?"

She drew herself up indignantly. "How dare you, sir!"

"Sheriff, I think your duty is clear," Caldwell said, dismissing Susannah by turning his back on her. "Marshal Brown has clearly compromised himself and his position by taking advantage of the young woman in his custody."

"What!" Susannah cried.

"You know your duty, Sheriff," the Senator continued.

MacElroy reluctantly stepped forward. "I'm sorry, ma'am," he said in a low voice. "I have to take you over to the jail now. We'll get this straightened out."

"I'm not going anywhere!" She whirled on the Senator. "You have a lot of nerve accusing Jedidiah Brown of any wrongdoing!" she snapped. "I've never met a more dedicated, honorable lawman!"

"I'm afraid your opinion carries absolutely no weight," the Senator informed her. "The facts speak for themselves. Sheriff?"

"He's right." With a shrug of apology, Sheriff MacElroy held out his handcuffs. "I'm afraid you have to come along with me, Miss Calhoun. Senator Caldwell and his party will escort you the rest of the way to Denver."

"But what about Jedidiah?" she cried.

"Jedidiah, is it?" the Senator sneered. "Your lover will learn what it means to trifle with a United States Senator."

Her protests went unheeded as the sheriff snapped on the handcuffs and escorted her to the jailhouse.

* * *

Doc Benson didn't like having his patients disturbed.

"This is completely unacceptable!" the wizened physician cried, as Jedidiah and Nate attempted to climb the stairs to the rooms above his office.

"We have no intention of disturbing your patients, Doctor," Jedidiah reassured him. "We're just looking for someone."

"You can't just barge in here like this!" the doctor protested, as Nate pushed past him to follow Jedidiah up the stairs.

"I'm calling the law!" Dr. Benson threatened.

"We *are* the law," Jedidiah returned, then entered the sickroom.

Neat beds lined the walls, three on each side. Four of them were occupied, and only one by a woman. Jedidiah's heart pounded as he approached the sleeping female. She had dark hair, that much he could see, but so did many women. It wasn't until she sighed and turned over in her sleep that he saw she was indeed Abigail Hawkins.

"It's her," he said to Nate, and his low-voiced remark woke her.

For a moment she stared at them in confusion. Then terror crossed her face. She struggled with the bedclothes as if trying to escape them, all the while whispering, "No! No! No!" in a weak, raspy voice.

"Mrs. Hawkins, don't be afraid." Jedidiah pulled aside his duster so she could clearly see his badge. "I'm a U.S. Marshal. My name is Jedidiah Brown, and I've been looking for you."

"Please don't kill me." The words shocked him.

"Kill you? Why would we do that? We just want to talk to you," Nate reassured her.

"No. He'll kill me."

"I have no intention of hurting you," Jedidiah said soothingly, pulling a chair up to the bed. "I just want to ask you some questions."

"Not you." She pressed her lips together and turned her head away.

Jedidiah sat back, tapping his fingers on his knee. "Mrs. Hawkins, do you know Susannah Calhoun?"

Silence.

"Susannah's been accused of killing Brick Caldwell," Jedidiah continued, watching the woman for any sign of interest. "I know she didn't do it, Mrs. Hawkins, but no one can prove it. Unless you saw something that night."

"Nothing. I saw nothing." She glanced at Jedidiah, resolve in her dark eyes. "I'm sorry about Miss Calhoun. She's a nice lady."

"If she gets convicted, she'll die, Mrs.

Hawkins. Do you want that on your con-
science?"

"I'm sorry," was all she said.

"You know," Nate mused, "we're sure Susannah didn't kill that Caldwell fellow. And Mrs.
Hawkins here was the only other person there
that night. How do we know she didn't kill
him? Might have been an accident."

"Is that how it happened?" Jedidiah asked
the woman. "Was there an accident?"

"It wasn't me," the woman said with such con-
viction that Jedidiah automatically believed her.

"Then who was it?" Nate asked. "We need
your help, Mrs. Hawkins."

The woman remained mute. Jedidiah pulled
Nate aside for a whispered conversation.

"She's not talking," Jedidiah observed as the
witness obstinately pressed her lips together.
"Maybe we're going about this the wrong way.
Maybe she'll talk to Susannah."

"Good idea," Nate said. "Why don't you go
get her, and I'll stay here with Mrs. Hawkins?"

"Good plan," Jedidiah approved. "Don't let
her out of your sight, Nate."

"You can count on me," Nate said.

Jedidiah clapped him on the back, then
headed downstairs. It would only take a few
moments to fetch Susannah—as long as she
hadn't bought out the whole mercantile.

* * *

Ten minutes later, Jedidiah stormed out of
the Benediction Hotel, his fists clenched with
fury. People cleared a path as he stalked down
the street. By the time he reached the sheriff's
office, he could barely see through the red haze
of rage.

Someone had taken Susannah from him.

Sheriff MacElroy looked up from behind his
desk as Jedidiah all but knocked the door off its
hinges.

"Where is she?" he snarled.

"She's in back," MacElroy said, standing.
"Now, Marshal Brown, just calm down."

"Calm down!" Jedidiah slammed his hands
down on MacElroy's desk. "You came into my
hotel room and removed a prisoner from my custody without any authority whatsoever, then put
her in the same prison as the bastard who tried to
kill her! Who the hell do you think you are?"

"I'm the sheriff of this town, and I was trying
to do you a favor." MacElroy folded his arms
across his chest and met Jedidiah's gaze evenly.
"Senator Caldwell was all set to remove her
himself. I convinced him to do it my way. At
least in my jail, she's safe."

"You had no right," Jedidiah said, straighten-
ing. "Now get her out of there."

"I'm afraid I can't do that," MacElroy replied.

"The Senator seems to think that you've taken advantage of Miss Calhoun, and the evidence seems to support his theory. Until I get word to the contrary, I'm afraid I have to keep her locked up for her own safety."

"You can't do this. She has to be in Denver tomorrow for a murder trial."

"Then my men will escort her there, along with Senator Caldwell's party."

"You're overstepping yourself, MacElroy," Jedidiah warned.

"I'm trying to protect Miss Calhoun," the sheriff corrected. "No one says you can't come with us to Denver, marshal. But you're not going to be alone with that gal anymore. It's for your best interest as well as hers. Senator Caldwell wants your badge. The way you're acting, he might just get it."

Jedidiah forced the anger back, forced himself to think. MacElroy was right. As long as Susannah was in jail, she was safe from anyone who might want to harm her.

"I'd like to see her," he said calmly.

"She's right back there," MacElroy said with a wave of his hand. "I'll give you five minutes, but that's it."

"I'm obliged." Jedidiah stalked back toward the jail cells.

Susannah, dressed in her new blue and white

dress, occupied the cell closest to the door, while Wayne Caldwell, surly and sulking, occupied the one farthest from it. Jedidiah looked at Susannah, a pretty picture of innocence in a place that routinely housed murderers and drunks, and he felt rage rising again. With effort, he restrained himself and stepped up to the bars of her cell.

"Jedidiah!" She reached for him through the bars, her long, slim fingers closing over his hands. "There was nothing I could do. The sheriff just took me away and brought me here."

"I know." He leaned closer, lowered his voice to a murmur. "I found Mrs. Hawkins."

She gasped with surprise, joy lighting her features. Then Jedidiah glanced at Caldwell, and she schooled her expression to sobriety.

"I'm going to get you out of here," he told her, reaching through the bars to touch her cheek.

"I know you will." The utter faith in those lovely eyes humbled him. She looked at him as if he were a hero, when instead he felt like a failure. He wanted to rip away the bars with his bare hands and carry her away from this foul place.

"Jedidiah, don't worry about me," she said, with a reassuring smile. "I'm not going anywhere, and I think Sheriff MacElroy is on our side. The Senator wanted to take me to Denver himself, but the sheriff wouldn't let him."

"Thank God for that."

"Do what you have to do to get me out of this place," she said meaningfully. "I heard the Senator say he wants to leave at one o'clock."

"That gives me about an hour."

"You can do it," she said, then whispered, "I love you, Jedidiah."

"I love you, too," he murmured in return. "You know, it's getting easier and easier to say."

"Keep practicing," she advised with a flirtatious grin.

He chuckled. "If you had agreed to marry me, you might not have ended up in here."

"If I had agreed to marry you, the Senator would definitely have had grounds to take your badge away," she retorted. Then her voice softened. "When I do marry you, Jedidiah, it will be forever. That I promise."

"I'll hold you to that." He drew her hand through the bars and pressed a kiss to her knuckles. "I'll be back before one o'clock."

"I'll be here," she replied.

"*Don't* say that!"

Chapter 21

Jedidiah's smile faded as he left the jail. Though he had put on a confident face for Susannah, he was worried. It struck him as just too coincidental the way the Caldwell family kept trying to take Susannah away from him.

He went back to the clinic and told Nate what had happened.

"She hasn't said a word," Nate said. "In fact, it's like she's pretending I'm not even here."

"She's going to have to start talking," Jedidiah said grimly. "I'm not letting Susannah leave with Caldwell at one o'clock. I've got a bad feeling about this whole situation."

"I trust your instincts," Nate said, "but what are you going to do? Break her out of jail?"

"If I have to."

"You must be in love," Nate teased, as he followed Jedidiah back to Mrs. Hawkins's bedside.

"I am." Jedidiah glanced at his friend. "I'll do anything I have to in order to save her."

Nate let out a low whistle. "Boy, when you fall, you fall hard."

"Tell me about it." Jedidiah sat down in the chair at Mrs. Hawkins's bedside. "Mrs. Hawkins, it's Marshal Brown."

The woman didn't respond.

"Mrs. Hawkins," he said again, "Susannah is in trouble. I need you to help me save her."

She looked at him this time, but still said nothing.

"This is getting us nowhere," Nate said, with a dark look at the uncooperative witness. "Maybe we should just put her in a jail cell until she's ready to tell us what she knows."

"No, not with Caldwell in there," Jedidiah responded.

"Yeah, I forgot about old Wayne," Nate replied.

"Wayne Caldwell is in jail?" Mrs. Hawkins blurted, surprising both of them.

"Yes, ma'am," Jedidiah answered. "I put him there myself. He tried to kill Susannah, twice."

"Susannah? Why in heaven's name would he do that?" Her voice rose with agitation. "She didn't see anything. Why would he try and hurt Susannah?"

Jedidiah leaned forward. "He can't hurt anyone anymore, Mrs. Hawkins, because I put him in jail. Now what did you mean, 'she didn't see anything'?"

"Well, she didn't. I thought he would come after me." She lay back on the pillow, staring at the ceiling. "Good Lord, all this time I thought he was after *me*."

Jedidiah and Nate exchanged glances. "Why would he do that, ma'am?" Nate asked.

"Because I saw him. I saw Wayne kill his brother." She looked from one to the other. "I ran away, and he shouted after me. I left town as quickly as I could. I thought he would kill me, too."

"Caldwell killed his own brother?" Nate exclaimed.

"Wayne said something strange to Susannah," Jedidiah reflected. "He said 'we both know you were the only woman there that night.' Could he have seen you running away, Mrs. Hawkins, and thought you were Susannah?"

"It's possible. It was very dark."

"That would explain a lot of things," Nate said.

"Yeah," Jedidiah agreed. "Wayne set Susannah up as the scapegoat, but he thought she had seen him, so he's been trying to kill her before she could talk."

"But why would Wayne kill his own brother?" Nate asked.

"Brick knew about the Senator," Mrs. Hawkins said.

Jedidiah leaned forward with interest. "What *about* the Senator?"

The woman bit her lip and looked from one man to the other. "Senator Caldwell will kill me, too, if I tell you."

"He won't hurt you." Jedidiah laid a hand on hers. "Please tell us everything, Mrs. Hawkins. If the Senator is involved in this, he needs to be punished just like Wayne."

"He's too powerful," she said, shaking her head. "Brick tried to take him on, and look where he ended up."

"What do you mean, Brick tried to take him on?" Nate asked.

She shook her head again. "I can't tell you. He'll find me and kill me, I know it. I'm sorry."

"Mrs. Hawkins," Jedidiah said quietly. "I can arrest you for withholding information about a murder. But I'm not going to do that. What I am going to tell you is this: an innocent woman is going to be convicted of a murder she did not commit if you don't help us. Senator Caldwell will get away with what he's done, and you will never be free of him."

"He might find out the truth someday," Nate added. "What if it comes out that it was you who was there that night, not Miss Calhoun? The senator is a powerful man. He'd be able to find you."

"He'll never be arrested," Mrs. Hawkins said sadly.

"It would be easier if we had proof," Jedidiah agreed. "Of course, if you could tell us why—"

"Oh, I have proof," she interrupted. "I took all Mr. Brick's letters, the ones he hid in the floorboard of the porch. I came back early the next morning and collected them. I was sure Wayne had gotten to them, but he hadn't found them."

"What letters?" Nate prodded.

She hesitated. "If I tell you, you have to promise to protect me," she said. "The Senator might still get away with what he's done. He has enough friends in high places to do it."

"I promise," Jedidiah said. "We won't let him get near you."

"We'll set you up with a fresh start someplace," Nate said. "But you'll have to testify in court."

"No." She shook her head vehemently. "I don't want him to see me. I can't do that."

"Mrs. Hawkins, please," Jedidiah said softly.

"If you don't do what's right, the woman I love is going to be convicted of something she didn't do. They will sentence her to hang."

She hesitated.

"Please, Mrs. Hawkins," Jedidiah pleaded. "Do the right thing."

"It's the only way this will ever end," Nate added.

The battle she fought with herself was clearly reflected on her face.

Jedidiah and Nate waited for her decision as the minutes ticked by, and it grew closer to the hour when Susannah would leave for Denver.

"Time to leave, Miss Calhoun," Sheriff MacElroy said, unlocking the door to the cell.

"Is it one o'clock already?"

"Closer to twelve-thirty, but the Senator's ready to leave," he said.

"But I can't leave yet!" She dug in her heels, resisting to the best of her ability. Still the sheriff managed to get her from the cell block to the main office.

"You've got to get to Denver," the sheriff reminded her.

"Not without Jedidiah." She grabbed his chair, holding it with both hands as he dragged both her and the chair toward the door.

"Sheriff, what is the holdup here?" the Sena-

tor asked, appearing in the doorway. He flipped
open an engraved gold pocket watch and noted
the hour.

"Just getting the prisoner ready to travel,"
MacElroy said, smiling politely despite his difficulty in removing Susannah from the room.

"I'm not going anywhere without Jedidiah!"
Susannah declared. She let go of the chair with an
abruptness that made the sheriff stumble. He lost
his grip on her, and she grabbed his keys off his
belt and darted back into the jail. As she passed,
she scooped the spare set of keys off the wall,
then shut herself in the cell and locked the door.

"Miss Calhoun!" the sheriff shouted, storm-
ing after her. "What do you think you're doing?"

She tucked the keys beneath the pillow on
her cot, then sat on it, arms folded. "I'm waiting
for Jedidiah. He'll be along directly."

"Young woman," said the Senator, following
MacElroy into the cell block, "you are embar-
rassing yourself with this display. Have you no
dignity?"

"Not a bit," she replied.

The Senator whirled on the sheriff. "Get her
out of there!" he demanded.

"I can't. She's got the keys."

"Then get her out another way. I don't care
how you do it, just get her out of there!"

MacElroy stared at the Senator with angry

eyes. His lips parted as if he wanted to say something, but then he spun on his heel and stalked from the jail.

Senator Caldwell turned to look at Susannah. She met the blazing hate in his eyes with a fulminating glare of her own.

"You have been entirely too much trouble, Miss Calhoun," the Senator said, in a silky tone that sent dread twisting down her spine. "When this is over, you will regret ever crossing me."

"I already regret it, Senator. You've turned my life upside down with your false accusations and pushy ways."

"We'll see how haughty you are when you're convicted of murder," Caldwell hissed. "I intend to put all the power at my disposal behind the prosecution."

Fear slithered down her spine at the evil twisting his features.

MacElroy came back into the cell block. "I sent for the blacksmith," he said. "He ought to be able to take the door off the hinges so we can get both Miss Calhoun and your nephew out."

"Excellent." The Senator consulted his pocket watch again. "Perhaps we will get to Denver on time after all."

"I'm afraid you may have to delay your trip, Senator," Jedidiah said from the doorway. "I don't think you'll be going anywhere today."

Susannah sprang to her feet and gripped the bars of her cell. Jedidiah sent her a quick, reassuring glance, then fixed his attention back on Senator Caldwell.

"What nonsense is this?" the Senator exclaimed, his silver brows arching. "Have you come to rescue Miss Calhoun, marshal? I assure you, she's no longer your concern."

"I've come to take you into custody, Senator," Jedidiah replied.

The Senator laughed. "If this is some deluded attempt to stop me from reporting your activities to your superiors, Marshal Brown, I must say it is a pitiful endeavor on your part."

"No, Senator, this has nothing to do with me. And I doubt my superiors will listen to a word you have to say once the truth gets out." Jedidiah held up a packet of letters tied together with a worn red ribbon. "Do you recognize these, Senator? You should, since you wrote them."

The Senator paled, but he maintained his air of bravado. "I don't know what you're talking about, marshal."

Jedidiah stepped forward. "Senator Morris Caldwell, I'm placing you under arrest as an accessory to the murder of your nephew, Brick Caldwell."

"This is preposterous!"

"These letters are proof that your nephew

was blackmailing you. He knew about a certain young lady—a *very* young lady, in fact—who had given birth to your child. Had this knowledge become public, your career would have been ruined." Jedidiah tapped the bundle of letters with one finger. "There is also an allegation that you forced this young lady, who is a member of a wealthy family in Washington, D.C., to have a relationship with you by threatening to ruin her father's reputation and his political career."

"Lies!" the Senator cried. "I'm a United States Senator. There are always young women accusing powerful men like myself of such things."

"As I said, this is currently an allegation. However, we have letters written to your nephew," Jedidiah stated, his voice calm, though his eyes blazed. "Letters written in your own hand in which you threaten your nephew with bodily harm when he tries to blackmail you. We have a witness who was there the night of the murder, who saw Wayne stab Brick—*after* Miss Calhoun had left for the evening. A witness who overheard Wayne admit to another man at the scene that the killing was done on your orders."

"A witness? Produce this witness!"

"In due time," Jedidiah said. "In the meantime, Senator, you are under arrest."

"Are you sure of your facts?" MacElroy asked. "Those are serious charges, marshal."

"Very sure. Sheriff, perhaps you can take the Senator into custody and hold him for a while?"

MacElroy hesitated. "I don't know, marshal. Suppose this is just some trick you've cooked up because the Senator wants you fired?"

"What if I'm right?" Jedidiah asked softly. "What if the Senator here is responsible for both the murder of Brick Caldwell and the attempted murder of Susannah Calhoun? These charges have to be investigated, sheriff."

Sheriff MacElroy thought the matter over, then gave a short nod and approached the Senator. "Sir, why don't we all sit down and talk this thing out?"

"Get away from me!" the Senator cried, backing away. "Marshal Brown, this has all been very amusing, but I am due at a dinner party in Denver this evening."

"You'll have to send your regrets."

MacElroy reached for the Senator again, but he twisted away. When he turned back, he had a tiny derringer in his hand.

"I'm not going to prison," Senator Caldwell declared, his voice tight with fear. He pointed the gun at the sheriff, forcing him to back away. Then he aimed it at Jedidiah. "You're not going to do this to me, Brown!"

"Senator, you can't get out of here," Jedidiah said, his tone even and reasonable. "That little gun only holds one bullet, and there's two of us."

Caldwell's eyes darted around the room as if seeking escape.

"Give it up, Senator," the sheriff said. "If the charges are false, you'll be released immediately. We just need some time to get this all settled."

"Of course they're false!" Caldwell shouted. "That girl is lying about the baby, and Marshal Brown has no witness. He's only doing this to get back at me!"

"You're wrong." Jedidiah took a step toward him, then halted as the derringer came up to point at his heart. "Wayne saw a woman running away from Brick's house that night, Senator. He thought it was Susannah, especially when Brick's neighbor corroborated that story. But it was a different woman who had witnessed the murder. Your nephew here has been trying to kill the wrong woman all this time."

"What!" Wayne shouted, coming to his feet in his cell. "You're lying! There wasn't any other woman there that night!"

"There was—and she saw and heard everything."

"You can't prove any of this," the Senator sneered. "No one will believe your insane accusations, especially when I go to your superiors and tell them about your improper conduct."

"Well, how about the fact that you're holding a gun on an officer of the law?" Jedidiah pointed out.

"This is merely a defense," Caldwell replied with a casual smile. "I simply wanted to get your attention."

"You have it," Jedidiah said. "Now give me the gun, Senator. You're just making everything more difficult on yourself."

"I can't be accused of murder," the senator replied. "I can't, don't you understand? I'm a United States Senator! My career will be ruined!"

"Give me the gun, Senator Caldwell."

The Senator laughed a little hysterically. "I'm sorry, marshal, but I can't do that."

Jedidiah knew what he was going to do. He saw it in Caldwell's eyes. He leaped forward as Senator Caldwell turned the derringer on himself.

Susannah screamed.

The gun fired, and a howl of pain split the air. Jedidiah sprawled on the floor atop the Senator, his wounded arm aching like the dickens. The gun slipped from the older man's fingers.

"Why?" Senator Caldwell asked in a defeated tone.

"Suicide's not the answer," Jedidiah replied.

"It is for me," the older man answered quietly. "My career is ruined. I have nothing now."

Jedidiah slowly got up, favoring his throbbing arm. MacElroy rushed forward, but Jedidiah held up a hand.

"He's fine," he said, rubbing his arm. "I think you should go check on Wayne, though. He's the one who caught the bullet."

MacElroy turned, and sure enough, Wayne lay curled on the floor of his cell, holding both hands against his bleeding leg.

"Crazy bastard shot me!" Wayne howled.

MacElroy glanced at Jedidiah. "Your lady's got the keys to both cells."

Jedidiah cuffed the Senator, then helped the older man to his feet and handed him over to MacElroy. Going over to Susannah's cell, he held out his hand for the keys.

Susannah gave him one of her flirtatious grins, then fetched a set of keys and dropped them in his outstretched palm. As he went to unlock Wayne's cell, Susannah used the other ring of keys to let herself out.

Sheriff MacElroy deposited the Senator in Wayne's cell, then he and Jedidiah helped Wayne onto the cot.

"He needs the doc," MacElroy said.

"I'll fetch him," Jedidiah replied. "I'm heading over there anyway."

Susannah came up to him and threw herself into his embrace.

"Ouch! Watch the arm, sweetheart." Jedidiah curled his good arm around her. "Sheriff, given the new evidence, I take it Miss Calhoun is free to return to my custody?"

MacElroy looked up from his examination of Wayne's wound, concern etching his features. "There's still that little matter of improper behavior, marshal."

Jedidiah grinned. "What if I told you that I had asked Miss Calhoun to be my wife, and that she's accepted."

A slow grin stretched across the sheriff's face. "I'd say that ought to settle things nicely."

Jedidiah tightened his arm around Susannah's waist. "Since it seems as if you have things under control here, sheriff, we're going to head out now. We have an appointment in Denver."

"Good luck."

As they left the jailhouse, Jedidiah released Susannah to scoop up the bundle of letters that had fallen on the floor during the scuffle. When they emerged onto the street, Susannah stared up at the bright blue sky with a smile of appreciation stretching across her face.

"It's over," she said with a huge sigh of relief.

"It's over," Jedidiah agreed. "But we still have to go to Denver and produce the evidence that's going to clear your name."

She stretched out a hand to him. "I'll go anywhere with you, Jedidiah Brown."

He took her hand. "Even to the altar?"

"*Especially* to the altar." Tears welled in her eyes, and she swiped at them before they could fall. "I'm just so glad it's over. I was so scared! And now we're talking about getting married."

"I love you, Susannah. And as soon as I can get you in front of a preacher, I'm going to make you my wife."

"But first we have to go to Denver." She sighed with disappointment.

"At least we know now what will happen there." He took both her hands in his, then raised them to his lips. "Susannah, I've never been a man for making promises, but I know now that there's no way I can face the future without you by my side."

"I can finally promise you forever," she whispered. "It seems like a miracle. Last night I had no future, and today I have everything."

They shared a sweet pledge of a kiss.

"I want to get married at home in Burr," Susannah said, smiling mistily at him. "My mother will make the dress. And I want my sister to be my attendant."

"Whatever you want." He grinned. "But first we have to go to Denver."

"I hope it doesn't take long," she grumbled.

"It shouldn't," Jedidiah said. "Nate's over at the doc's with Mrs. Hawkins. She's been feeling poorly, but he'll get her to Denver as soon as she's able to travel."

"I can't believe everything you've done," she said in amazement. "You risked your job for me. You found Mrs. Hawkins and her evidence. I can't believe it's finally over."

He took her hand in his and squeezed it. "No, sweetheart—it's just beginning."

Hand in hand, they walked toward the livery stable. And forever.

Epilogue

Burr, Wyoming Territory
Three weeks later

Someone was watching her.

Susannah peered over her dance partner's shoulder at the figure standing in the shadow of the huge crabapple tree. He stood unmoving near the white picket fence that encircled the yard, isolated from the revelry around him. She had sensed his eyes on her all through the wedding reception, and no matter how hard she tried to ignore it, she couldn't overlook the urgent response of her body to his intent regard.

"You look beautiful tonight," her partner said.

"Thank you." She barely heard him. Her entire being was focused on the still shadow of the man beneath the crabapple tree.

"You've always been beautiful," the man she danced with continued, "but tonight you're radiant. Love does that to a woman."

"Thank you," Susannah said again.

"Susannah, you're not listening to a word I've said," her brother-in-law, Jack Donovan, said with an indulgent smile. She caught the twinkle in his dark eyes. "You know, if you wanted to slip away for a while, I could make excuses for you."

She leaned up and kissed his cheek. "Thank you, Jack. I knew I always liked you."

Lifting her layers of snowy white skirts, she darted away, her attention fixed on the man who awaited her beneath the crabapple tree.

She slowed as she reached him, shaking out her skirts and brushing her lacy veil back over her shoulders. Casually, as if she had all day, she came to stand before him. "Good evening, Marshal Brown," she said with a soft smile. "Or should I say 'Sheriff Brown'?"

" 'Husband' will do well enough, Mrs. Brown." He took the hand she extended and raised it to his lips. His touch, as always, sent her pulse skipping. Then he turned her hand over and boldly licked her palm.

"Jedidiah!" The blush that crept into her

cheeks stemmed from arousal, not maidenly modestly, and he knew it, the odious man.

He tugged her closer until her thighs grazed his. His mustache brushed her ear in a most erotic manner as he leaned down to whisper, "What do you say we go on up to the house?"

"We can't leave yet," she protested half-heartedly, pressing her hands against his chest as if to push him away. But she found herself caressing the broad expanse instead.

He chuckled, and she felt the vibration against her palms. "Sure we can," he replied, encircling her with his arms. "We're the bride and groom. No one will think twice about it."

"Oh, yes, they will," she retorted. "They'll all know exactly why we slipped away."

"Of course they will." He pressed a tender kiss to her lips, then leaned his forehead against hers, looking deep into her eyes. "But your mama is busy bragging to her friends about this beautiful weeding dress she made you, and Donovan is over there with Sarah, showing off their new baby girl. With everyone making a fuss over little Cassie, this is the perfect time to sneak off and catch a few moments alone."

"Just a few moments?" she teased. "Is that all?" She gave him her best flirtatious pout, the one that had made grown men beg. "The people of Burr will be most disappointed in their new sheriff, Jedidiah ... as will your new bride."

He gave a bark of laughter at her audacious response. She covered his mouth with her hand and glanced around. "Will you hush? We'll never get away if you make so much noise!"

He tugged her hand away from his lips, kissing her fingers as he did so. "Sweetheart," he murmured. "I promised you forever, and that's what you're going to get."

She slanted a look at her new husband. "When does that promise start?"

"Right now." He gave her a kiss that made her head spin, then took her hand. "Let's go, Mrs. Brown. We have a lifetime of loving to begin."

She touched his cheek, her heart aglow from the tender emotion in his sherry-colored eyes. "We already have."

America Loves Lindsey!
The Timeless Romances
of #1 Bestselling Author

KEEPER OF THE HEART	0-380-77493-3/$6.99 US/$8.99 Can
THE MAGIC OF YOU	0-380-75629-3/$6.99 US/$8.99 Can
ANGEL	0-380-75628-5/$6.99 US/$9.99 Can
PRISONER OF MY DESIRE	0-380-75627-7/$6.99 US/$8.99 Can
ONCE A PRINCESS	0-380-75625-0/$6.99 US/$8.99 Can
WARRIOR'S WOMAN	0-380-75301-4/$6.99 US/$8.99 Can
MAN OF MY DREAMS	0-380-75626-9/$6.99 US/$8.99 Can
SURRENDER MY LOVE	0-380-76256-0/$6.50 US/$7.50 Can
YOU BELONG TO ME	0-380-76258-7/$6.99 US/$8.99 Can
UNTIL FOREVER	0-380-76259-5/$6.50 US/$8.50 Can
LOVE ME FOREVER	0-380-72570-3/$6.99 US/$8.99 Can
SAY YOU LOVE ME	0-380-72571-1/$6.99 US/$8.99 Can
ALL I NEED IS YOU	0-380-76260-9/$6.99 US/$8.99 Can
THE PRESENT	0-380-80438-7/$6.99 US/$9.99 Can
JOINING	0-380-79333-4/$7.50 US/$9.99 Can

And in hardcover

THE HEIR
0-380-97536-X/$24.00 US/$36.50 Can

HOME FOR THE HOLIDAYS
0-380-97856-3/$18.00 US/$27.50 Can

....